Sommerhjem Journeys Series:

Journey's Middle: 2012
Winner of the Author Project 2018 Best Self-Published Young Adult Fiction Author in the State of Minnesota Award.
Winner of the Midwest Independent Publishing Association (MIPA) 2012 Midwest Book Award for Young Adult Fiction and finalist in the Fiction: Fantasy and Science Fiction category.

Journey's Lost and Found: 2013
Finalist of the MIPA 2013 Midwest Book Awards in both the Young Adult Fiction and the Fiction: Fantasy and Science Fiction categories.

Journey's Seekers: 2014
Winner of the MIPA 2014 Midwest Book Awards in both the Young Adult Fiction and the Fiction: Fantasy and Science Fiction categories.

Journey's Crossroads: 2015
Finalist of the MIPA 2015 Midwest Book Awards in the Young Adult Fiction category.

Journeys Chosen: 2017

Sommerhjem Tales Series:

Thorval's Tale: 2019

Perrin's Tale: 2021

PERRIN'S TALE

B. K. PARENT

iUniverse

PERRIN'S TALE

iUniverse books may be ordered through booksellers or by contacting:

iUniverse
1663 Liberty Drive
Bloomington, IN 47403
www.iuniverse.com
844-349-9409

Cover Artist: Katherine M. Parent

ISBN: 978-1-6632-3228-1 (sc)
ISBN: 978-1-6632-3227-4 (e)

Library of Congress Control Number: 2021923965

Print information available on the last page.

iUniverse rev. date: 12/09/2021

Acknowledgements

Many thanks to Celeste Klein who encouraged me daily and to my sister Patti Callaway who insists I read each chapter to her. They have been my main readers, critics, suppliers of ideas and support, and have kept me on track.

Once again, many thanks to Katherine M. Parent for her cover and interior art. I can only hope the inside of the book is as good as the cover she has designed.

A special thanks to Steven Freund, who took copious notes on all of the books, and created a detailed map of the country of Sommerhjem. The map contained in this book is a simplified version of the map Steven created, redrawn by Katherine M. Parent.

A special thanks goes to Linne Jensen for surviving editing yet another book with me. I am extremely grateful for her knowledge of grammar, punctuation, and the ability to make sure the stories have consistency.

Introduction

All of the books in the Sommerhjem Journeys Series and the Sommerhjem Tales Series were written originally as serials. A cliffhanger was written into the end of each chapter in order to build anticipation for the next chapter or, in some cases, merely to irritate the reader. You, as a new reader, have choices. You can read a chapter, walk away, and then later pick the book up and read the next chapter to get the serial experience. Another choice is to just read Perrin's Tale as a conventional book and "one more chapter" yourself to three o'clock in the morning on a work or school night. Whichever way you choose, I hope you enjoy the adventures of Perrin and Kipp.

Check out Neebing, Ontario, Canada

In 2019 the Municipality of Neebing, Ontario, Canada, commissioned the building of a rover homewagon and placed it in the park next to their municipal building. They have named the park Journey's Middle after the first book in the Sommerhjem Journeys Series. Neebing, Ontario, could be Sommerhjem, for it has the rolling landscape that you can see a homewagon traveling across, the large body of water with various bays, the high tree-covered hills where foresters could live and work, and the cliffs that would attract a finder looking for tyvfugl bird treasure. Definitely a place worth visiting.

In memory of Gail (Flika) Gardner and Michael M. Cassidy

To CEK, always.

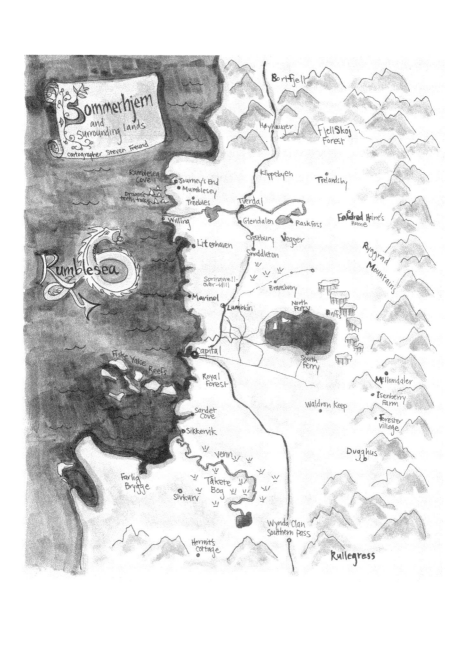

CHAPTER ONE

I hurried as fast as I could over the wet, slick, moss-covered stones which formed the floor of the open portico that ran alongside the old keep. I would have cut across the garden from the newer buildings had there not been a raging spring storm tearing up the night sky. My mood matched the storm, and the rumble of anger inside of me matched the rumble of thunder overhead. It had been a longer day than usual, and for once, I was glad I knew about the long-forgotten sleeping cupboards in the keep. I sorely needed to get away for a while, and no one would realize I was gone from the family wing.

As I hurried along, I noticed a brown-striped cat was keeping pace with me, swiftly slipping from shadow to shadow, sometimes ahead, sometimes behind me, but always close. I quietly let myself through the small side door that few even remembered in the oldest section of the sprawling manor house. The great hall had been the original keep long ago when my ancestors first came to this region. They had named their landholding surrounding the keep Nytt Heimili. The great hall had once housed all the members of the clan. The old keep had kept them warm and safe from the harsh cold months and the harsher marauding nomads that once roamed the territory. Over time, the clan had grown and expanded, spreading out over the landscape, just as the keep had been added to time and again. It had reached its present sprawling state with family, guest, and servant wings, summer and cold month kitchens, gardens, herb house, stables, and troop barracks. The great hall was rarely used these days, for there were now grander, more ornate rooms for official occasions, banquets, and ceremonies. The great hall was only used now for those ceremonies or occasions where tradition, or the appearance of tradition, was called for.

The large stone room was long, dark, and cavernous, with huge smoke-stained timber beams supporting the slate roof. Fireplaces large enough to roast a whole deer filled most of each end. Tapestries so old, dusty, and faded that it was hard to tell what tales they once told hung along the upper reaches of the room. The two long sides of the room were framed with rough stone pillars creating openings to the arched corridors that ran the length of the great hall. At first glance, the age-darkened wood along the long walls looked like rough-hewn wood paneling. Most folks paid little attention to the walls, and few remembered that the wood was not paneling at all, but rather formed doors to sleeping cupboards tucked away under the arched corridors that ran along the walls. In the early times, clan members of rank slept in the cupboards, while the rest of the clan slept in the great hall.

Nona had been the one who had first shown me the little-remembered sleeping cupboards. It had been our secret. I sighed softly thinking about Nona. I wished the old dear woman were still alive. Nona had come to Nytt Heimili as a young girl, accompanying her mother who was first lady to the woman who married my great grandfather. In time, Nona came to oversee the nursery and had had a hand in raising three generations of my relatives, ending with me. Nona had been a small woman who had broadened with age. To the children she had helped raise, she was pillowy softness, a haven of comfort, in a clan that demanded toughness of its members.

My father, Leifur, was the second child born to my grandparents. His older sister would have been the laird of the clan had she not been thrown from a horse shortly before she was to have been married, leaving no heir. My father had been away at the time, serving in the border guard. When he returned to become clan leader, he brought with him his bride, Helka. I know little about my mother other than my father had adored her. All Nona could tell me about my mother was that she had been from beyond, meaning she had been from beyond the borders of Bortfjell.

Unfortunately, my mother had withdrawn from the world after the birth and loss of a child when I was about ten years of age. She kept to her rooms, or could be seen wandering the corridors at night, a pale woman in a pale flowing night dress, a living ghost, who barely acknowledged my father's existence much less mine. She died when I just turned thirteen. My memories of good times as a family have faded over time.

After my mother died, my father had had little to do with me. His grief over the loss of my mother had carried him away from me. I often wondered if he saw too much of my mother in me, and then, in my bitterest moments I would laugh, thinking he would have to notice I still existed to see her in me. Nona had raised me.

As heir to the ruling clan laird, I should have been schooled in letters, arms, diplomacy, and statecraft by my father. Instead, Nona had seen to the teaching of my letters. Jard, the elderly stable groom, had taught me riding at Nona's urging. Arnar, who had once served in the border guard until an accident had left him too crippled for active duty, had taught me the short bow, throwing knives, and the discipline of kazan, which is part meditation and part martial arts. One of my grandfather's counselors had taken it upon himself to teach me the rudiments of statecraft and diplomacy. My education has been as piecemeal as the patchwork quilt on my bed. I spent my days with former members of my father's staff who most felt no longer had any use. They were too worn, too old. They were the redundant folks who were kept on because of past loyalty but were not thought of as useful. I could tell them different.

As I grew older, my days were filled with the lessons Nona arranged. Nona, who no longer had youngsters to look after in the nursery, spent more and more time in the stillhouse, and there I would find her at the end of each day. Nona insisted on an hour a day of my time to help her in the stillhouse. She showed me how to cut, prepare, and dry the herbs and medicinal plants, all the while teaching me their uses. I often fretted at being inside on warm summer days, but I never minded the stillhouse during the cold months. The tidy stone building with a cozy fire lit against the cold was warm, dry, and often smelled of summer.

Nona had been gone now three full turnings of the moon, and I missed her more each day. While Nona had been alive, I felt that at least I had a home for my heart. With Nona gone, I worried that there were few within the household who would notice if I suddenly were to disappear. Certainly not my father, who was way too busy these last years with his new family. Upon the urging of his advisors, he had remarried three years past, and his new wife, Lady Kolbrun, had given him a male child one year ago. This day had marked the child's first birthday, and it had been duly celebrated in the clan tradition with a naming ceremony in the great hall.

Bunch of fuss and bother. He was just a squalling stinky baby, not much use for anything, and yet such a to-do was made over him. But that was not what was causing my anger to resonate with the thunder. This night, my stepmother had stood there, her arms crossed over her reed-thin body, her lips pinched as if she had just swallowed something sour, and declared that starting on the morrow, I needed to spend my days in the women's workroom doing what my stepmother claimed was learning a woman's role and woman's work.

"Perrin, I have talked to your father about how you are spending your days, and I told him it is not suitable for a young woman of this family to spend her time in meaningless pursuits such as brushing down the horses, fooling around in the stillhouse, and sitting around talking to old retainers. Even worse, I told your father, is the way you dress. Certainly, pants and a tunic are not suitable for a young woman of your rank. We have an image to maintain after all."

I could have sworn at that point I heard my stepmother sniff disdainfully. When I had pointed out that it would be difficult to practice arms or to ride in a dress, my stepmother had informed me that "a true lady" did not need to know or do those disgustingly dirty things. "After all, your father is noble, and his children and his lands are well-tended by the servants and well-protected by the home guard." She had gone on to say that I needed to learn the gentler pursuits of a lady so as to appear attractive when suitors came to call. Also, I needed to learn to dress as a proper lady, do needle point, and be able to have genteel conversations with ladies my age at court when we traveled there this summer. In addition, I must learn all these things so as not to embarrass my father. After all, who I married was important to the strength and wealth of the holding. The worst part of this conversation was that my stepmother had gone on to say that my father agreed with her.

I could not believe what I had heard. I was the heir to this landholding, so suitors should be falling all over themselves to make themselves presentable to me and not the other way around. What use would I be to our folk if the land came under attack and all I knew how to wield was an embroidery needle? I had almost laughed out loud, as my stepmother droned on and on, having the mental image of walking into battle, because ladies did not ride, slashing at my foes with a tiny shiny needle. *Oh yes,* I had thought, *that would put the fear on them so that they would turn and run.*

My thoughts had taken me across the keep hall to the east wall. I went to the southeast end, placed my hands on the wooden paneling where the seams met, gently inserted my fingers beneath the slats of wood, and pulled. The cupboard doors swung soundlessly open. I crawled through the opening and pulled the doors behind me, placing the stout wooden bar in the metal brackets and thus locking myself in. I unshielded the glow lamp which cast off a feeble light. I reminded myself that I needed to take the glow lamp with me in the morn and set it in the light outside so it could renew. I glanced up from the lamp and jumped just slightly at the sight of a brown-striped cat sitting at the foot of the bed calmly cleaning his paw.

"How did you get in here?" I asked as if I expected an answer. "Oh good, now I am talking to cats."

That there was a cat in the sleeping cupboard with me did not really surprise me. It seemed lately that everywhere I went, a cat or two was usually close by. It was not always the same cat or cats, but when I would look up from whatever I was doing, there would be a cat sitting or lying nearby and watching me. At least, I thought they were watching me. The company would be welcome on this night, when it seemed that my world had just gotten too strange by far. It was cold in the cupboard now, and a cat on my feet, or curled against the small of my back, would bring a bit of warmth. I knew I would have been quite warm in my suite of rooms in the family wing, but I had had more than enough of my family this day.

Several weeks later, I sat by the open window of the women's work room, looking out over the gardens feeling more miserable by the minute. Day after day, I felt like a prisoner of both my new circumstances and my new clothes. I felt like I was being strangled by the high collar of my dress. Added to that was the smell of the fresh spring air coming in the window. This day was the first really warm, sunny day of spring. The rains were over, and the leaves were almost growing right before my eyes. What I really wanted was to be outside riding, taking in the fresh air.

Each day since my little half-brother's birthday, I had tried to speak to my father about my stepmother's proclamation that I had to "grow up and learn what a true lady of the realm needed to know." I could not believe my father was really going along with this decision. Each time I had tried to see my father, someone always intervened, sending me circling back to where I had come from. Even though I had not always been at the center of what was happening in my father's court, I had grown up knowing his advisors and other important folk that surrounded him. Lately it seemed that the folks bustling hurriedly and importantly around the manor were strangers, or somehow connected with my stepmother's retinue.

"Well, fettle ferns and nettles," I exclaimed when I stuck my finger with a needle for the fourth time in as many minutes. Lady Marsham gave me a scalding look, but then Lady Marsham was always finding reasons to show disapproval of me.

"You are late," she would exclaim when I came in each morning whether I was late or not. "You are not dressed properly, your hair needs to be neater, your stitches are too big, too little, too tight, not tight enough."

The high point of each day had become the cats. Lady Marsham seemed to truly loath cats. Saying that they were dirty creatures, she did not allow them in the women's workroom. Each morning she would storm through the room with her broom, chase cats off chairs, out from under tables, and brush them all out of the room. Lady Marsham would then shut the door and briskly announce "Well, that's that." As the day dragged by, soon one cat and then another cat and then another cat would somehow just show up on an empty seat or on a window ledge, even if all the windows had been closed. Or the cats would show up on the rug by the fire. I had started watching for them to see how they were getting into the room, but so far I had not been able to figure it out. Neither had Lady Marsham, who would get all red in the face and demand that everyone stop what they were doing so she could shoo the cats out again. I always thought the cats left the room with great dignity and perhaps a twinkle in their eyes. This seemed to be a grand game with them.

It was only after the evening meal that I was able to slip away and have some time for myself. No one seemed to notice if I showed up to eat, unless it was a banquet or other important dinner. I often ate in the common kitchen, or grabbed something the cooks had set out, and then went to try to fit into what remained of the day some lessons with Jard and Arnar. I also tried to get to the stillhouse and keep up what Nona would have been doing. No one had taken over the gathering and drying of plants and herbs, nor had anyone been working on replacing the salves, liniments, or syrups needed. I had tried to talk to my stepmother about the need to find someone to take over the stillhouse, but my stepmother told me to quit bothering her with trifles and silliness and those commoner home remedies. She had said her brother had trained with the royal court physician and would be arriving shortly to take care of everything.

Where does she think the medicines for the folks and the animals here come from? What would happen if we ran out of medicine, if the spring cough hit again like it had several years back? What if a horse came up lame and there was no liniment? Was that brother of hers bringing medicines for all the folks who would need it, and would he have what was needed to care for the animals? Was he going to be helping with the birthing of the lambs, calves, and foals? Those were the questions I asked, but I had been told that it was none of my concern. It seemed to me that on the surface the holding was doing all right, but underneath, common everyday tasks were being neglected.

As soon as I escaped the women's workroom this day, I quickly hurried to my room. For some reason I felt a sense of urgency. Each day over the last fortnight, I had been gathering my clothes and other personal items and moving them to one of the sleeping cupboards. I had just returned to my room after taking the last of my riding clothes, the ones my stepmother had forbidden me to wear, when my stepmother swept into my room followed by several of the servants.

"My brother Grimur and his family will be visiting shortly, Perrin, and I will need you to give up your suite of rooms and move temporarily. I thought this would be a good time to go through your things and sort out what is suitable and what needs to go into the rag bag."

"I think you will find that there is not much left to sort, for I cleared everything out shortly after you told me to." *Perhaps not quite the way you think, but it is in the strict sense not a lie*, I thought.

It did not surprise me that I was being moved from my rooms. What hurt was I seemed to be being moved from my place in the family also, and my father did not seem to notice.

CHAPTER TWO

With the arrival of my step-uncle, Grimur, my situation went from bad to worse. When I went to attend the formal welcoming dinner, I was not seated with the family, but rather I was seated at a nearby table. Not quite below the salt, which would have been an even bigger insult. When I finally got away from the dinner and headed to the stillhouse, I found my step-uncle Grimur there. He did not resemble his sister, my stepmother, very much. He was somewhat short and squat with a pasty complexion. It looked as if he spent little or no time out-of-doors. While he was dressed well, as befitted a gentleman of his station, the clothes looked a bit worn. He had a swagger about him and a smug look which spoke of being overindulged and feeling entitled. I found him boxing up all of Nona's salves, liniments, tinctures, and syrups.

"What are you doing?"

"Nothing you need to worry your little head about, my dear. I am cleaning out the stillhouse in order to set up a place to receive those of the manor who are ill and in need of my services."

"What are you going to do with all that you are boxing up?"

"I will have the servant take it away and dispose of it. Now run along. You are not needed here."

I schooled my face so as not to betray how truly angry I was. *I need not worry my little head, indeed. I should just run along, should I?* Walking a short way away, I waited for the servant who had been at the stillhouse to walk by pulling a hand cart piled high with the contents of the stillhouse.

"Gallagher, isn't it?" I asked, signaling the young lad to stop.

"Yes'm," he said shyly.

"Where did the gentleman in the stillhouse tell you to take what is in your handcart?"

"He didn' really say. Just tol' me ta get rid of it."

"Do you know Elder Nambi, the woman who lives near the edge of the forest just beyond the rye fields?"

"Yes'm."

"Take what is in your handcart to her. Tell her where it came from, why you have it, and that I sent you. I will try to get to visit her soon. If there is a second load or more, take those to Elder Nambi also. Can you do that?"

"Yes'm."

"Good. You had best be on your way."

Gallagher tipped his hat to me and continued on down the lane leading off the manor house grounds.

The next day when I was free from another miserable day in the women's workroom, I headed to the stables to visit with Jard. I hoped that a little time with the old stable groom would help ease the loneliness of my day. I was disappointed to discover that he was not in his usual spot working on repairing some tack or cleaning a saddle. Concerned, I sought out the marshal, the man who oversaw our horses and stable. Upon finding him, I asked where I might find Jard.

"He's no longer here, or more correctly, he's no longer allowed here," the marshal informed me sadly. "Orders came through her ladyship's brother that Jard was no longer fit for work because he was too old, and I was to send him packing. That Grimur suggested that Jard was a burden on the manor. I am sorry, I had no choice. A burden indeed. So, he didn't muck out stalls or do any heavy lifting. So maybe he couldn't handle the newer, friskier horses. However, he had a soft and gentle hand, and it almost seemed that he could calm a frightened horse just by talking. He also was good at cleaning and repairing anything made of leather. He was a valuable folk around here, but those who surround your father and make the decisions did not view him as such."

"Where did he go?"

"I called in a favor from the owner of the stable in the village. You can find Jard there. He's made himself a place in the stable loft in return for a meal a day and taking on night duty. Not ideal, I know, but better than nothing, which is what Grimur left him."

"I just do not understand what is going on. Yesterday Grimur cleaned out the stillhouse. He told the servant helping him to get rid of everything, that he would be using the stillhouse to see folks from the manor. I do not think that healing help will be available to anyone who works for the manor. Also, he made no mention of dealing with any animals. So basically, he threw out all the liniment and salves that you might use. I asked the servant lad to take everything to Elder Nambi, who lives near the edge of the forest just beyond the rye fields. She and my Nona used to exchange information and sometimes would work together. I think she is as good an herbalist as my Nona was."

"Thank you for saving the liniments and salves we'll need here. I'll get in touch with Elder Nambi."

"I hope to go visit her on the morrow. Could you have a horse ready for me?"

"Once again, sadly I cannot. I have strict orders that you're not allowed to ride unless you are accompanied by someone chosen by your stepmother, Lady Kolbrun."

"I see. I need to think on that. Before I go, have you seen Arnar around lately?"

"Once again, I don't have a good answer for you. According to the captain of the home guard, orders came from your father, the Laird, that Arnar was dismissed and could no longer live in the barracks. I don't know where Arnar went."

I thanked the marshal and headed to the manor garden. I needed a place to sit and think about what I had just learned. Something was just not right. Why had Jard and Arnar been dismissed? Each day it seemed there were fewer and fewer familiar faces in the manor house. Those folks who surrounded my father were different from the ones I had known all my life. Outwardly, it still appeared that my father was in charge of our clan, and as far as I could tell, that was still true. He still met with the reeve, the captain of the home guard, the bailiff, the marshal, the constable, and others. Who was in charge within the manor was another matter. My stepmother, Lady Kolbrun, had brought with her a number of retainers who over the last year or so had quietly taken over key positions and duties.

When I settled into the small room I had been assigned, since Grimur had taken over my suite, it occurred to me that his visit was going to be an extended one. I began to question if it was just a visit, or a more permanent move. I knew he was not in line to inherit Lady Kolbrun's landholding since her older brother was first in line, and there were several other older siblings. It did seem to me that since he had studied with the royal physician, his own family could use his skills, rather than ours.

Just before I fell asleep, it struck me that I needed to figure out a way to get to the village, find Jard, and find out had happened to Arnar. When morning came, I was no closer to a solution. As the days droned on, I became more and more discontent with my new role in life. Each day I was forced to sit all day in the women's workroom working on what I considered frivolous tasks and lessons. The other young women seemed to relish the lessons on how to be a proper young lady. I, personally, was bored nearly to tears.

A break finally came from the tedium of my days when Lady Markham announced that we were to have a fortnight break, for she was departing to visit her family. With less supervision and no major evening events or formal dinners looming within the next fortnight, I felt it was time to get away from the manor. I had a plan.

CHAPTER THREE

It was a sad comment on my life that I learned more about what was going on in the manor and on the landholding when I chose to take my meal in the kitchen than I learned from my family or my family's advisors. I had discovered one evening that the porter's niece, Rosilda, was home from duty as a border guard. Rosilda and I had both done our early training with Arnar and had been friends. I hoped that friendship still held. I had to do something before I went quietly mad.

Several days later, I met with Rosilda near the archery range. "Well met, Rosilda. It has been a long time."

"Well met, Perrin, or do I need to be more formal and call you Lady Perrin?"

"Considering that we have spent hours tossing each other in the dirt practicing kazan, I think you can just stick with Perrin, old friend."

"Father suggested that this meeting was not to be a public one. What is going on?"

Now that I was face to face with Rosilda, it was time for me to make a decision. I was surprised to see the changes in her that had occurred in the years she had been away. The young, somewhat pudgy, woman who had left our landholding years before was now lean and fit. Her brown hair, tied back in a severe bun, was streaked with blond from spending time in the sun. Her gray eyes were less warm than they had been when we were younger. I suspected what she had seen and done while in the border guard may have had something to do with that. Despite the outward changes, I hoped the woman who had been my friend was still standing before me.

I had trusted her uncle, the manor porter, to set this meeting up. Now I was faced with making a decision about whether or not to trust Rosilda.

"Much has changed since you left to serve with the border guard. Father's new wife has had a child, a male. As you know, Nona died. Lady Kolbrun's brother Grimur has recently arrived and has apparently become the manor physician. Many of the old advisors and retainers are no longer here. Worst of all, Lady Kolbrun has declared that I need to be relegated to the women's workroom to learn needle work and how to be a lady. I am no longer allowed to take lessons. I am not allowed to ride without a proper escort. I am no longer seated at the family table for formal dinners. My suite of rooms has been reassigned."

"I had heard some of this from my father. I am so sorry. What is it you need from me?"

"I need to get to the village and make sure Jard is all right. I also want to find out what happened to Arnar. In addition, I would like to visit Elder Nambi. I am worried that the medicinal supplies that Nona provided, and I tried to keep up, will no longer be available to the folks and animals of our landholding as they always have been. I was hoping if I suggested you as a suitable escort, Lady Kolbrun would not object."

"I would be happy to be of service. I do have a question, however. With all this shunting you aside, are you concerned for your safety?"

The question took me aback for a minute, for it had not occurred to me that I might be in danger from anything other than sheer boredom.

"To be honest, I have not thought on that. While I have felt for some time that there is something not right going on, that Lady Kolbrun and those close to her seem to be subtly more and more in charge of decisions in the manor, especially concerning me, I have not felt in danger. Perhaps I had best think about that."

I left my meeting very troubled by my conversation with Rosilda. While I had been angry concerning the restrictions that had been placed on me, and I had been extremely disappointed that my father appeared to go along with my stepmother's decisions, I had not been concerned for my safety. Was there something more sinister going on? Was this gradual removal from my rightful place in our family just the beginning?

I approached Lady Kolbrun later in the day to broach the idea of my riding into the village with an escort.

"Lady Kolbrun, might I have a moment of your time?"

"What do you want? Be quick about it!"

"Since Lady Markham is gone for a fortnight, I would like to take this opportunity to ride into the village and to visit with some of the elderly crofters. It has been my habit to do that in the spring. Border guard Rosilda has returned home on business. Might she meet your approval as a suitable escort?"

Just as I finished talking, Lady Kolbrun was distracted by the approach of her brother and several other gentlemen I was not familiar with. "Fine, fine, arrange it. Be off now."

I left quickly before Lady Kolbrun could change her mind. I went directly to the porter's station and asked him to get a message to his niece, Rosilda, asking her to meet me the second hour after dawn at the stables. Then I went to my room to figure out what Lady Kolbrun might deem suitable for a young lady of the manor to wear while riding a horse. I did not want to be kept back from my ride should she see me and disapprove of my clothing. I found a riding outfit which certainly was not going to be as comfortable, nor as practical, as what I was used to wearing, but it would have to do.

Rosilda was waiting for me at the stables the next morning. One of the stable lads had my favorite horse already saddled and ready to mount. The extra material of the riding skirt was cumbersome, and my mounting the horse was less than graceful. I probably looked like I was a beginning rider. I did not care, for this was the first time in months that I had been able to leave the manor.

As we rode, I told Rosilda that I wished to head into the village first to see if we could find Jard. I hoped he might know where to find Arnar. I also wanted to visit Elder Nambi.

When we arrived at the village stable, Jard was sitting out front cleaning a bridle. I felt a pang of loss, for his pose and position were the same as they had been each day at the manor stable, and yet I could no longer visit with him as easily as I had in the past. I did not realize how much I had missed him, missed lessons with him, and missed him telling me tales of times past.

Jard stood up at our approach and reached out to take the reins of our horses. It took him a moment to recognize us.

"My, my, look what the wind has blown down the street. The returnin' border guard and the missin' Lady. Ya two just gonna sit up on them fine horses or are ya gonna slip off and set a spell with ol' Jard?"

My slipping off my horse was a bit more graceful than my mounting the horse had been. Not by much, however, if Jard's raised eyebrow was any indication.

"I am so sorry you can no longer work at the manor stable and that you were kicked off the manor grounds …."

"Now, donna ya worry none. 'Twasn't yer doin'. Marshal found me this work, and it suits me jus' fine. I do miss seein' ya and others though."

"I do not really know what is going on, and I am certainly not consulted. Did you know Arnar was also dismissed? Do you know where he is?"

"Aye, I can tell ya about Arnar. He and a few others of the ol' home guard have made camp up close ta Tumble Falls. They'll be all right through the warm months, bein' good at huntin', fishin', and gatherin'. Donna know what they'll do come the cold season."

Rosilda and I spent a bit more time with Jard, then we left our horses with him and took a stroll through the village. In times past, I had been greeted cheerfully or kindly by the village folk. This day, that did not happen. The villagers looked wary when I stepped into their shops. In some shops, I did not feel welcome. Not knowing what had caused this change in attitude and beginning to feel uneasy, I suggested to Rosilda that we move on and go visit Elder Nambi. She readily agreed.

When we reached Elder Nambi's cottage, we found her sitting out front in a patch of sunlight, resting, with a ginger cat curled up on her lap. Elder Nambi was a tiny woman, skin brown and wrinkled from years in the sun, her silver-gray hair tightly braided and wound like a crown around the top of her head. Upon our approach, she opened her eyes and straightened up.

"Well met, Lady Perrin, Rosilda. You both are a most welcome sight."

After we returned the greeting, Elder Nambi invited us into her cottage. The smell of drying herbs hanging from the rafters swept me into memories of the hours I had spent with Nona harvesting herbs and bundling them for drying. I had to give myself a swift shake to return back to the present.

"I have to thank you for sendin' the contents of the manor's stillhouse to me. The folks of the landholdin' thank you also. There's a rumor in the village that you are responsible for emptyin' out the manor stillhouse, and thus denyin' them what they might need. I have tried to tell them that you dinna do so. They are hurtin' since they lost their herbalist this cold season past and have found no replacement. They also have found no help from the manor. Some have found their way to me, but not many."

"The rumor you mentioned might explain why at some shops I did not feel welcome."

"That and your absence from the village. Many of the villagers and crofters are feelin' shut out of what is happenin' in the landholdin'. Your father, our laird, is rarely seen outside the manor walls. The new reeve has been quite harsh and that has folks grumblin'. The Laird has also increased the cost of rent for the land and placed a charge for goods and services on the village shops."

I felt ashamed, for I had been so wrapped up in my own misery, that I had not thought much about those who lived and worked on our landholding. Folks who live on our land depend on us for protection and fair justice. In return, we expect payment of some kind from the folk, which might be in the form of military service or the regular payment of produce or coin. We had always tried to be fair and reasonable with our folks and maintained a good relationship with them. From what Elder Nambi was telling me, that had changed and obviously not for the better.

It was a quiet ride back to the manor house. I had decided that I would not seek out Arnar this day. I had much to think about. I wanted to see if I could find a way to speak to my father privately. I arranged to meet up with Rosilda at the same time on the morrow.

I was unsuccessful in my efforts to meet with my father when I arrived back at the manor. I was turned away from his wing of the manor by some officious man I did not recognize.

"The Laird is quite busy this afternoon. I do not recall he had an appointment scheduled with you, Lady Perrin."

"You do understand I am his daughter. I should not need an appointment."

"Ah, yes, well," the stern thin man stated coldly. "The Laird is quite busy this afternoon. Perhaps you should try another time."

I decided to head back to my quarters to change out of the horrible riding outfit and think of a different way to reach my father. As I paced my small room, I tried to figure out how I could get past the thoroughly awful gatekeeper outside my father's wing. I tried to recall if my father had any routines he followed daily, and I could not. It was then that I remembered that he often would stroll through the back garden and stop at my mother's grave towards dusk. I determined to try to catch him there.

I found my father that evening sitting alone on a bench near the hedge maze. Seeing him there brought back memories of the two of us wandering through the hedge maze and of my father making up tales of what might be around the next corner. We had not shared very many moments of late, and I found myself feeling immensely sad.

When I reached the bench, my father turned toward me. I was struck, now that I was able to see him up close, how he seemed to have aged. He no longer was the tall, barrel-chested man of my youth. His flame-red hair was streaked with gray, as was his beard.

"Daughter."

"Father."

"What brings you out on this chilly night?"

"I was hoping to find you. I tried to see you this afternoon. However, I was told I needed to schedule an appointment."

"Why is it you wished to see me this afternoon?"

"I finally was allowed to ride to the village this day …."

"What do you mean, you were finally allowed?"

"I have been told I can no longer ride without an escort. In addition, Lady Kolbrun has told me I am no longer allowed to take lessons from Jard, Arnar, and others, and that I need to spend my days in the women's workroom. I have been moved out of my suite of rooms and am no longer seated with the family at formal dinners. I am not allowed to work in the stillhouse, which by the way has been cleaned out of all of Nona's work and taken over by Grimur. And I have been told you have approved of all these changes."

"You did not wish to be finished with your lessons?"

"Of course not. How can I serve the members of our clan and land if all I know how to do is to stitch patterns on cloth? Which by the way, I am abominable at."

My father sat for a long time in silence, not responding to what I had just told him. Instead, he said, "You started this conversation telling me you finally rode to the village. Were you concerned about something in the village?"

"I went to the village to check up on Jard. Marshal told me that Grimur had told him to dismiss Jard because Jard was too old. Marshal also told me that you sent word down that Arnar was no longer allowed to live and help out at the barracks."

When I paused to take a breath, my father told me to continue.

"The villagers seemed wary of me and less than friendly. They are concerned that they rarely see you, that the new reeve is quite harsh, and that you have increased the cost of rent for the land and placed a charge for goods and services on the village shops. They are also without an herbalist and are getting no help from here."

Before my father could reply to what I had just told him, Lady Kolbrun hailed him as she came striding forward.

Chapter Four

"Ah, my Lord, there you are. I wish to discuss the upcoming opening of the spring market days. I am concerned about having it on the grounds near the manor. Mayhap we should move it to an empty field closer to the village."

I was having trouble with the conversation that Lady Kolbrun just started for two reasons. The first was the fact that she had barely acknowledged that I was present, and she had interrupted my conversation with my father. The second was that she was suggesting that we change an eon long tradition by moving where the spring markets were to take place. And perhaps there was a third troublesome reason. I suspected what she was not saying was she did not want the spring market anywhere near the manor because she held the villagers and others who worked and lived on the landholding in great disdain, not to mention the traveling merchants and traders who came to the spring markets.

I had just begun to step back from my father and stepmother when my father spoke.

"Perrin, please wait." Turning to my stepmother he said, "My dear, I will talk to you when I return to our chambers. In the meantime, I would like to continue my conversation with my daughter."

I wished I could somehow preserve the look of disbelief and anger that passed quickly across Lady Kolbrun's face when she was dismissed by my father. I did not wish to preserve the look of pure loathing that was on her face when she turned and looked at me before marching away, her back rigid.

I had to keep my face turned away from my father for a few moments because I was trying so extremely hard to quell the bubble of laughter that was trying to escape. Lady Kolbrun's angry march away from us was being hampered by cats. There had to be six or eight different cats that darted out of the flowerbeds one after another, causing Lady Kolbrun to halt and start, sidestep, weave, and sometimes jerk back or jerk to the side. The cats certainly spoiled her exit. When I turned back, I thought I saw a look of amusement on my father's face, but I could not be sure.

"Daughter, come close, for we have very little time and much to discuss. When Prince Mallus ascended the throne, he made it clear that only those whose family line came from the first settlers would have standing in our land, those of pure Bortfjellian blood. Any member of a family who did not fit those criteria, could not be a clan leader. He made that declaration to make sure several of his siblings from his mother's second marriage could not claim the throne. Unfortunately, that directly affects you, since your mother came from beyond our borders. I have tried to protect you by going along with Lady Kolbrun's actions toward you."

When I gave my father a quizzical look, he continued.

"I felt if you were, in a sense out of sight, out of mind, you might be safer. I am worried that might not be the case. You need to be ever vigilant. Our new ruler, Prince Mallus, and those who surround him are against anyone whom they deem of foreign birth or to have foreign blood in them. They are placing many restrictions on those folks. There are rumors that some folks of foreign birth have mysteriously disappeared. There is a shadowy group who call themselves The Rensing who are rumored to be hunting down foreign-born folk. I am worried about your safety."

At that moment, my father looked beyond me with a look of grave concern on his face.

"The porter is walking slowly this way, so I must assume he has been sent to fetch me. You need to have a plan if the situation becomes worse. I suggest you begin to gather what you might need to flee. I am so sorry this has come to pass. I have left some resources at the tree we call the wishing tree in case the danger to you grows too strong. Seek out Arnar, for he will help. Again, I am sorry I have treated you badly, Perrin. I was trying to keep you safe. Know that I love you."

I had no time to ask questions or talk further, for the porter had arrived.

"Your pardon, Laird. I have been sent to tell you that Laird and Lady Nagranni have arrived."

"Thank you, Porter, I will be right there." Once the porter was out of hearing, my father continued. "I must go. Remember all the lessons that you have been taught. If you do have to leave to be safe, please leave me some type of message that you have disappeared of your own accord. Stay safe and stay well."

With that said, my father turned and swiftly walked down the garden path away from me.

I sat down hard on the bench my father had just vacated. I was having difficulty gathering my thoughts on what he had just told me. I had been raised all my life to understand I would be the next clan leader. I had been trained to take that position up until the time my stepmother's child had turned one year of age and I was relegated to the women's room. It was now clear to me from my father's conversation that under Prince Mallus I could not be a clan leader. For that matter, I was not even sure I was a member of our clan. The clear message from my father was that I was in danger.

I needed a plan, it would seem. First, I needed to return to my sleeping quarters and remove anything I had left there that I wanted or needed and move it to the sleeping cupboard in the old keep area. I did not think I was going to feel safe in my sleeping quarters anymore. They were in an isolated corridor in the family wing of the manor. The sleeping quarters near mine, now that I thought about it, were all empty. My sleeping quarters were certainly not defensible. It would be easy for someone to come in the night and dispatch me.

I also needed to sort through my possessions and winnow out what I really needed and what I could leave behind if I had to flee. As I was thinking this, I realized I had been petting a large, brown-striped cat that had settled himself on my lap. I also realized that there were several other cats gathered in the area around the bench. Most of them were napping, but a few were sitting up looking very alert. I wondered if these were the same cats that had impeded Lady Kolbrun's progress down the path. I wondered if I should thank them for providing a bit of humor amid a very worrisome conversation with my father.

I realized I was becoming chilled and needed to return to the manor. However, before I headed back into the manor, I decided to seek out the wishing tree my father had mentioned. The wishing tree was an incredibly old tree in the walled garden next to the old keep wall. My father had told me his mother had told him that if you placed a small coin or gift in the tree and made a wish, it might come true. When I was younger, we would leave a coin or gift in a deep hollow in the tree. I suspected that what my father had left for me would be hidden there in that deep hollow.

It was just a short walk to the walled garden from where I was sitting. I gently removed the now sleeping cat from my lap and placed him on the ground, quietly thanking him for his company and comfort. As I started forward, he fell in step with me. I noticed that the other cats who had been nearby stayed near, darted ahead, or followed behind. I caught them out of the corner of my eye, weaving in and out of the foliage.

I arrived at the wishing tree without incident. After looking around to make sure I was alone, and seeing no one, I went to the back of the wishing tree, which is tucked into a corner of the stone garden wall. Stepping between the trunk and the wall, I stood on my toes to make myself tall enough to reach into the hollow in the tree. I felt around until my hand found what felt like a leather pouch. Slowly I drew it out and put it in my pocket. I put my hand back into the hollow to see if there was anything else hidden there and discovered there was something else at the bottom of the hollow. I slowly drew that out as well.

I could only hope no one was nearby to hear the gasp I made when I looked at what was in my hand. My father had left me my mother's medallion. I had seen it only once before when I was much younger. I had gone to wish him a good night and had found him holding the medallion. He had explained it had been my mother's. He told me she had always worn it under her clothes and had never taken it off. He did not know its significance. For that matter, my mother's past was very much a mystery to me. I have never known if he did not talk about my mother because her loss was too painful, or because he just did not know very much about her. I think the answer lay somewhere between those two ideas.

I placed the chain holding the medallion over my head and tucked the medallion under my shirt. I did not want anyone to see me wearing it and then need to explain what it was or where I had gotten it. Just as I was about to slip out from between the garden wall and the wishing tree, I heard folks talking as they entered the walled garden. I did not know if

I should reveal myself or stay where I was. When I heard one of them say "We need to talk about the Laird's daughter, Perrin," I decided I was not about to step into view at that moment.

"Quiet, let's make sure we are alone here."

I held my breath and scooted even farther back into the corner of the garden wall, hoping whoever was checking to see if anyone was in the garden did not find me. I heard the sound of footsteps coming closer and closer to my hiding place. I stopped breathing.

The man I had heard before spoke with a gravelly voice. "Come on back. I do not see anyone else here, unless you count the cat. Let us have our conversation and then move back into the manor. We really cannot chance being caught talking to each other here."

"Fine," stated the second man. I recognized the voice as belonging to my stepmother's brother, Grimur.

"Your sister has certainly done what she needed to do by having a child by Laird Leifur. Now that Prince Mallus has declared that foreign born folk, or those having foreign blood, cannot hold any title in our land, that certainly clears the way for your nephew to one day become the clan leader here. Unfortunately, as you know, anything can happen, and something could happen to Prince Mallus. Then a new ruler would emerge and may change the rules of succession."

"Ah, I see where you are heading," said Grimur. "Since we cannot control who sits upon the throne, my nephew's eventual clan leadership is in peril as long as Perrin remains alive."

"She needs to be taken care of, yet it should not happen right away."

"And why is that?"

"Because Lord and Lady Nagranni are here for a fortnight before they move on to the capital city, Fyrstaborgin. It would not do to have Perrin disappear or have a tragic accident while they are here. A tragic accident after Lord and Lady Nagranni, your sister, and the Laird leave would be most suitable. We should wait about a week after they leave, and then arrange for something very dire to happen to Perrin."

I really did not like the sound of the idea that I would meet with a tragic accident, nor did I like the relish I heard in the other man's voice when he talked about my demise.

"You are right. If something were to happen to Perrin after my sister and the Laird are already in Fyrstaborgin, it would take over a fortnight for the message to get to them, and for them to return, if they chose to do so."

"Then we are agreed. Now, we have been here far too long. We should leave."

"Right."

"Remember, this meeting never happened."

I listened intently as the men walked away from my hiding spot. Though there was now silence in the garden, I stayed in the corner next to the garden wall behind the wishing tree for quite some time before I moved. Finally, when I felt I was alone in the garden, I slipped out from behind the wishing tree. I started when I caught movement out of the corner of my eye, only to realize it was the brown-striped cat I had sat with earlier. Once he saw I had seen him, he turned, stuck his tail straight up, and began walking down the path that led out of the garden. When I did not move, he stopped, looked over his shoulder, and gave me a look that seemed to suggest he was impatient.

"Fine, all right, I am coming."

The cat then turned and walked through the walled garden gate. He waited until I too had exited the walled garden before he started walking again. He was not heading in the direction I had intended to go, but something about this cat made me curious to see where he was heading, so I followed him.

The cat continued along the wall of the old keep and then just simply disappeared between one eye blink and the next. I cautiously walked to where I had last seen him, thinking he had just slipped into the jumble of hedges next to the wall. Moving the branches of the hedge apart, I peered into the shadowy interior and saw the cat's tail disappear through a gap in the stone wall.

Fortunately, before I had gone to find my father, I had changed out of the ridiculous riding outfit, and I was thankful I had put on something more comfortable and easier to move in. Pulling the branches back farther to allow me to slip in between, I worked my way to the portion of the wall where I had last seen the cat's tail. I knew I needed to look around quickly, for the evening light was fading fast.

Crouching down, I saw that a stone had fallen out of the wall about a foot up from the ground. I was a bit wary about putting my hand in the opening in the wall. However, I wanted to see if the cat was hiding inside the area where the stone had been. I could not see within the opening, for it was dark inside the hole. I could however feel a slight draft coming from the opening, and it smelled a bit stale and of dust. After a few moments of indecision, I slowly stuck my hand into the opening. No cat. I reached farther and farther into the hole, until my arm was up to my shoulder. Past my elbow, I found that my arm was not confined by stone at all. I could move it around without touching anything.

I slowly eased my arm out of the hole in the wall and backed out from the hedge. Now I had even more to think about this night. First and foremost, my life was in danger. In addition, I needed to see what was in the pouch my father had left me in the hollow of the wishing tree. Finally, I wanted to think about the hole in the wall the brown-striped cat had disappeared into.

CHAPTER FIVE

Once I was back inside the manor, I moved quickly to my sleeping quarters. It did not take me long to go through what was left of my belongings, to sift out what I really wanted or needed. If I were going to have to flee, I certainly would not be dragging along the frocks my stepmother had insisted I wear. In addition, I would certainly not be running off wearing the ridiculous riding outfit I had worn this day.

Next, I mussed up the bed covers to look like I had slept in the bed this night, just in case someone looked in in the morning. Since I had been moved to this room, I no longer had a lady's maid or even a housekeeping servant. This night I was thankful for the fact that no one would know if I slept here or not.

Giving the room one last glance, I hurried down a back stair and made my way to the great room of the old keep. I met no one on the way, for which I was thankful. Upon reaching the great room, I stepped into the shadows of the archway and listened. All was quiet and still. It took all my control not to jump or make a noise when something brushed against my leg. My heart rose to my throat and was beating quite fast. When I heard a faint purring sound, I relaxed a bit.

I do not know what was going on with all the cats that kept appearing wherever I was. When I stopped to think about it, while there had always been cats about in the manor, I had noticed more of them nearby since I had been moved out of my suite. When I reflected on that idea, I realized I had found comfort in having a cat or two nearby. Odd.

I knelt and gave the cat a scratch between its ears and then moved down the corridor to the second to the last sleeping cupboard. Earlier, when Lady Kolbrun had announced that I was to spend my days in the women's workroom, I had removed those items I wished to keep that she might deem unsuitable for a young lady of standing. I had moved them to the sleeping cupboard for fear she would throw my possessions out. Now I needed to take the time to sort through what was sitting in a jumble in the sleeping cupboard.

After I had spent several moments standing still and listening to make sure no one was in the great hall besides the cat and me, I moved and opened the sleeping cupboard's doors. Reaching in, I pushed the jumbled pile aside and climbed in. I could only hope the glow lamp I had set inside the sleeping cupboard earlier had retained some light. Quietly closing the cupboard doors behind me, I set the bar across the metal door brackets so no one could enter. Opening the glow lamp, I was relieved that it gave off a decent light. I was a little disconcerted when I saw two eyes glowing from a darkened corner of the sleeping cupboard, until I realized it was the brown-striped cat.

"How did you get in here?" I whispered.

The cat did not answer. He just settled in for a nap.

I realized that the first thing I needed to do was to see what my father had left me in the leather pouch. Pulling the pouch out of my pocket, I tipped the contents out into my slouch hat so I would not lose anything. My father had put a veritable fortune in the pouch. There were bits of gold and silver, a large number of coins, and an amazing number of jewels. I certainly needed to think about what to do with what was in the pouch, for I did not think it was going to be safe keeping it all in one place. If someone were to steal the pouch from me, I would be left with nothing.

Setting the slouch hat aside in a space I cleared near the foot of the bed so it could not get tipped over, I sorted through the jumble on the bed until I found my riding boots. There were places in my boots where I could hide some of the precious metal and some of the jewels. I also slipped a knife into the sheath built into each boot. The belt I wore with my favorite riding outfit also had hidden places where I could stash more of the pouch's contents. I pulled out my pack and hid some more coins and metal bits away in it.

Then I found my cloak and my blanket roll. I began to quietly laugh at what I was going to do next. I was going to use what I had thought were worthless skills that I had learned in the women's workroom. I was going to sew some of the gems into the hem of my cloak and the border of my blanket roll. I wondered if Lady Markham would approve of my careful stitches.

Once I had finished distributing the pouch's contents as best I could, I sorted through the remainder of the jumble on the bed, setting to one side what I wanted to pack and discarding the rest. I packed several changes of clothing, the rest of my throwing knives, rain gear, a small pot, a cup and spoon, several glow lamps, and other things I deemed I might need while running for my life.

I thought about grabbing up the pack and trying to slip out this night. I realized that would be very foolish, since while I was packed to set out, I had no plan as to where I would go. I also had not gathered any travel food. Besides, leaving right now would certainly raise an alarm. I needed to wait until my father, stepmother, and their guests left for Fyrstaborgin before I departed.

I spent the next little while once again going through what I had not packed, folding, straightening, and putting the items in neat piles. I found a few more items I had missed and packed them. With nothing left to do, I once again shielded the glow lamp, very slowly lifted the bar off the door brackets, and opened the cupboard door a crack. After a long while, I eased the door open enough to slip out. Turning back, I reached for my pack. I suggested to the cat that he might want to leave with me. My pack was where I had left it. The cat was nowhere within the sleeping cupboard.

I shut the cupboard doors and moved to the next sleeping cupboard, opened the doors and climbed in, pushing my gear ahead of me. I turned back and reopened the other cupboard to grab my riding boots, riding clothes, cloak, and the glow lamp. I quickly transferred these to the other sleeping cupboard, closed the doors of the cupboard that held my remaining possessions, and climbed back into sleeping cupboard that held my pack. After placing the wooden bar across the metal brackets to lock myself in, I cracked opened the shield of the glow lamp and let out a sigh of relief. I heard a soft sigh from the shadowy area at the foot of the bed. When I looked closer, it was the brown-striped cat. I was way too tired to try to figure out how he had gotten into the sleeping cupboard.

The next morning, I was up and at the stables by the second hour after dawn. Rosilda was waiting for me with both horses saddled and ready to ride. I did a little better mounting the horse in my awkward riding outfit, but not much. Once we were away from the manor grounds, I halted my horse.

"Jard told us that Arnar was in an encampment up near Tumble Falls. It is a several hour ride. Are you up for it?"

"I would be happy to accompany you. Do not look over your shoulder, but I think we are being followed. I would suggest we head away from the direction we wish to go along this lane heading north. There is a heavily wooded area a few minutes from here. Remember how we used to get away from my pesky younger brothers on that hidden animal path?"

"If I recall, we rode over a stretch of solid rock on this lane which would not show our horses' hoof prints, then after rounding a bend, we came to a small creek. Didn't we then ride a short way up the creek to where there was a nice flat rock? We left the creek on that rock and then traveled on the animal path."

"Ah, you do remember. Let us try that."

When we had traveled halfway to where we would leave the lane, Rosilda informed me that we were indeed being followed. We urged our horses into a trot and were soon around the bend in the lane. Slowing the horses, we turned them down into the creek which led us away from the lane and around another bend. Because of the trees, brush, and tall ground cover, I was sure that whoever was following us could no longer see us. Since the water was very swift and tumbled quite noisily over a series of rocks on the opposite side of the lane where we had left the lane, I did not think whoever was following us could hear our movement down the creek, up out of the creek, and down the animal path.

After we had traveled quite a distance, Rosilda signaled that we should stop.

"I think we probably have lost whoever was following us. If I remember right, this animal trail will take us to the path to Tumble Falls. It will take us a bit longer this way."

"I have all day since I have no duties at the manor this day." *And I will have even less duties after my father leaves for the capital, Fyrstaborgin, since I will either be running away from home or I will be dead,* I thought. I wondered if I should let Rosila know about the conversation I had heard last night in the walled garden.

As we rode, I had time to ponder my situation. From what my father had told me and what I had overheard in the walled garden, I knew my life was in danger, and I needed a plan to get away. The more I thought about it, the more I came to the conclusion that I might not be able to do it alone. Now, I just needed to figure out who I could trust.

As we drew closer to Tumble Falls, I got the distinct feeling that we were being watched. I also noticed that Rosilda was sitting up straighter in her saddle and appeared even more watchful. Suddenly, an elderly man stepped out from the trees holding a bow nocked with an arrow.

Rosilda, who was ahead of me, halted her horse and held her hands out in front of her in a gesture of peace.

"No harm here, Elder. We have come seeking Arnar."

Just then another older man stepped out of the trees and gently placed his hand on the bowman's shoulder.

"It is all right, my friend. I know these two. Well met, Rosilda. Well met, Lady Perrin. What brings you here to our camp?"

"We came to find you, Arnar."

"Well, you've found me. Why don't both of you dismount and come sit a spell?"

We did as he asked and followed Arnar down a short path to a well-established camp. Semi-permanent shelters ringed a communal cookfire. Camp chairs were set about the cookfire, and a pot hung from a tripod over the fire. Arnar led us to the chairs and suggested we take a seat. I looked around, but I could see no one else in the camp.

"Are there others camping here besides your sentry?" I asked.

"Yes, but they are all out foraging or hunting at the moment. Again, I ask, what brings you here?"

There was a touch of something in Arnar's voice that caused me to pause before answering. I looked at Arnar. He was the same man who had patiently taught me warrior skills from the time I was young. While he looked as fit as he always had, he also looked as if he had aged. His hair had grown longer and grayer and his beard was long and bushy, no longer neatly trimmed. It was his eyes that bothered me the most, for they did not look at me with welcome, but rather with suspicion. I watched him reach out with his gnarled right hand to rub his right knee. I knew when he did that, that his old wounds were bothering him.

I took a moment to think about what I would say next. "Up until this week, I have been forbidden to leave the manor grounds. I have been stuck in the women's workroom by order of my stepmother. Once I was able to leave the grounds, I went into the village to check on Jard and find out where you had gone after you were summarily dismissed and sent packing. I am here because I wanted to see for myself that you are all right."

Arnar was silent for a long moment before he spoke. "That explains much. I had trouble believing that you were part of that group that gathers around the Laird and your stepmother. I and the others here are fine for now. Hopefully, we will have something figured out by the time the cold season comes. My hope for now is that no one at the manor decides that we are not allowed to hunt or fish in these woods, or to gather firewood."

"You should know that my father and stepmother are traveling to Fyrstaborgin in less than a fortnight. You might want to be extra vigilant once they leave."

The conversation at that point turned away from me as Arnar addressed Rosilda, and they began to talk about her recent assignment with the border guard. My mind wandered back to my need to plan what I was going to do when my father's entourage left the manor heading to the capital. The question of whether I was safer trying to go it alone or whether I should ask for help kept tumbling over and over in my head as rapidly as the water tumbled over Tumble Falls.

"Have you drifted off there, Perrin? Bored with our conversation about guarding the border?" Rosilda asked.

"No, just juggling a problem in my mind, trying to figure out what to do."

When both Rosilda and Arnar looked at me quizzically, I knew I needed to make a decision.

Chapter Six

I hesitated a moment longer, once again weighing both sides of the issue of whether or not I needed help with my escape from what would surely be an attempt on my life.

"Arnar, can we check that there is no one in the camp who might overhear our conversation?"

Arnar must have correctly read the seriousness of my request, for he stood and motioned we should follow him. He led us down a path toward Tumble Falls. When we reached the bottom of the falls, he turned left and started up a rock-strewn path that led to the top of the falls. He stopped about halfway up, stepping onto a large flat boulder.

"The sound of the falls should cover our talking. In addition, we will be able to see anyone approaching. What is it you need?"

"I am going to need help from those I can trust."

Arnar brought his left fist to his chest and bowed his head. "I am always at your call, Lady Perrin."

"As am I," stated Rosilda firmly.

I looked hard into the faces of these two who had been part of my growing up years. I was surprised by the fierceness I could see in both of their faces.

"I thank you. I am not sure where to start."

"Does this have something to do with the edict our new ruler, Prince Mallus, has put out concerning who is pure enough to hold the title of clan leader among other posts?" Rosilda inquired.

I looked at her in surprise. "Yes. It seems that my father has been trying to protect me by allowing Lady Kolbrun to shunt me aside. He had hoped that once I was basically banished from the workings of the clan, and no longer training for my rightful place in line for succession, I would be safe. His justification was that if the rule changed hands again, the new ruler might not care for his or her predecessor's rulings and might change things once again."

"Risky, but possible, the way rulers change in our country," suggested Arnar.

"Lady Kolbrun and her brother Grimur do not want to take that risk. I was in the walled garden next to the old keep and heard folks approaching. I ducked between an old tree and the corner of the wall, for I really had no desire to talk to anyone just then. I overheard Grimur and another man, whose voice I did not recognize, discussing my demise. They plan to stage some type of tragic accident about a week after my father and the rest leave for the capital."

"Clever. By the time your father got back, the tale about what happened to you would be spread across the landholding, twisting and changing with each telling so that getting to the truth would be harder," suggested Rosilda.

"That is not the biggest problem," stated Arnar. "The biggest problem is that once your father and the rest leave, you do not know when or how, not to mention who, will strike. That will be the most dangerous time."

"Unfortunately, you are both right. I am as prepared as I can be for now. I have a travel pack hidden, along with traveling clothes. I still need to gather food. But that is as far as I have gotten. I have no plan as to where to go from here, or how to get there without getting caught. I have concluded that I will need help. I would ask that of you. You have a right to say no, for what I am asking will certainly put you both in danger."

Rosilda was the first to speak up. "Loyalty to clan always comes first. The danger to our country does not always come from across our borders. Sometimes it comes from within. I stand with you and will help you."

"I was getting pretty tired of all this fancy living here at the camp so I suppose I can tear myself away from here for a while," Arnar stated. "Would feel good to be useful again."

"Now all we have to do is come up with a plan," I mused. "Arnar, I appreciate you wanting to help and would welcome it …."

"I hear an objection coming."

"No, I am just concerned that you live with others that I do not know ..."

"... and don't feel you can trust them," stated Arnar. "I understand. However, I have been known to wander off for days at a time, so it would not be unusual for me to pull on my pack, grab my walking stick, and go off on a solitary hike. I will leave just after you leave this day. I think a show of anger toward you and your visit will set the right tone that I want nothing to do with you. Your meager extremely late apology was less than sincere. Harrumph!"

I found myself smiling. Arnar had always taught me that misdirection was a helpful strategy. I could just see him throwing suspicion away from himself by stomping away from the camp, angry.

"And what of you, Rosilda? You need to return to your post with the border guard, do you not?"

"Actually, I don't. My time with the border guard has been served. I returned home to gather up what little was left of mine from my mother's cottage, now that she has remarried. I have not decided what I want to do next, so I too can leave at any time. And I think you should be prepared to leave the night of the day your father leaves, since you do not know how or when your deadly accident might occur," Rosilda stated.

"Wouldn't Grimur be forced to send someone after my father right away?"

"Not necessarily. Since you are not really a part of what is going on in the manor, many might not even know you are missing. In addition, if someone inquired as to where you might be, Grimur could suggest you had gone to visit someone, or were out riding, or ...."

"Hum-m-m, that is true. They could cover up for my not being there for a while. Then they could make up some sort of tale about my unfortunate tragic accident. It could be horrible enough that they would bury me right away."

"I agree with Rosilda. The night of the day your father leaves would be the best time for you to leave. It would certainly be unexpected by Grimur. Besides, he and others involved in this plot might not even know you are missing for several days. You will not be able to count on that though. However, the search for you would have to be very discreet," suggested Arnar.

"I agree on when to leave. What both of you have said about leaving the night my father leaves makes sense. The next question that needs answering is where do I go?"

"I have a thought," answered Arnar. "Why not head to the country your mother came from?"

I was quiet for a long time. It had not occurred to me to head south to the country of my mother's birth. Rosilda interrupted my musing.

"Your mother was from Sommerhjem, was she not?"

"Yes, at least I think so. My father did not talk much about my mother's past. I only know that she was from beyond our southern border."

"The idea of heading to Sommerhjem might just work. We could head to the border town of Høyhauger. The main southern pass into Sommerhjem is there," stated Arnar.

"Both of you could head that way and no one would question you on the road. Someone might recognize me."

"True, but you could travel as a border guard and folks might not give you a second glance," said Rosilda.

"And just how might I do that?"

"As I said, one of the reasons I came back to Nytt Heimili, besides to see my family, was to clean out some of my belonging I had stored at my mother's cottage. I have not gotten around to that yet, thankfully. I know there is my first border guard uniform in a trunk I stored under the eaves. It will certainly fit you."

"Hum-m-m, that might work. For folks might not even give two border guards a passing glance. Only one problem. I do not have a horse, nor do I think taking one from the manor's stables would be a good idea."

"Maybe folks would not give a passing glance at three border guards traveling together. I still fit my border guard uniform, which I still have," stated Arnar. "In addition, while my two horses are old, they still have a few long travels left in them. I have them pastured at Elder Nambia's cottage."

I asked if they were both sure they wanted to help me. Both said that they were. We agreed that we would attempt to meet up at the site of the broken mill several miles south of the manor on the night that my father and his group left for the capital. By Arnar's calculation, it would be a waning full moon night, so we would have some light to travel by. They would wait all night for me. I told them I would try to leave about an hour after full dark and meet them there. Meanwhile, I would try to gather travel food and, if they would each do the same, we would have enough supplies that we could stick to the back ways if we needed to.

On the ride back to the manor and before we parted, I gave Rosilda some of the coin my father had left me. I told her to buy any supplies she thought we might need. I suggested to Rosilda that we continue to ride each day while Lady Markham was still away.

"Only this time when we ride, we need to let whoever is following us be able to follow us."

Rosilda gave me a questioning look.

"They can then report back where we go and who we see. I still want to see some of the crofters, check back in with Jard, and visit Elder Nambi again. Some days we could just ride leisurely about the landholding. Just very innocent, expected trips away from the manor to give the impression that I am totally oblivious to their plot to kill me. I also suggest once Lady Markham returns, and I am stuck in the women's workroom once again, that we not meet again before you leave, unless something comes up that would cause a change to our plans."

"I agree. I will say goodbye to my family several days before the day your father and his party leave. I will find a safe place to wait. I have learned how to stay undetected and am good at it. The night we are to meet, I will await you at the old, ruined mill along with Arnar."

Rosilda and I parted ways at the gate to the manor. I slowly rode to the stable, dismounted, and left my horse with the stable lass. I decided not to go inside right away. I wanted to wander the grounds. I was in a very melancholy mood.

In a short time, I would leave this place, my home, and all that was familiar, perhaps never to return. As I wandered through the gardens, I tried to breath in the scents of spring flowers and damp earth. I wandered the orchards, knowing I was going to miss the colorful bloom of the apple blossoms and other fruit trees, which made me think of fall and the fall harvest smells. I wondered where I would be in the fall. Hunger finally sent me back to the manor. I decided I would be better off filling my stomach with food than to continue filling my mind with sad and fretful thoughts.

The next morning, Rosilda and I took a leisurely ride to check out the northern spring plantings. From time to time on our wanderings through the countryside, either Rosilda or I would spot what appeared to be someone tailing us.

When we stopped beside a stream to rest and water the horses, Rosilda remarked that this day's tail was better than the one yesterday. I suggested we go a bit farther along this lane and then find a high meadow to stop at and have our lunch. That way we would have a good view if someone tried to approach.

Once we had settled into our lunch spot, I asked Rosilda what, if anything, she had told her family.

"I told them I was not sure where my life was taking me. I was not sure I wanted to stay at the landholding, or whether I wanted to see what else was out there in this country of ours. Since I had saved all my pay from my time with the border guard, I do not need to decide right away. I also told them that I was getting restless and would probably be off on a walkabout fairly soon, once you no longer needed an escort."

"Thank you so much for reminding me that Lady Markham, the supreme ruler of the women's workroom, will be returning soon."

"You are so very welcome, m'Lady," Rosilda said with a mock bow. "On a more serious note, I have had good success with gathering the supplies we need for travel. I left my young nephew this morning with the task of tending to the smoking of meat jerky. Hopefully, there will be some left when I get back. Knowing him, he will tell me that some fell in the fire and was no good and other strips needed to be tested to make sure they were curing properly. He is a bit of a scamp with two hollow legs."

It struck me at that moment how extremely complicated life can be. Here I was having a lunch in a spring meadow with an old friend talking about her nephew, the rascal, all the while being on the lookout for someone who had been tailing us and could cause both of us harm. I was sitting here talking about normal goings on, all the while knowing that my very existence was in peril. I decided to just lean back and soak up the bright sunlight, listen to the bird song and the buzz of insects, and try to relax for a moment. Rosilda and I remained quiet for a time before I suggested we move on.

The days passed too quickly, and all too soon Lady Markham returned, and the days were again filled with tedium in the women's workroom. I missed my daily rides with Rosilda. I missed the freedom I had had.

Finally, the day arrived for the departure of my father and the group heading to the capital with him. I had gone to stand on the manor front terrace to see him off. He did not approach me or even wave farewell. I knew he was just ignoring me to try to keep me unnoticed and safe. It hurt none the less, for were it not for Prince Mallus and his new ruling, I would have been traveling with him to the capital, as would be proper for the heir to the laird of our clan.

After the entourage had all passed through the manor gates, I turned and reentered the manor. I knew I needed to stick to routine so no one would suspect that I planned to leave this night. I needed to be extra vigilant and careful during the time between now and full dark.

Chapter Seven

Not wanting to raise the suspicion of anyone who might be watching my actions, I headed to the women's workroom to try to survive another day of tedium, other than the continual removal of the cats. Lately there seemed to be more of them, and so, Lady Markham interrupted our demure conversations and her constant scolding of my work or appearance with more frequent removal of the cats. It was hard not to laugh.

Finally, it was time to leave. I took my time walking back toward my room. I changed into old clothing, which I would be discarding once I met up with Rosilda and Arnar and put on the border guard uniform. I left my room quietly and slipped down a hidden servant's stair, carefully making my way to the great room in the old keep. I really did not want to take any chance of being caught or delayed for any reason. Fortunately, I met no one along the way and arrived safely at my sleeping cupboard. I quickly crawled inside. I tipped the hourglass over and settled in to wait out the five hours to full dark. I was not at all surprised when the brown-striped cat appeared and settled in next to me.

"Well now," I whispered, "are you thinking of coming along on my upcoming adventure?" The cat did not answer.

Really looking at the cat, I realized that this brown-striped cat was the cat that always joined me in the sleeping cupboard. He had very green eyes and a distinctive ringed tail. In addition, his dark stripes were unbroken, and the very tips of his fur and his whiskers were cream or silver. It was difficult to tell in the light of the glow lamp. The more I looked at him, I began to remember other places I had seen him nearby. He always showed up in the women's workroom. I had noticed him there because he was a third larger than the other manor cats. He was also the cat I had followed from the walled garden. Interesting. I did not really know what to make of it.

Since I had hours to wait, I checked through my pack one more time. I also tightened the knot on the satchel of supplies that I had gathered over the last few weeks. It was mostly dried travel food that would not spoil. I hoped no one had noticed me taking things here and there.

Time seemed to crawl along very slowly. I was tempted to shake the hourglass, thinking something must have clogged it up so the right amount of sand was not falling. I restrained myself. Finally, I opened my pack and pulled out a small bundle wrapped in a waterproof cloth. I debated opening the bundle and then decided against doing so. Carefully I placed the bundle back into my pack. I hoped that at some point, I would have a chance to spend time deciphering what was written within.

One day on our ride about the landholding, Rosilda and I had stopped once again at Elder Nambi's cottage. She had informed me that more and more of the villagers were beginning to seek her out. In addition, she had taken on an apprentice. She then motioned me to follow her to the stillhouse. Rosilda had stayed behind with the horses, saying she needed to check a back hoof on her horse.

"I found something in the boxes that you had sent over from the stillhouse at the manor. It was in a box that contained neat rows of crocks of horse liniment. I think the woman you called Nona might have hidden away what I found, and fortunately, that scoundrel Grimur did not discover it."

"What was it?"

"It looks to be a journal. It is written in a language I am unfamiliar with. I suspect it might have belonged to your mother. I was hopin' you would come by so's I could give it to you."

"I wonder, if the book was my mother's, why did Nona not give it to me herself?"

"My feelin', lass, is that Nona may have wanted to, but was waitin' to see which way the wind was goin' to blow upon the arrival of Lady Kolbrun. Or she may have thought to give it to you when you were older. We may never know. Here, let me fetch it."

The book was leather bound with a leather strap around it to keep it closed. It was a book that looked well worn, scratched, and stained on the cover. When I heard Rosilda approaching, I quickly tucked the book into the cloth bag Elder Nambi handed me, saying, "Now you take those two pots o' liniment to the marshal. He'll be needin' 'em now as spring has arrived."

Later that evening, I had taken a closer look at the book. I decided I needed to wrap it in some waterproof cloth and tuck it in my pack so it would not be harmed more than it already had been. I just did not have the heart to look at it with all that was going on. I hoped I had not made a mistake and would have a chance to figure out what was written in the book once I found a place of safety, far from here.

I had just tipped the hourglass over for the fourth time, when I heard loud voices that sounded like they were coming from the opposite end of the great hall. I leaned closer to the cupboard doors to be able to hear better.

"Spread out. Check all the nooks and crannies. She has to be somewhere."

I had to stifle a laugh, for I had always found the phrase "it has to be somewhere" ridiculous because of course something must be somewhere. For something really cannot be nowhere. Sobering up, I continued to listen, hoping whoever was out there did not know about the sleeping cupboards. If they did, I would be trapped.

"There's no one here, sire."

"Did you check the fireplaces?"

I could hear the sound of running footsteps. Moments later, a voice called that the fireplaces hid nothing but ash and bat droppings.

"Where could she have gone? I have had all of the exits from the manor watched ever since the Laird's party left. Even the small side one from this hall. Perrin could not have left the manor."

A small trickle of dread crept over me. I had hoped they would not notice I was missing until several days hence. Apparently not, and I do not think this search for me was because of an overly large amount of love or concern for my wellbeing. A small part of me was surprised that they were looking for me at all, this close to the time my father had left.

"We have systematically searched this manor from top to bottom with no sign of her. What are we missing? You, go up on the balcony and check if there are any hidden nooks or secret stairs up there. You two, go and tap on the wooden walls on this level. Sometimes in these old keeps, they had storage areas and sleeping cupboards built into the side walls."

I could feel the panic rise up within me. If they discovered the sleeping cupboards, it would take them very little time to find the one I was in. Though I had it locked from the inside, it would not take much effort for them to find something to pry it open with. I was trapped. I held my breath, hoping against hope that they would either not find that there were sleeping cupboards built into the side walls, or not find how to open them. Unfortunately, they discovered both.

"Sire, you were right. It looks like the side wall here does indeed contain sleeping cupboards. I have found one."

"Well, do not just stand there, see if there are more. You by the fireplace, go check the other side."

I was so intent listening to the men make their way towards my end of the great hall, so frozen in place, that at first, I did not feel the brown-striped cat pawing at me.

"I am sorry, I cannot open the door and let you out," I whispered to the cat.

He then headbutted me and turned, walking toward the back wall at the foot of the bed. I turned back to listen and heard one of the searchers open the door of the cupboard next to the one I was in.

"Sire, come look."

"What have you found?"

"Small piles of clothes and things."

"Hers?"

"Donna know. Belong ta a female."

I could hear someone walking swiftly toward the cupboard next to mine. I was kicking myself for not getting rid of what I had left behind, not that that would have made a difference once they discovered the sleeping cupboards. Maybe they would think I had been in that cupboard and not try to open the one I was inside.

"Check if there is one more cupboard beyond that one," the voice I now recognized as Grimur's said.

I held my breath, hoping the wooden bar would hold. It did.

"There's another cupboard here. Either stuck or something else is keeping it closed."

"Well, you, run and get an axe."

Now what was I to do? I certainly did not think it was going to bode well for me to open the cupboard doors and step out. Having an axe swing at the door with me right behind it also did not feel safe. I quickly scooted back. The cat came to me, pawed at me, and gave me a headbutt. Then the cat put his paw on my arm and pulled. I turned to look as the cat walked to the end of the cupboard and slipped through a crack where the cupboard and the back wall met.

I quickly and quietly scrambled to where the cat had disappeared. The crack ran from about eight inches above the mattress to the top of the cupboard and was wide enough for me to put my hand in. I could feel cool air flowing from the other side. I reached my hand around the wood and pulled. A panel swung inward toward me, but stopped, caught against my pack. I moved my pack and my satchel of supplies behind me, scooted back a bit myself, and pulled again. What was before me was an opening. I grabbed the glow lamp and thrust it into the opening. I realized I was looking at what must have been a storage cubby. It would certainly be big enough for me and my gear.

As quickly as I could, I grabbed my pack and set it inside the cubby, followed by my satchel of supplies. After that, I crawled through the opening and lifted the glow lamp overhead to see back into the sleeping cupboard to make sure I had not left anything behind. I realized I had left the hourglass, so I snatched it up. Then there was nothing left, for I had removed the covers and linens earlier and left them rolled up in the cupboard where I had left my discarded possessions.

Taking a deep breath, I made a decision that was either going to get me caught or allow me to escape undetected. Just as I quietly partially reentered the sleeping cupboard, I heard Grimur holler at the servant to hurry up with the axe. I reached out and silently lifted the wooden bar off the metal brackets and then retreated into the opening, closing the panel behind me. In the soft glow of the lamp, I could see that there was not a bar that could be swung down across a bracket, effectively locking the panel from my side.

I heard the muffled sound of an axe hitting the sleeping cupboard door and then one of the men exclaimed, "The door musta been stuck, sire." A moment later the man announced, "There's nothin' inside."

Just as a precaution, I began to back toward the back stone wall of the cubby. I had almost reached the stone wall when I heard a sound behind me. It was a soft mer-reef. I had forgotten all about the cat. It was then that I realized that I had not seen the cat when I had held the glow lamp up to see into the cubby before I entered it. Where had the cat been?

Suddenly I had more to worry about, for I heard Grimur tell the servant to climb into the sleeping cupboard. I scooted even farther back until my back was pressed to the stone wall, which to my great surprise moved. I quickly shifted so I could see that the wall behind me had swung partly open. When I pushed on the wall, it created an opening that I could go through. I quickly cracked open the glow lamp and swung it through the opening. How had no one ever even suggested that there was a stairway leading down from a sleeping cupboard? I did not know where it went. I did not care.

"Did you find anything?" I heard Grimur say.

I did not wait around to hear more. I placed my pack on my back, hung the glow lamp off the shoulder strap of my pack, grabbed up the hour glass and my supply satchel, and carefully started down the stairs. Turning around, I pushed the stone wall closed. I heard a click which I hoped meant that the wall had locked behind me. I had no idea where the stairs would lead me. I just knew that for now, I had escaped the hunt for me, at least temporarily.

I took a moment to readjust my possessions. I unhooked the glow lamp and set it on the step behind me. I placed the strap of my satchel over my head and across my chest. After putting the hourglass into my pack, I put the pack on and adjusted the straps. Picking my glow lamp up, I started down the stair steps, following the brown-striped cat.

CHAPTER EIGHT

I could only hope that my glow lamp did not dim on me, for there was no other light in the narrow stairwell. I had just enough light to see several steps down, and that was all. I noticed the brown-striped cat was traveling down the steps at the same speed as I was and staying just at the edge of the light given off by the glow lamp.

The steps only went down about eight or so feet before I hit a narrow level corridor, which only allowed me to turn right. I felt at this point, after turning right, I must be walking parallel to the sleeping cupboards. After walking a short way, I thought I could smell green growing things and rain. In the light of the glow lamp, I saw a slightly damp spot on the floor. I stopped, stooped down, and reached out. I moved my hand near to what I thought might be the opening in the keep wall that I had noticed the brown-striped cat disappear into the day I talked to my father. I could feel cold damp air on my hand.

As I moved on, I was glad the glow lamp continued to give off a soft light, for the narrow corridor I was walking down did not stay level. Every twenty feet or so, there would be stairs leading down eight or ten more feet. After descending several more times, I came to a branch in the narrow corridor. I could either move straight ahead or turn to the right. The brown-striped cat stood several feet ahead of me in the corridor that went straight ahead. I was also surprised to see he had been joined by several more cats.

I surmised that I was at the end of the great hall, and if that were true, if I turned right, I would be heading under the fireplace. If I walked in the direction of the cats, I would be under the manor grounds. When the cats turned tail, I followed them. It was as good a choice as any.

As I walked, I noticed the corridor was no longer made of blocks of stone. Rather it was carved out of bedrock and became a tunnel, which was narrower and lower than the corridor I had previously been walking down. I wondered how old this tunnel was. I hoped it had not collapsed somewhere ahead. The cats seemed to know where they were going. That did not, however, necessarily mean that I could go where they went. I was also fearful that the tunnel might lead to an opening that would expose me to anyone who might be looking for me.

If I had figured out the direction I was heading right, we were on our way toward the river that ran at the edge of the manor grounds. I could only hope that I came out in the large grove of ancient trees rather than somewhere on the groomed grounds. Coming out among the trees seemed reasonable to me. I would think if the exit to this tunnel were on the groomed grounds, it would have been found and known. Added to my worries of collapsed tunnels or exiting in full view of those who were looking for me was the fact that my glow lamp was beginning to dim. I picked up my pace.

I had only gone a little way when I heard something behind me. Turning around, holding the glow lamp aloft, I saw dozens of glowing eyes. It took a scary moment or two to realize I was looking at a gathering of cats. I knew there were always cats around in the manor, on the grounds, and at the stables. I had never seen this many all in one place. One stepped forward, and I recognized her as the cat Nona had named Thistle, for she was prickly with most everyone except Nona. I had always seen Thistle in or around the stillhouse. I felt ashamed that I had not looked for her after Grimur had taken over the stillhouse.

"Thistle?" I whispered softly. She came forward, rubbed against my legs and then went forward to join the cats up ahead. The rest followed. I do not think the scene ahead of me would even be believable in a tall tale told by the traveling taletellers. I was being led through a previously unknown tunnel, heading to who knew where, by a clowder of cats.

A short while later, I began to hear the sound of water running and to smell greenery. I noticed that the temperature in the tunnel had also begun to drop. I quickly closed the glow lamp down so that it only let out a very small amount of light. I began to shuffle forward. The sound of running water became louder. I crept forward until I came up against a small opening that was covered with vines. The cats had all disappeared.

I pulled a few of the vines apart and found I could see out. I was looking at the river flowing by. I knew where I was. The tunnel I had followed the cats through ended at the river under the bridge. How clever, I thought. As long as I could remember, vines had grown up all over the bridge to the point it was hard see the stone underneath. I realized in the thin sliver of light from the glow lamp that there was a door that could be swung closed to cover the opening into the tunnel I was in. From the looks of the hinges, it had not been closed in a very long time.

After closing the glow lamp, I moved a bit more of the vines, enough so I could see better. The rain had stopped, and I could see moon sparkles dancing off the fast-flowing water. I realized that the tunnel opening just under the bottom of the arched bridge was above the high-water line and left me with a bit of a drop down to the edge of the river. I guessed the cats had jumped. When I looked down, I could see them milling around below me.

I took the time to reach into my satchel and pull out the coil of thin rope I had placed on top. I had enough length to lower my satchel down, then my pack, and finally the closed glow lamp. Dropping the rope down after the glow lamp, I followed. It was not difficult to climb down the vines, for they were thick and sturdy. Once I reached the riverbank, I recoiled my rope and put it back in the satchel. I packed the glow lamp in my pack after removing my cloak, for the air had grown cold.

Now that I knew where I was, I just needed to follow the river several miles downstream to the old broken-down mill. The problem was that the mill was on the other side of the river, which meant I either had to cross this bridge or I would have to cross the river near the mill. The first option would expose me if someone was watching the bridge. The second option would have me swimming in the icy river, which was flowing quite fast due to the recent rain. Before I could move, I heard voices coming from overhead.

"Well, at least it's stopped rainin'. Donna knows how longs we's supposed to stay watchin' this bridge. What are we watchin' for anyway?"

"Dinna tell me. Just says we's supposed ta stop anyone from crossin' and bring 'ems to that Grimur fella."

"So we's just stuck here?"

"Seems so."

"May's well settle in."

I knew I could not cross the bridge with those two up there guarding it. I also was reluctant to move out from under the bridge, for there was no cover on this side of the river near the bridge. If I tried to swim across the river here, I would have trouble doing so with the backpack and the satchel. I knew I would have that problem further downstream also. I was loath to have to give up what I had so carefully packed.

My thoughts were interrupted when one of the cats nudged my boot. I looked down just as the brown-striped cat jumped up on my shoulder and launched himself onto a decorative arch that was under the bottom of the bridge. He made his way across the arch to the other side of the river and looked back at me before jumping off onto the bank on the other side. A number of other cats followed him.

I took a few moments to look at the archway the cats had crossed. It was just possible that I would be able to crawl along the inside edge under the archway. The outer edge was covered with vines so I might not be noticed. I took off my cloak, for it would only get in the way, and put it back in my pack. I tightened my pack straps and made sure the satchel was knotted closed. Climbing back up the vines, I reached the under archway. It was very dark and difficult to see. I hesitated just a bit before starting off. Trying and falling, being swept away by the fast-moving river, seemed a better alternative than being taken back to the manor and delivered to Grimur.

It was very slow going, crawling practically on my stomach, inching my way across the expanse over the river, which sounded louder and faster with each passing minute. After what seemed like an hour or so, but was probably only a few minutes, I reached the other side. I could not reach the riverbank fast enough. Now that I was on the other side of the river, there was more cover, and yet, I was hesitant to move out from under the cover of the bridge. Before I could decide what to do, I heard a shout from the top of the bridge. I froze.

"What was that?"

"What?"

"I saw movement at the other end of the bridge."

"Whadda ya see?"

"Shadows. Something low ta the ground and running."

"Come on. We'd best check it out."

I heard the sound of running feet above me and quickly moved out from under the bridge and along the riverbank, clinging to the shadows. I climbed over a tree that tilted out over the water and ducked down behind it. Looking back, I could see the two men heading back toward my side of the river, taking up their post, each leaning against the railing. Unfortunately, one was looking my way. I ducked farther down, but not so far that I could not see them. Suddenly the one on my side ran to the upstream side. The men's voices carried even over the sound of the river.

"What dida ya hear?"

"Rustlin' over there in that brush. Go down there and look."

"Why do I has ta look?"

"Cause I tolds ya ta."

I did not wait around for them to decide who was going to go check out the rustling in the brush. I suspected it was a cat or two. I was not going to question why all the cats were with me and distracting those watching me. I was just going to be grateful and move as fast as I could downstream, away from the bridge.

I had another frightening moment when my path along the riverbank brought me too close to the lane. The sound from the rapids at this point of the river had obscured the sound of several horses until they were almost upon me. I ducked down behind what meager cover there was, hoping the riders neither stopped nor spotted me. I felt exposed. Suddenly, there was a weight on my back accompanied by a soft purr. Then another, and another, plus a cat just plopped itself down in front of my head. A dark cat tail flipped in front of my nose, making my nose itch. If I were going to blend into my surroundings by being covered in cat fur, I could only hope that none of the cats on my back were white or cream colored. In addition, I hoped the cat's fur did not make me sneeze and give me away.

Unfortunately for me, the riders chose that moment in time to slow their horses, stop, and dismount.

"It feels good to stand and stretch for a moment. I think we should head back. It is going to rain again soon, and quite frankly, I cannot imagine that Lady Perrin would have come this way. She normally rides toward the village or heads out to visit the crofters."

"There is something off about this whole idea that Lady Perrin rode off alone late afternoon and didn't return. I thought she was not allowed to ride off unescorted."

"I wondered about that myself. She had been escorted by the border guard Rosilda who left several days ago."

Just then a ginger-colored cat who had been hunkered down under a bush by the side of the lane, streaked out, ran right past the nose of one of the horses who was munching grass. The cat's sudden appearance startled the horse who lifted his head and pulled the reins out of his rider's hand. The rider quickly caught the reins and calmed the horse down.

"What is it with all the cats this night? It seems like every cat that lives in Nytt Heimili is out on the prowl. Let's head back. I have had enough of this. Besides, it is starting to mist, and soon it will rain. Maybe if it rains, the cats will all go back to where they belong."

After that narrow escape, I picked up my pace as much as I could, considering clouds were flying by covering the moon momentarily and then moving on. It was very disconcerting to have light one moment and dark shadows the next.

I finally drew close to the old mill. I slowly crawled up the bank, a few feet at a time, stopping to listen. I halted my forward movement when I saw a dark figure move near the broken-down water wheel. Just then, the moon moved out from behind a dense cloud and lit up the landscape. I let go of the breath I did not know I had been holding when I recognized the dark figure was Arnar. Still, I held my place. As I watched, to my astonishment, first one cat and then another cat, and then more the cats who were still accompanying me, left the shadows and walked toward Arnar, except for the brown-striped cat.

As the two of us continued to watch, I saw Arnar motion for someone else to step out of the shadow of the old mill. It was Rosilda. I could not hear what they were saying. Arnar was pointing at the line of cats who walked past him and into the ruins of the old mill. I was distracted when I heard the rumble of thunder, and it sounded closer than it had only moments ago. The storm was approaching fast. The cats had the right idea since they were seeking shelter. It was time to move.

Still hugging the shadows, I made the five-note whistle call of the flautfugl, an uncommon bird in Bortfjell. I was answered back. Arnar would not have answered back if it were not safe to move up to the mill. I stood up and quickly closed the distance between us. I saw both Arnar and Rosilda move ahead of me into the mill ruins.

Once I entered the mill ruins, I was greeted by Arnar and Rosilda. Rosilda handed me two large saddlebags and led me to where the horses were standing.

"Head behind that crumbling wall behind you. You can just see it by the dim light of the glow lamp. Arnar will keep watch outside and signal us if we need to close down the light. Empty your pack into the saddlebags. We will strap your satchel, empty backpack, and blanket roll across the back of the horse. Here are the clothes you need to change into. Cloak and rain gear are included. We need to travel while it is raining and put as much distance from here as possible. The rain will cover our tracks, wash away any scent, and confuse any tracking dogs they might send out to find you."

I did as I was told, and soon had repacked my gear, changed my clothes, and was ready to ride. Just as I was about to mount, the brown-striped cat jumped up and settled on my satchel.

"Who's your fellow traveler?" asked Rosilda.

Chapter Nine

I was not sure how to answer Rosilda. The brown-striped cat had certainly been present in my life over these last few months. A constant shadow in a way. Always appearing in the women's workroom each day, showing up in the sleeping cupboard and the walled garden. This night he had led me out of the sleeping cupboard, down the flights of stairs, through the tunnel, and showed me how to cross the river undetected. I suspected he was also the cat who had plopped in front of my face when I was hiding on the riverbank from the two riders. Before I could answer Rosilda, Arnar spoke up.

"We had best get on our way. I want to be well beyond the borders of Nytt Heimili before first light."

I nodded my agreement, not that anyone could see me in the dark, since I had closed down the glow lamp. I did not mount right away. I was trying to figure out a way of mounting my horse without knocking the brown-striped cat off. I finally made it into the saddle and settled my boots into the stirrups. I grabbed the edge of my rain cloak and lifted it to make sure I was not sitting on it, when I felt the cat settle in next to my back. I could feel his purr. It seemed, for the moment, he was intent on riding along. I wondered if he would stay on the horse once it started moving. In any case, I needed to get going. I draped my rain cloak over the back of both of us and urged my horse forward.

The rain started in earnest, slowing our travel. It was difficult to see in the rain and the dark. Our only light was during flashes of lightning which were becoming more and more frequent, and closer and closer. Of course, the advantage of traveling on a night like this was we probably would not run into anyone else on the lane. The disadvantage was we should not be out on a night like this. By first light, the only warm spot on my body was where the cat had nestled against my back.

Dismounting was easier, since the cat leapt off first. Once I was on the ground, I had to lean against the horse for a moment while I got feeling back in my legs. It had been quite a long time since I had ridden nonstop for hours. We had pulled off the lane and down a side trail in order to rest our horses and get to something to break our fast. There would be no fire, no warm tea this morn. Just a brief rest, and then back on the road.

Arnar handed me a hard biscuit and a piece of dried meat. I looked around for the cat and noticed he was getting a drink from the small trickle of water that ran down the side of the hill over some rocks. I thought there might be a spring higher up.

"So, it would seem that your traveling companion stayed with you," stated Rosilda.

"So it would seem. I do not know quite what to make of it."

"What is even more interesting than the fact that this cat is traveling with you, is what type of cat he is," suggested Arnar.

"He's just a rather large, brown-striped cat who I have seen frequently in or near the manor."

"Not so. What has been hitching a ride with you is one of the very elusive wild hill cats. They are rarely seen outside the forests of the high hills. You can tell he is a wild hill cat by his ringed tail and very thick coat. He is probably doing better in the rain than we are, for that thick coat keeps out the rain. Did you know they are also good swimmers and good hunters? Hunt mostly at dawn and dusk. And they are very quiet, and only hiss or yowl if they are in a fighting mood."

"How come you know so much about wild hill cats?"

"Spent part of my misspent youth in the high hills. Learned about them then. If he is going to continue with us, you need to find a name that suits him. You cannot just keep referring to him as the brown-striped cat. We had best mount up and be on our way. Your traveling companion is already settled in."

Before I mounted up, I set half of my dried meat by the cat. I watch his paw swiftly snatch the dried meat. As we continued down the lane heading ever south, I tried to come up with a name for the cat. The word "kipp" floated into my head and got stuck there. I had no idea if "kipp" was even a word. I just know that when I would try out another name for the cat, the word "kipp" came to the forefront of my thoughts each time.

We traveled on through the intermittent rain showers. Several hours after dawn's light, Arnar signaled we should pull down an overgrown side lane. The side lane was just two faint wagon ruts winding through scrub brush and gnarled trees. We traveled down the lane looking to find some type of shelter. Luck seemed to be riding with us, for after rounding a bend in the lane, we came upon a falling down two-story fieldstone byre-dwelling. The roof was mostly gone over the upper story living quarters. We would have to take a closer look to see if the floor between the living quarters and the area below where the farm animals had been kept was also gone.

The door to the lower level of the fieldstone byre-dwelling was hanging open. We dismounted, moved to the open doorway, and looked in. While there was water coming in through holes in the ceiling, there was a section on one side of the large open room that seemed dry. More important was the fact that the dry area was large enough to hold all four us and our horses.

"This looks like a good place to hold up for the day," suggested Rosilda. "It does not look like anyone has been here in years. Let's get the horses inside before the next heavy rain starts."

I was more than willing to follow Rosilda's suggestion. For the next little while, we were all quiet, wiping down the horses and the tack. We did not remove the saddles, saddle bags, or tack in order to be able to leave quickly if we had to. Once the chores were done, we turned to look for reasonably clean places to sit down.

"I would be happy to take first watch," I suggested to the others. "So much has happened in the last twenty-four hours. I need some time to just sit and think."

The others agreed, and I settled in close to the door so I would have a good view of anyone approaching down the lane. I set the hourglass up so I would know when my three hours were up. I settled in with my back to the stone wall, drew my cloak tighter around myself, and gave a small sigh of relief that I was sitting on something that was not moving. I think every one of my bones ached. I realized I was a bit out of shape.

The brown-striped cat came and settled in next to me, taking time to give himself a swift cleaning. He had disappeared after we had moved inside of the byre-dwelling. I guessed he had probably been hunting. Once he had finished his ablutions, he folded his paws under his body and stared alertly out the door.

"Standing guard duty with me, are you?" I whispered. "Would be glad for the company. I have been thinking. I just cannot continue to refer to you as cat, or brown-striped cat. How do you feel about the name Kipp?"

The cat swiveled his head toward me, and I would avow to anyone who might ask me that he nodded his head.

"Kipp it is then." I tentatively reached out to run my hand over Kipp's back. I was comforted at having him close. Here I was running for my life away from all that I had known. The sorrow of that loss hit me hard. I was glad that Arnar and Rosilda were asleep and could not see the tears that ran down my face. For a long moment I was overwhelmed by the enormity of the loss of my home, my family such as it was, and my position in the clan. All that I had grown up knowing about where my life was going was now gone with only the slimmest of hopes that someday I could return to my rightful place in Nytt Heimili. Sitting there feeling sorry for myself was not going to change any of the circumstances I now found myself in. I sat up straighter, readjusted my rain cloak around my shoulders, and settled in to wait out my time on watch.

We left the fieldstone byre-dwelling ruin at dusk and continued heading south toward the border town of Høyhauger. Travel was easier, for the sky had cleared and there was a bright moon lighting the way. We traveled all night without meeting anyone on the road. When dawn began to break, we again pulled off the lane, following a deer trail into a densely wooded area. We had to walk our horses until we found a sheltered glade. Before we settled in for the day, we sat down to discuss what our plans should be for the next few days.

"I think we should continue to travel by night for the next three nights," suggested Arnar. "That should get us far enough from Nytt Heimili to begin to travel by day. Once we begin to travel during daylight hours, we should continue to travel disguised as border guards."

"I am not sure traveling all the way to Bortfjell as border guards might be the wisest choice," I responded. "We might want to change our disguise along the way."

"Why do you think that?" asked Rosilda.

"I am hopeful that those who might be trying to find me think I am traveling on my own. The heavy downfall of rain will have washed away both our horses' hoof prints and our scent, so even good trackers and scent dogs will have an exceedingly difficult time finding our trail."

"I know there are some decent trackers living in Nytt Heimili, but I know of no one who raises or trains scent dogs there," suggested Arnar.

"So, as I was saying, I am hoping we got away without leaving obvious tracks. We have been lucky so far not meeting folks on the road at night. That could change at any moment. The idea of traveling as border guards when we start traveling during daylight hours is a good one. If folks are looking for me, they might not suspect that I am traveling with anyone, much less that I might be disguised as a border guard. Which brings me to my idea that once we have established ourselves as three border guards, we should then change our looks again, especially as we draw closer to Høyhauger. How fond are you of that scruffy beard, Arnar?"

Arnar gave me a mock look of disgust, while stroking his long beard before he spoke.

"Scruffy beard? Ha! I'll have you know that this magnificent beard should never be mocked. Why do you ask?"

"Because a clean-shaven older gentleman traveling with his two nieces to visit some ailing relative near Høyhauger might throw any would-be searchers off once again."

"Your idea has merit, Perrin," stated Rosilda. "Let us think on it. I will be happy to take first watch."

After more discussion the next evening, before we took to the road once again, we decided that we would follow my suggestion. The final days of traveling under the cover of darkness were uneventful. We passed quietly through a vast forested area and entered more rolling farmland before we began to travel by daylight.

It was going to be a very long day since we had already travelled all night. I was also feeling more anxious since we were now more exposed. I was glad the weather was cool, and I needed to wear my cloak. I had realized that a border guard traveling with a wild hill cat behind her was going to be noticeable. Fortunately, Kipp was content to ride snuggled up behind my back under the cloak, and so was not noticeable to those we passed on our travels.

We did not stop in any of the villages along the way and continued to camp at night rather than stay at any of the wayside inns. We avoided making a fire, for we did not want to attract the attention of fellow travelers who might wish to share our campsite.

Finally, we had traveled far enough and long enough that it was time to change out of our border guard uniforms and change into traveling clothes, which would make us indistinguishable from others on the road. I had chosen my traveling clothes carefully when I had packed my knapsack. With the possible need to flee in mind, I had chosen plain clothing, rather than finery. Though the clothing was of good make and material, it was not newly made, rather it was clothing I had had for some time.

Fortunately, our campsite the night before we were to change out of our border guard uniforms and into our traveling clothes had a clear, clean river running next to it. We decided to delay our departure the next morn so we could bathe, clean and repack our gear, and so Arnar could shave. I have to say that the river was more than a bit brisk, and Rosilda was heard to remark when she came back into the campsite that she thought that having a decidedly blue skin color due to the frigidly cold bath might make her more memorable.

I heard someone approaching out of the woods behind me when I was tying down my blanket roll on the back of my horse. When I saw a stranger approaching, I turned and set my feet ready to defend myself. It was a man of later years with graying hair pulled back and tied with a leather thong. He had a rather full mustache and was dressed in well-made traveling clothes. I was taken aback when he laughed.

"Good fighting stance. I taught you well, Perrin."

"Arnar?"

"Ayup. I know I am not quite as clean shaven as you suggested. Just couldn't do it."

"I think this look will work just fine. I have known you all my life, and I did not recognize you. Good look, by the way."

I had to admit that we all cleaned up well. We no longer looked like border guards who had been on a long march. We looked like experienced travelers who were just a bit road weary. Nothing out of the ordinary. I thought we would fit right in with the other folks traveling this road. By the time we began looking for a place to camp for the night, I was feeling less stressed. Those we had passed during the day did not seem overly curious about us. Everyone seemed to have a destination in mind and was determined to get there.

It was late afternoon when we rounded a bend in the road and came upon an odd-looking wagon. It looked more like a small cottage on wheels than a hauling wagon. It was very colorful with beautiful designs painted and carved on the sides and the trim. There was a man sitting in the driver's seat holding his horses steady. Peering out the backdoor of the wagon was the frightened face of a young lad. Surrounding the wagon were three dismounted riders who were shouting rude comments at the folks in the wagon. The mounted rider looked to be about to grab the reins of the wagon's horses. Two of the other three were spread out along one side of the wagon with their hands placed on the side wall and were starting to rock the wagon. The third man had a long sturdy tree branch partly under the wagon and was using it as a lever. It looked like they either intended to shake up what was inside the wagon or simply push it over.

When the riders saw us approaching, one of them yelled at us. "Just move along folks. Nothin' to see here. We's just lettin' this foreigner know that he and his donna belong here. They's need to leave our land. We's just gonna give them a little lesson so's they's never come back."

Without taking time to stop and think, I urged my horse forward.

Chapter Ten

In that moment when I urged my horse forward, the sadness that had been riding with me since I had left Nytt Heimili turned to rage. Just with the stroke of a pen on a declaration, Prince Mallus had not only changed my life, but he had also given permission to these four to prey on any folks they deemed foreigners.

I reached the wagon, slid off my horse, and had the long sturdy tree branch out of the man's hands and out from under the wagon before he could register that I was by his side. When he took a swing at me, I blocked it as Arnar had taught me, and then I swept the legs out from under the man. He went down with a thud, knocking the wind out of him. I turned toward the next man, only to find he was also on the ground, and Rosilda was hovering over him. The second man who had been pushing at the wagon's side had retreated all the way to his horse and was mounting. The man who had been reaching for the wagon horses' reins was backing his horse away from Arnar, arms out in the gesture of peace.

"Hey, hey, sir. No calls for fightin', ya know. We's was only tryin' ta put a little scare in these folks. Just tryin' ta scurry thems along ta the border. Youse wants ta take over, we's gots no problems with that. I's just collect my mens and leave."

Just as I was about to speak, Arnar held up a hand and addressed the men. In a voice that was as cold as ice, Arnar said, "Now why would you be stopping and hassling this rover family? It is obvious that they are already heading south, most probably heading to Sommerhjem for the spring markets. What you were doing was not showing them anything but misguided cruelty and, if you had succeeded in tipping their homewagon over, you would have delayed them from leaving the country rather than getting them to scurry on. Now go on, get, before I turn my nieces back on all of you."

I had to put my hand over my mouth to cover a pretend cough as I watched the two unmounted men run to their horses and ride away. One almost made it onto his saddle before the horse took off, leaving him draped over his saddle. Another had one foot in the stirrup and was holding on to the front of his saddle for dear life when his horse took off. It was quite entertaining. I was distracted from the amusing sight when Arnar called my attention back to the matters at hand.

"Are all of you all right?" Arnar asked, directing his comment to Rosilda and me in addition to the driver of the homewagon. Rosilda and I acknowledged that we were fine.

"I think so," said the homewagon driver. "Thank you for intervening. Let me quick check on my son and my mother."

"Well, four against two and a half didn't seem quite fair."

"Who's the half? Me or Amma?" asked the lad who I had seen earlier. There was a decided look of mischief about him.

"Probably you, son. Pardon my manners. I am the rover Wright and this young rascal in my son, Lakyle. The woman Lakyle calls Amma is my mother and Lakyle's grandmother. Her name is Burle. Again, I do not know how we can thank you."

"There is no need for thanks. We were just glad to be of service," Arnar stated, moving to change the subject. "So, what brought you to Bortfjell?"

I was glad Arnar had changed the subject before we had to introduce ourselves. We had not discussed what we would call ourselves if asked. I did not think that giving our real names at this point would be a wise idea, since we had gone to so much trouble to get this far undetected.

"I am a woodcarver by trade," stated Wright. "Merchant Handelsmann, a wealthy merchant here, saw my work and commissioned my sister and me to do the woodcarvings on her summer house trim and some of the interior wood such as the mantle piece and doors. It was a fine commission for the cold months, but now it is time to head back to Sommerhjem."

"Your sister? Is she with you also?" I asked.

"No, when we heard that the new ruler of Bortfjell was neither particularly fond of nor kind to those not from Bortfjell, my wife," our young daughter, my sister, and her husband packed up my sister's homewagon and left several weeks ago. Hopefully, they did not run into any trouble. We are supposed to meet them about two days' ride across the border into Sommerhjem."

"Why don't we ride with you a while? Just to make sure those men do not return," suggested Rosilda. "I am called Brina. I will let the others introduce themselves."

Taking our cue from Rosilda, I told the rover family that my name was Milva, and Arnar introduced himself as Raxit. Before I could mount my horse, Lakyle spoke up.

"You have a cat on your horse."

"Why so I do. I apologize for forgetting to introduce the fourth member of our group. This is Kipp. He has chosen to travel with me for a while. I noticed that you and your father speak the language of Bortfjell very well."

"Aye, my uncle and others of our family have worked here during the cold months on commissions before. My father got the commission from Merchant Handelsmann very early last spring. Knowing we would be traveling here late fall, my father asked my uncle who knows your language to teach us. If you are traveling to Sommerhjem, do you speak our language?"

"When I was young, I was taught your language by an old, retired border guard. I will admit I am a bit rusty. Perhaps if we continue to travel together, you will talk to me in your language so I will be less rusty."

Before Lakyle could give me an answer, his father admonished him to climb into what they called a homewagon. "Get in and close the door now, Lakyle. The shadows are growing long, and the air is cooling down. We have lost time, so we had best get moving. Mayhap, Milva will tell you more about Kipp when we stop somewhere up ahead."

Wright gave a snap to the reins, and his horses began moving. Arnar, Rosilda, and I saddled up and followed behind. While we might have been able to travel faster on our own, I saw the wisdom of traveling with the rovers. We were now a party of seven, counting Kipp. It is not unusual for folks traveling along the major roadways in Bortfjell to travel in groups or caravans. Safety in numbers. If anyone picked up our trail, I hoped our joining the rover family would confuse them.

As we rode, Arnar, Rosilda, and I talked about what we should do next. Should we ride on with the rovers? Should we only go a little way and then ride ahead of them, putting distance between us? Or was it time to change tactics? We talked about whether it would be more beneficial for us to become the folks we had introduced to the rovers and stick with them. We decided we had hidden and confused our trail as well as we could. Now, since we were drawing closer to Høyhauger, no matter how hard we tried, we were going to have to come out of hiding. We decided to ask the rover family if we could continue to travel with them toward Sommerhjem. We would have to give them some reason for why we were heading there. We decided to share a bit of the truth and hoped for their discretion. They could then make a choice if they wanted us with them.

Several hours before dusk, Wright stopped the homewagon and stepped down. We also stopped and dismounted from our horses. It was nice to stretch.

"About an hour's ride from here is a wayside next to a spring. It is a bit off the road and sheltered. I am hopeful that we will not meet any hostility there this night."

"We were wondering if we might camp with you this night, and on the morrow continue to travel with you toward Sommerhjem. Before you answer, you need to know why we are heading there. My mother's folk may have been from there. No one thought very much about it until Prince Mallus began his campaign against foreign born folk. It became quite uncomfortable for me on our landholding. It began to feel unsafe. Some of the folks back home threatened to chase me all the way to the border and do me harm. We have covered our tracks as best we could. However, know that us joining you might draw danger to your doorstep."

"What of the other two who travel with you?" Wright asked.

"Our Laird declared that I was too old and unfit to remain at the barracks where I have been living. That left me with no place to be except a summer camp in the forested hills with others who had also been summarily dismissed from service. One last adventure seemed a better choice than staying there," Arnar stated frankly.

"I just finished my service as a border guard and really do not know what I want to do next. Milva and I have been friends since childhood, so I decided to travel with her for a while," said Rosilda.

"Please talk over what we have told you with your family and let us know your answer when we get to the turn off for the wayside," I suggested.

Wright nodded his head and climbed back onto the driver's seat of his homewagon. When we arrived at the turn off for the wayside, he gave us his answer.

"We have talked over what you said and asked. We have decided it is probably in our and your best interest for us to continue to travel together. After the incident yesterday, we decided we are already traveling a dangerous road, and that we can help each other out. Will that suit?"

"It will suit us fine. Now what can we do to set up camp? Raxit is actually the better cook amongst the three of us. We have mostly travel rations, but we would be glad to share. Brina and I would be happy to forage for firewood and any spring greens we can find."

"Any help would be gratefully accepted."

We turned down the lane and traveled the short distance to the wayside. There was one other wagon there. The couple who was sitting by the cookfire hailed us and asked us to join them.

"Finished dinner, we have, but yer welcome to the fire," the woman called. "Headin' in to sleep soon. Leavin' at the crack of dawn. Have a ways to travel on the morrow so as we can get home. Been visitin' our daughter. Have a new grandson, don't yer know."

Wright answered that we would be glad to take them up on their offer of the cookfire. He asked where home was, and they told him. I knew of the town. They would be heading back in the direction we had come from.

"Be glad to be home. Just as I am sure you are anxious to be heading back to Sommerhjem. Donna like what's goin' on, no, I donna. Never heard of such a thing as this nonsense that our new ruler and his like are spreading about that foreigners are dangerous," the man stated. "We've seen small groups the looks of which I would not want to meet in a dark alley, asking us if we've seen any foreigners. You folks had any trouble?"

"Now, you hush, ol' man. Donna know who might be listenin'. Donna want to get us in trouble," the woman admonished her husband.

Not deterred, the man went on. "And then there were those two, that man and woman, who was askin' about some poor gel they says wandered off … where was that from … oh yes, that landholdin', Nytt Heimili. If I had someone likes thems two lookin' for me, I would wander off too."

I hope I schooled my face well enough and did not give anything away, when I heard that the search for me had reached this far. I would need to be the least interactive with these folks. Keeping my head down, I led my horse to the line we had tied between two trees and tied my horse's reins to it. I heard Rosilda come up behind me.

"Are you all right?"

"Just a little shaken up. I think I will just slide into the shadows, so these folks do not get too good a look at me. Stretching out the duties of taking care of the horses and gathering wood and edibles in the forest until near dark, in addition to putting my hood up to keep off the night's chill will also help. I just hope they did not notice Kipp."

I realized now that I had mentioned Kipp, I was not aware of where the wild hill cat had gone.

"I saw him drop down off your horse just before we entered the campsite. He was next to the lane one moment and disappeared the next. With his coloring, he blends into the woods quite easily."

"I guess I have been surprised he has traveled with us for all this time. I've gotten used to him being behind me when we ride."

Rosilda must have heard the sadness and longing in my voice, for she quickly said, "Now don't you go getting all weepy and sentimental, and don't you go giving up on Kipp."

"Right, no more foolishness. Arnar did not train me all those years to be a whiney, sniveling, soft-hearted ...."

"Enough. Go gather wood. Look for some early mushrooms. I will finish with the horses."

I left the horses in Rosilda's hands and wandered off into a nearby grove of trees. As I gathered wood, I tried to spot the mushrooms she had mentioned. I had good luck finding plenty of dry wood and no luck finding the mushrooms. I was just about to enter the campsite when I heard loud voices. I set the firewood I was carrying down and crept forward, sticking to the shadows, and hiding behind a tree.

"You filthy rovers need to pack your things and move on. You're not welcome here."

In a very reasonable calm voice, Arnar spoke up. "Think, man. If you want the rovers to leave Bortfjell, sending them out in the dark on unfamiliar roads is only asking for their homewagon to break down, or their horses to slow due to exhaustion. You will then delay their departure from our land rather than speed them on their way. Besides, you have us. We have taken on the task to ensure they travel the shortest route to Høyhauger and not take any side trips. Do you not think two former border guards cannot handle that task? That we cannot handle one old woman, one man, and a small lad?"

I could hear the cold iron in Arnar's voice, and the riders who had entered the camp while I was gathering wood must surely have heard it also. I had seen hale and hardy folks quail at the sound of that voice when Arnar oversaw the training of our home guard. I froze when I felt something touch my shoulder.

CHAPTER ELEVEN

I slowly turned my head to see what was resting on my shoulder. What I saw was a tannish colored paw which, even in the dim light, I could see belonged to Kipp. He then jumped down, walked a few feet farther into the forest, stopped, and looked over his shoulder. With an impatient flick of his ringed tail, he walked a few feet farther and stopped once again. I got the message. He wanted me to follow him.

We did not walk more than one hundred yards before I noticed a large burnt-out tree stump. Kipp walked straight up to it and around to the back side. I cautiously followed. Tucked within the open hollow of the large tree trunk, curled into a ball, was Lakyle.

"Lakyle," I whispered gently, "it is Milva and Kipp. Do you mind if we join you?"

He nodded no, he did not mind, and I moved to slip in beside him. At the last moment, I slipped off my cloak. Once inside the tree hollow, I put the cloak over the two of us. I was not sure if Lakyle was shaking because he was cold, or because he was afraid. Just then I heard loud crashing sounds through the underbrush, and two men arguing.

"I donna care whats that old man said back there. There's gots to be another folk or two hidin' around here."

I could feel Lakyle begin to move, and I laid a hand on his shoulder. "Stay very still," I whispered. "Let's scoot as far back into this hollow as we can. Then I will make sure my dark cloak covers all of us, hiding us from view. Hopefully, they will walk right by. If not, I still have a few moves that might surprise those blundering through the underbrush."

Lakyle did as I asked, and we waited in silence, listening hard. As

I tried to make myself as small as possible, I realized that Kipp had not followed us into the hollow. Rather, he had climbed to the very highest part of the tree trunk and lay in wait.

I heard the two men move closer to our hiding spot. As they drew next to the tree trunk, still arguing, suddenly their argument stopped when Kipp let out a menacing yowl. I could hear the sound of his claws as he dug them into the wood of the tree trunk and launched himself into the air. After that, all I could hear was yelling, yelps of pain, and expletives that I wanted to cover Lakyle's ears to keep him from hearing, followed by the sounds of men crashing and blundering through the woods, retreating.

"I guess I did not have to reach into my bag of tricks in order to keep those men away from us. Are you all right?"

"Yes," Lakyle said in a quiet voice.

"We'll just stay here for a wee bit more time, just to be safe."

As the time passed, I could feel the lad begin to relax a bit. The silence stretched out, and finally Lakyle quietly spoke up.

"Are you mad at me?"

"Now why would I be mad at you?"

"I ran away. I was scared, and instead of staying with my father and Amma, I ran."

"That was probably a wise choice."

"How can you call running away a wise choice?"

"Answer me a question. What does your father love above all else?"

"Our family."

"Right. If those men had been able to get past Raxit, Brina, your father, and Amma and snatch you right up, would any of those grownups have been able to refuse those men any request to get you back? I will answer that question for you. The answer is no. So, you see, by finding a place to hide, you took away the opportunity for those men to use you as a hostage."

Before Lakyle could speak again, I heard his father calling his name.

"Wait here while I make sure your father is not being forced to call out for you. Do not worry, I will slip through the shadows. I am very good at it, so I do not expect to be seen. I'll be back soon."

As I slipped through the trees, I thought about what was happening in Bortfjell. I had never really thought about how rulers frequently came and went. It had never bothered me, for it had never really impacted the clan or the landholding. Our clan was a strong one, and we were united by marriage or blood to the surrounding landholdings. It never had occurred to me that the change of rule might affect others outside of our clan. I had been quite narrow-minded, it would seem.

I quickly located Wright and saw that Arnar was with him. Having known and been trained by Arnar, I could see he was alert but fairly relaxed. That indicated to me that he was not being forced to come into the woods looking for Lakyle.

"Raxit, Wright, if you would follow me, I know where Lakyle is. He is quite safe and fine, if a little shaken up. Before we go fetch him, you need to know he is thinking he is a coward for having run away. I have suggested to him that he did the right thing, for he could have been held as a bargaining hostage if he had been snatched by the two threatening men."

"Thank you, Milva. I had not thought of that," Wright stated. "I will reinforce what you have told him. Let's quickly go find him. His Amma is quite worried, as am I."

"Why don't you two go on?" suggested Arnar. "I will get back to the campsite and back Brina up, should those two men decide to return. I think that is unlikely after what Kipp did to them."

"Kipp?"

"He is fine, Milva. We will tell you about it when you return to the campsite."

Arnar turned and headed back the way he had come. I motioned to Wright that he should follow me. We took a more open and more direct route to the large hollowed-out tree trunk. I called softly to Lakyle.

"It's all right to come out, lad. Your father is here with me. If you could please bring my cloak out with you, I would appreciate it. The dusk draws chilly."

Lakyle's father reinforced what I had said to his son, coaxing him with a quiet, calm voice. Once Lakyle was in his father's arms, I moved a little farther away to give them some privacy. I would not have minded the comfort of my father's arms around me right now. I knew that longing for home and hearth, for the comfort of my father's presence, had not faded over the years since my stepmother's arrival. I realized it had only intensified since leaving Nytt Heimili.

Once we were all back in the campsite, Burle fussed over all of us. Even though it was late, we all sat down to have dinner. For Arnar, Rosilda, and myself, it was the first hot meal we had had since leaving Nytt Heimili. I think it was the most delicious soup I have ever eaten.

While we were eating, Arnar regaled us with a description of the two men running out of the woods, screaming that they had been attacked by a huge mountain cat or a vicious hunting cat. They warned us that the cat probably had a litter hidden in the woods and was defending it. They said they were lucky to be alive. Arnar suggested that they had ridden off faster than was safe in the darkening conditions.

Just before it was time to turn in, Lakyle asked if he could talk to me. I said yes. He motioned I should follow him away from the cookfire. I guessed he wanted what he had to say to be just between the two of us.

"Milva, I want to thank you for saving me. You and Kipp," Lakyle said quietly.

"I actually think you saved yourself, and possibly me, since you were the one to find the hollow in the tree trunk. I will agree that Kipp caused a grand distraction," I said, smiling down at the lad.

"I have a favor to ask of you."

I realized that Lakyle was being very serious, so I put on a serious face and told him to continue.

"I want to be prepared to be able to get away if someone were to snatch me. I saw how you and the others moved, and what you did when those men were trying to tip the homewagon over. Can you teach me what to do, some kind of move, if someone tries to grab me or gets ahold of me?"

"I could, but …"

I watched his face fall as if he thought I was going to refuse him.

"… but I think you should ask Raxit, for he was the one who has been teaching me since before I was even as old as you. I think he would agree to teach you while we are with you. Shall we go ask him?"

I had insisted that Lakyle be the one to ask Arnar. Lakyle was hesitant at first. I assured him that Arnar did not eat half pint lads for breakfast. Arnar quickly agreed to give Lakyle kazan lessons. I think he might have been secretly pleased to be asked.

Dawn arrived much too soon. Our camping companions were up and had their horses hitched to their wagon at first light. They wished us a safe journey. I think they were happy to be on the road and heading home, away from all that had happened last night. Travel in Bortfjell had become a bit too harrowing for them.

I worried that travel was going to become hazardous for many in the next few years, unless Prince Mallus reined in the forces he had let loose. Since he appeared, so far, to condone harassing and hassling foreign travelers, what was to prevent folks from expanding who they would stop along the roadways? I could only deal with the moment, however. Arnar, Rosilda, Kipp, and I needed to make it across the border into Sommerhjem.

I realized I was being presumptuous concerning Arnar and Rosilda. When Arnar had suggested that I travel to the land of my mother's birth, or at least what I assumed had been the land of my mother's birth, he had not committed to come with me into Sommerhjem. Neither had Rosilda. I would need to talk to them sometime this day, for the thought of them not being with me was making me anxious. If they were turning back at the border, I needed time to prepare for that.

We made swift work of saddling up, checking the campsite to make sure we had not left anything behind other than firewood for the next folks who would camp here. After about an hour or so of traveling, the road widened out, and the three of us could ride side by side following the homewagon. It was then I broached the subject of what Arnar's and Rosilda's plans were for when we reached Høyhauger.

"I've got nothing holding me here in Bortfjell," Arnar answered. "Never married, don't have any children, don't really have a place at Nytt Heimili anymore, and probably won't be missed by many. I was thinking I had never actually been very far into Sommerhjem, and perhaps going on one more adventure might be as good a plan as any. Was hoping you wouldn't mind if I kept tagging along once you crossed the border."

I told him it might be a wee burden to have him along, but I would try to bear it. I could not keep the joy out of my words and was not able to be convincing about what a burden he might be. He just nodded, smiled, and urged his horse forward, leaving Rosilda and I alone.

"And what of you, Rosilda? What are your plans once we reach the border?"

"When I joined the border guard, I went against my family's wishes. They had wanted me to stay and work the land with them. I knew it just wasn't for me. I have a wanderlust in my blood, I guess. When I went home this last time, my experience there only further convinced me that Nytt Heimili is no longer home to me. I also know that under Prince Mallus, the Bortfjell border guard is also not something I would be comfortable being part of. So, the call to travel to a new place appeals to me. I have never been across our southern border, so if you have no objections, I too would like to continue on with you to wherever this adventure leads us."

"I can honestly tell you, I cannot think of a single objection to your continuing to travel with me. Well, except that there might still be folks out there who are trying to kill me. This journey might be filled with unknown peril and danger."

"Pish tosh, what is a little unknown peril and danger between friends?"

What indeed? After we talked a bit further, we urged our horses to catch up with the others ahead. It was with an extremely glad and grateful heart that I traveled through the rest of the day.

Over the next few days, the scenery began to change as we headed into the mountains that divided Bortfjell from Sommerhjem. The road to the pass was well maintained and became more and more crowded as we traveled closer and closer to Høyhauger. There were no more incidents of folks threatening the rovers.

Once we reached the walled city that guarded the southern pass, the chance of being spotted would increase. I could feel the tension begin to build, and I was worried that even though we had escaped detection so far, something might happen in the last moments before we crossed the border that would make all our deceptions for naught.

CHAPTER TWELVE

When we were about two days out from Høyhauger, we pulled off the main road down a little used lane. There was just enough room to turn the homewagon around and for us to camp. Arnar suggested we take a day to get organized and to prepare for what might possibly happen at the border.

Once we had settled in, I approached Arnar. "I do not feel the rovers will have difficulty crossing over the pass to Sommerhjem. How do we explain why we are traveling there?"

"I have an idea. You still have the border guard uniform that Rosilda lent you, do you not?"

"Yes, but …."

"Hold on, lass. I'm not going to suggest that we try to pass as border guards. No, I am going to suggest that we mix and match our clothing so that we look like rag tag mercenaries. When asked why we want to cross the border, we will tell them that the rovers hired us to make sure they got to Høyhauger safely, got over the pass, and made it down the mountains. That they had experienced too many incidents of folks trying to either harm them or hurry them along to feel safe on their way here."

"That makes sense. I have a few other concerns. I know each of us have some resources that will help us survive for a time in Sommerhjem. However, some of that is in Bortfjell coinage. I do not know if it will spend across the border."

"Perhaps we should ask Wright, since it sounds like he has worked in Bortfjell before," suggested Rosilda, who then walked over to where Wright was checking the cart behind his homewagon to make sure nothing had shifted.

When she returned, Rosilda told us that Wright always asked to be paid in precious metals rather than coin. If he were paid in coin, he would spend it here for supplies that he might need. If he needed to exchange Bortfjell coins for Sommerhjem coins, he said that he always lost value.

"It seems perhaps one of us should ride ahead and gather any supplies that we might need before we cross the border," Rosilda suggested.

"If I leave now, travel as far as I can this night, and leave early in the morn, I can meet you day after tomorrow. There is a wayside about a half day's ride just north of Høyhauger. Let's figure out how much coin we have, and what we might want to spend it on. I, for one, would like to have something to camp under other than the night sky," suggested Arnar.

"Why do you think you should go?" Rosilda asked.

"Because most folk don't give an old crippled-up man much notice. And I once served in Høyhauger with the border guard. I know many of the ins and outs of the place."

Arnar spent time with Rosilda and me making a list of what we might need for our continued travels. He then spent a short time with Wright and Burle, to see if they needed anything.

Once Arnar was done getting his list together, he stepped off into the woods for a moment. When he emerged, I had to look twice, for standing before me was a man of the mountains.

"I's just down from the high reaches fer ta gets me some supplies. Sold me furs. Thems big towns folk just has goods thats ta fancy fer the likes of me. I knows I can finds what I's needs in Høyhauger. Ah, lass you should see the look on your face," said Arnar, after he had stopped laughing.

I bid Arnar luck and safe travels as I watched him ride off. I hoped all would go well, and we would all make our rendezvous in two days' time.

The next morning, we began our climbing back up the mountain on the main road. Several hours into our travel we came upon another rover homewagon pulled over to the side of the road. The driver greeted us. She told us she had pulled over to check one of her horse's hooves and rest the horses since she and her brother had been driving since first light. Wright asked if they wished to join our group. There was a look of what I could only interpret as relief on her face.

When we settled down to camp that evening, Rosilda and I went to talk to the two new folks. We felt it would be unfair if the two new rovers were not informed about the potential danger I might put them in. When they heard us out, they said that they had great sympathy for anyone who was labeled a foreigner, for they had felt the growing anger and distrust toward themselves.

I felt like we could trust the two. When we explained to them the idea Arnar had come up with concerning us dressing up as mercenaries and acting as their escort out of Bortfjell, they agreed to go along with our ruse.

The trip towards Høyhauger was uneventful. We arrived at the wayside where we planned to meet Arnar by midafternoon. Fortunately, there was room for both homewagons and their carts. As I looked around the campsite, I became worried because Arnar was not there. The hours passed by with agonizing slowness, and still, no Arnar. After a while, it was all I could do not to get on my horse and ride toward Høyhauger. Finally, I saw a rider heading down the road, followed by a small pack horse. The closer the two horses and rider came, the more I became convinced it was Arnar.

Rosilda had come up beside me to watch the approach. "Ayup, that's Ar, um, Raxit." She moved forward to greet him and show him where we were camped.

Once Arnar dismounted and tied up his horses, he explained why he was late. "I took a little extra time to check out the pass. I wanted to see if those who were crossing over to Sommerhjem met with any difficulty. I also wanted to see if I could hear any gossip that might pertain to you or Nytt Heimili. Stopped in at a pub that those of us from our area used to frequent. Appears that some things do not change. I was a bit worried I might be recognized. Most of those in the pub were much younger than me. Did hear some interesting tidbits."

"What did you hear?" I asked.

"One of the men in the pub was just back from Nytt Heimili. Apparently, he had gone home on leave. Seems there has been a hue and cry about your disappearance. No one seemed to be able to explain to your father, who came back early from the capital, just when you had gone missing, or what had happened to you. Grimur had not been expecting the Laird back early, and thus had not put anything in place. I suspect he was still looking for you discreetly, so not many knew you were gone."

"I wonder why Father came back early."

"I believe he wanted to make sure you were safe."

"On the day I was to leave, I left him a note in a place only he and I knew. I hope at some point, I will be able to get a message to him that I am in a safe place. So, what is happening now at home?"

"I just happened to snag a bench next to the young border guard and kept his mug filled with ale, which I should tell you definitely encouraged him to talk freely. Told him I was from his area, and I was a wee bit homesick for news from home. He and I had a grand time talking of the changes back home. The Laird has sent Grimur packing along with a number of Lady Kolbrun's retainers. He has begun to travel out about the land and to visit the village. It sounds like he has taken back his rightful place in the landholding. Unfortunately, that does not change anything for you."

"Speaking of me, what is happening about my disappearance?"

"Your father has sent out search parties to no avail. Even though Grimur has been sent packing, I have a feeling he and his ilk have not stopped looking for you. Seems our young border guard was encouraged by Grimur and the promise of a bit of coin to keep an eye out for you. I imagine there are others besides the young border guard who are also looking for you."

"The news about what is going on at our landholding is good news. The fact that I cannot return, and there may still be folks looking for me with the intent to harm me, is not so good news."

"Before we finish this conversation, I have a bit of strange yet strangely funny news. It seems that the night you disappeared so did all the cats at the manor house, and they had not been back by the time our young border guard had left to head back here. Cats can be found everywhere else in Nytt Heimili. Not at the manor house, however."

"Lady Markham must be delighted. Or will be until she discovers vermin making nests in her sewing materials." The whole idea made me smile. "Changing the subject, you, I am sure, have observed that we have been joined by another rover homewagon. Rosilda and I gave them the same account of why we are going to cross the border as we gave Wright and his family. We also told them how we were going to cross the border disguised as mercenaries they had hired to escort them safely across the pass into Sommerhjem. They were anxious to have the help, for they have been harassed along the way too and just want to go home."

We spent the rest of the afternoon sorting through what Arnar had been able to purchase and repacking the packs to go on the sturdy little pack horse. Wright and his family took the supplies Arnar had purchased for them and packed them away in their homewagon and cart. I approached Wright later in the afternoon, carrying my empty pack and my empty satchel.

"I was wondering if you might have some way of hiding these two items in your homewagon or cart where they might not be found easily. I am not asking for you to give up any secrets about your homewagon if there are any secrets …." I trailed off, for I realized I had begun to babble and was sure my face had turned a lovely shade of red with embarrassment.

"I think we can find someplace to put both of those items where they will not be easily found."

"Good. Should something happen to me before I can get them back from you, will you give them to my friends?"

"Of course."

With that taken care of, I found a comfortable log next to the fire and settled in. When night fell, I rolled up in both my cloak and my blanket roll, for it was quite cold this high up in the mountains even though we were sheltered by pines. I knew that the higher we went, the land would become rockier and that there would be less and less vegetation to shelter us from the wind.

As I lay in my blanket roll, I felt something pawing at my shoulder. It was Kipp. I opened up the covers, and he crawled in. I found great comfort in him being beside me. If anyone had asked this night how I felt about heading into Høyhauger, and if I answered honestly, I would tell them I was terrified. As I lay there, I thought about what I knew about the border town.

Høyhauger, the southernmost town on the border of Bortfjell, is situated at the mouth of the pass to the country of Sommerhjem. Part fortress and part town, it is a place of contrasts. In times of peace, a brisk trade moves through the pass, and the wealth of that trade is reflected in the richness of the merchants' homes. Part of the town is still fortified and houses the barracks of the border guard, representatives of the reigning prince, and the administration overseeing the town. In a time of unrest, Høyhauger could still be defended.

Even in the best of times, Høyhauger was not the most peaceful and certainly not the safest town in Bortfjell. Like many towns, and most especially border towns, there is an underside where folks, some with and some without the blessing of the current ruler, cater to the seamier wants of either the folk who live there or are just passing through. A border town set to regulate or monitor a pass through the mountains also attracts its share of smugglers, who pass between the two countries by ways other than the main, more well-traveled, pass.

In other words, besides having to be wary of being spotted by those folks who might still be looking for me at the behest of Grimur, I and the others felt we did not need to linger in Høyhauger. On the morrow, we decided we would begin traveling at first light and hopefully reach the pass close to noon. None of us had any need to pick up more supplies or stop anywhere in the town. Rather, we planned to travel straight through to the pass and hoped to be a half day's ride into Sommerhjem before we stopped for the night.

While we woke up to sunshine, the day turned gray and windy about an hour after we started. By the second hour, a drizzle had begun. By the time we approached the main gate into Høyhauger, it had begun to rain steadily. Høyhauger was certainly not an attractive town even in the bright sunlight. Through the rain and the gray light, it looked cold and uninviting. The gray, dull mountain rock it was built of gave the formidable wall surrounding the town a forbidding look. I could only hope we could pass through quickly.

Just as the second homewagon rolled through the border town's main gate, the icy cold rain turned to a mix of rain and snow. Not unexpected for this time of year. Not ideal for traveling. As we moved down the main thoroughfare through town, I noticed that travelers who had been in front of us and behind us began to turn off onto side streets or pull outs. I imagined those who left the line heading toward the pass either had business in Høyhauger or had decided to wait the weather out.

Arnar rode quickly up past Wright's homewagon to speak with Rosilda, who was leading the way, and then rode back to Wright's homewagon. After holding a brief conversation with Wright, he then waited for the second homewagon to come abreast of his horse and repeated the conversation. Then he returned to me.

"I have told the rovers that even though it is beginning to snow, we should continue on through the pass. I am hoping that the swirling snow will discourage folks from paying too close attention to us. We need to go while the snow is light. If we cannot cross the pass now, if they close the pass because of worsening weather, we would be stuck here in town until we could move on. Being in this town for any amount of time would increase the danger to you."

Chapter Thirteen

As we wound our way through the town, the snow did not increase. Then again, it did not decrease either. With little traffic in front of us, we reached the entrance to the pass quickly. Arnar and I rode forward to join Rosilda at the head of the little group.

The wet weather had certainly increased the down-on-your-luck, bedraggled look of the three of us. With some of the items Arnar had picked up from a rag picker in Høyhauger, we had been able to cobble together our disguises. Once again, Arnar had outdone himself with his disguise. He had worn a threadbare old uniform coat with the insignia removed, a tattered cloak, his regular riding pants, and muddy boots. He had covered his head with a floppy hat and had added an eye patch to cover his left eye. Rosilda was wearing her border guard pants and boots, a raggedy old coat, and a rain cloak that hardly kept the rain and snow off. She had pulled her old, battered guard hat down on her head and tucked her hair up under it. I had also cobbled together a disguise. I had chosen to do as Arnar had done, minus the eye patch. The snow that was beginning to swirl around due to the wind picking up had the added benefit that I could tie a scarf across my face, further disguising me. I could only hope what we had done was enough. As we approached the guard station, a single guard stepped out and called us to halt.

"State your business."

"We're escortin' thems rovers behind us across the pass and beyond. Theys hired us'n 'cause theys been, let us say, hurried on theirs way none too gently by others. Gives us'n a bit o' coin, if'n ya knows whats I means."

There was such a sly twist to what Arnar just said that if I had not known it was all a ruse, I would have believed he had some mischief in mind. Just as he finished speaking, the wind picked up. I saw the guard pull his cloak closer around himself and glance over his shoulder.

"Go on. They sent me out to close the pass. Seein' youse are getting these rovers out of Bortfjell, go ahead. Know that yer traveling at yer own risk. No one is gonna helps ya out if ya gets in trouble."

With that said, the guard whirled around and headed back into the guard station. We wasted no time signaling that the homewagons should move ahead. Arnar took the lead, I slipped my horse followed by the pack horse in between the two homewagons, and Rosilda took up the rear. Fortunately, the pass ran between the mountains along a river and provided some relief from the swirling snow. As we slowly moved through the pass, the snow began to accumulate. I began to become fearful that we were going to have trouble with the homewagons making it across the pass. At one point about halfway through, we all dismounted and walked our horses. When we reached the slight crest of the pass, all the rovers except the drivers, got out and walked. A number of nail-biting, teeth-clenching minutes passed as we traveled downhill, until the road leveled out once again.

By the time we reached the guardhouse on the other side of the pass, I could not feel my hands, and I was convinced they were frozen to the reins of the horse. I worried about Kipp, who had been riding behind me. I was not sure with the blowing wind whether he had been covered by my cloak. Even though his thick fur probably provided better protection from the snow and rain than the cloak I was currently wearing, I still worried.

We received a more cordial greeting when we arrived at the guardhouse on the Sommerhjem side of the pass. A border guard, hastily pulling on his cloak, stepped out of the guardhouse.

"Hadn't expected anyone to be coming through the pass in this weather. We have closed it from our end, not that we have many heading into Bortfjell. Spring storms are often harsher and more dangerous than the cold month ones. You all will not be traveling any farther this day. The road down the rest of the way out of these mountains is too treacherous right now. The storm seems to be tapering off. I suspect the snow will quickly melt on the morrow, and you should be able to be on your way late morning. Please follow me, and we will get your homewagons into a sheltered spot and your horses settled. Once that is done, I will escort you to the barracks, and we can get the formalities sorted out."

We did as the border guard requested and followed him down a lane and into a small, sheltered valley. This valley held what was obviously a border guard encampment. There were a number of long, timbered buildings which probably housed the border guards. I suspected there was a dining building among the outbuildings. Also, a smithy, supply buildings, and a granary. We rode beyond most of the buildings until we reached the barns. Our guide showed the rovers where they could put their homewagons. He then directed us to a timber-framed barn where we could quarter the horses.

"Your horses and gear will be quite safe here," he told Arnar, Rosilda, and me. "You are welcome to bunk in the barracks, or you are welcome to the hay loft. It should be quite warm this night due to the number of animals in the barn. I will be right back, for I forgot to tell the rovers where there is a supply of wood that they can use to heat their homewagons. Please wait here until I pick you back up."

I was more than glad to wait in the barn. The border guard was right, the barn was significantly warmer that the outside. I was grateful for the warmth. My hands almost worked again. Glancing around, I noticed that there were several border guards in the barn with us, so I felt it would not be prudent for us to speak of anything other than taking care of our horses and equipment. While Kipp had jumped down from my horse when I dismounted, he did not wander off. Rather, he perched upon the pile of our belongings that we had removed from the pack horse so I could rub him down and move him into a stall.

We had just finished our chores when the border guard returned. He was accompanied by Wright. Just as I was about to step out into the blustery cold, I felt something land upon my back.

"You would be much warmer if you stayed in the barn, Kipp. No? Well, you are welcome to come along."

Once we had reached the barracks, a small, diminutive border guard stepped out of the barracks. I hoped we would not be facing problems on this side of the pass. It was Wright who stepped forward and addressed the new border guard.

"It is good to be on the Sommerhjem side of the pass. It was worth the worry and a few very scary moments crossing through the pass just to stand on home soil once again. As I am sure you are aware, Bortfjell is a much less welcoming country this day than it was when we crossed the border in the fall. Each of us driving a homewagon is returning from our cold months' commissions in Bortfjell. Can you tell me, did a rover homewagon pass through here several weeks past? Would have had a man, two women, and a small girl."

"I am Captain Shala. I suggest we move this conversation into the barracks and sort things out."

We did as the captain asked and followed her into the barracks. The blast of warm air that hit me as I entered the barracks was almost too much, even after the warmth of the barn. Nevertheless, the heat was so welcome that I took a moment just to absorb it, little thinking that the next few moments could seal my fate one way or the other. I was pulled out of my reverie when the captain spoke up, directing her questions to Arnar, Rosilda, and me.

"I clearly understand why the rovers might risk traveling through the pass this day. What I want to know is just what role you are playing in their journey."

Wright spoke up before any of the rest of us could answer. "Our three companions on horseback are the reason we have arrived in one piece. Do not let their rag-tag appearance fool you."

I was grateful for Wright's support, for Captain Shala's tone of voice had not been quite neutral. I think our disguises may have been too good, for she was looking at us as if we were mercenaries and just might be taking advantage of the rovers or might intend to do something nefarious to them once we were off the mountain. Before Arnar could speak, I spoke up.

"May we have this conversation away from listening ears?"

The captain suggested we follow her to her office. Wright asked to be included. Once we were all in Captain Shala's office, she closed the door and settled behind her desk.

"Let me address Wright's concern first. Your wife, child, sister, and family traveled safely through the pass about a fortnight ago. They met with some small nuisance trouble along the way, nothing that did much harm or delayed them. They asked me to tell you that they would wait for you at the campsite you had agreed on. They are well supplied and are looking forward to a time of rest. Your daughter asked that you specifically be told not to dawdle or lollygag. She is quite something," the captain said with a kind smile.

Wright thanked the captain for the information and sagged into his chair. I could only imagine the burden of worry that had been lifted off his shoulders upon hearing that his family had made it across the border safely.

The captain then turned her attention to Arnar, Rosilda, and me. "You all speak the language of Sommerhjem passably. Would you like to continue in our language or the language of Bortfjell?"

I spoke up first. "The language of Sommerhjem will be fine. Wright's young son has been giving us lessons to refresh our use of your language in exchange for lessons in kazan, for he wanted to know how to defend himself against bullies."

The captain gave me a quizzical look, and I worried that she might be questioning how we might know her language. I hoped I had not made an error. I rushed right on.

"We may look like former guard mercenaries, which was intended by our outfits. While it is true that the other two of us are former border guards, we are not mercenaries, nor have we charged the rovers to travel with them. On our way to the pass, we had the occasion to help Wright and his family out and prevented their homewagon from being tipped over by folks who had taken up Prince Mallus' cause against foreigners. After that, we asked to travel with them because there is always safety in numbers."

"Is that correct, rover?" Captain Shala inquired.

"Yes, Captain."

"Go on," the captain requested of me.

"I am heading to Sommerhjem because I am no longer safe on the landholding I grew up on. While my father is of Bortfjellian birth, my mother was not. What I know of her was that she came from beyond, as they say where I am from, meaning beyond the Bortfjell border. It has been suggested to me that she came from Sommerhjem. Since I could no longer remain in Bortfjell, I headed this way." I hoped further details would not be required.

"And what of you?" the captain asked Arnar.

"As you can see, belonging to the guard is long in my past. I had found a place in Milva's landholding up until recently. The Laird's new wife and retinue had great influence on the Laird and had me dismissed as being old and not of much use. I felt one last adventure was better than trying to survive in the forested hills come the cold months."

"And you?" the captain asked Rosilda.

"Milva and I have been friends since childhood. I was back at the landholding when she told me she had to leave. Having just mustered out of the border guard, I had not decided where my life would lead me next, so I decided to tag along with her. Always wanted to see Sommerhjem."

"I will tell you now that I hear truth in what you have told me," suggested Captain Shala. "I also surmise that I am not getting the whole truth, so until I am satisfied that I have the whole truth, we will remain in my office. I would sincerely like to hear the whole truth. One additional question is for Milva. I want you to tell how you managed to have a wild hill cat cradled in your arms. Until all that is accomplished, none of us is going anywhere. You might as well sit and make yourselves comfortable. Please know that the only way out of here is the door behind you and through my border guards. Wright, you are welcome to stay or to go, as you wish."

"Oh, I think I might like to stay."

Suddenly, any continued conversation was halted when there was a caterwauling that could be heard from behind the door into the captain's office.

"Good gracious, what is going on?" Captain Shala said just as there was an urgent knocking on her door. She rose and moved to the door, opening it a crack.

I heard someone say from the other side of the door, "Yer pardon, Captain. Don't understand it, but it would seem every blame cat in the valley just rushed into the barracks when Sarge opened the door to come in from his rounds. They are now all gathered at my feet and pushing on your door to get in."

"Try to hold for a moment," Captain Shala suggested, as she closed the door. "You heard," she said, directing her comment at me. "Will this be a problem, if the cats make it in here?"

"I have no idea. However, back home, Kipp got along well with the other cats."

"Well, either we sit here and listen to the cats howling, or I open the door and we let nature take it's course. You choose."

"Actually, I think Kipp has chosen, since he is sitting patiently next to the door."

The captain went over to the door, opened it, and let the cats in. Kipp touched noses with each cat that entered the room as if he were greeting them. Once the last cat entered the room, and there had to be at least a dozen of them, Kipp returned to my lap, circled twice, and settled in. The cats who had entered the room chose various folks' laps, window ledges, the captain's desk, vacant chairs, or the hearth to settle in on. I had a hard time not bursting into laughter. Here we were about to be judged as to who we were, what our intent was, and most probably whether we could continue into Sommerhjem or whether we would be sent back to Bortfjell, and we were surrounded by cats.

"Now then, now that we are all settled, I think I would like first to start with you, Raxit. No wait, that is not the right name, is it, Arnar?"

CHAPTER FOURTEEN

You could not even hear a cat's whisker twitch, the room had fallen so quiet. I think even the roaring wind outside the window paused. The stunned silence was broken when a log in the fireplace crackled, shifted, and dropped farther into the coals.

I hoped I had schooled my face to give nothing away. I tried not to look at Arnar, instead I looked down at Kipp. I could feel Rosilda stiffen slightly next to me. A moment passed, then two, before Captain Shala broke the silence.

"It was a very, very long time ago, Arnar, but I still remember it as if it were yesterday. I was so new to the border guard that my boots were not even scuffed. Guarding the pass into Bortfjell was my first assignment. I had arrived just days before I was sent on my first patrol. There had been an increase in smuggling in the area. The then Prince of Bortfjell was cracking down on the smuggling traffic between our two countries."

I chanced a look at Arnar at this point and saw he was sitting quite still and attentive.

"My fellow border guards took the opportunity of my first patrol to see if they could ruffle me. They sent me off on a side trail, knowing full well it would lead me onto a trail that crossed the Bortfjell border. They wanted to see how I might handle running into a Bortfjellian border guard. And run into a Bortfjellian border guard I did, literally. Unfortunately, our collision made enough noise that we alerted a small band of smugglers who were on a cliff above us. They had rigged boulders on the edge of the cliff, and thinking they had been discovered, they pushed the boulders off the cliff. The Bortfjellian border guard's quick actions saved my life, and I was unharmed. Unfortunately, he was not. His right hand had been crushed under a large rock, and his right leg was twisted at an odd angle."

Arnar had never talked about what had caused the injuries to his hand and leg. I knew it had caused him to return from the border guard and become a trainer for Nytt Heimili's home guard.

"My patrol caught up with me, not too long after the boulders had rained down on us. We carried Arnar to safety, and our healer did the best he could to put him to rights. To make a long tale short, no matter how clever your disguise, Arnar, I would have recognized you. I owe you a debt that can never be repaid. Having said that, I owe my allegiance to Sommerhjem ...."

"Would you give me a moment to talk to my two traveling companions?" asked Arnar.

"Of course. Wright, perhaps you would help me gather some tea and something to eat from the cook."

"I would be glad to."

Once Captain Shala and Wright left the room, Arnar turned to the two of us.

"There is some irony in this present situation. We have made it all the way from Nytt Heimili to here without giving away who we are. I even took the calculated risk to enter a pub in Høyhauger frequented by folks from back home and appeared to escape unrecognized. Now the one folk in Sommerhjem, the only one who might have the slimmest chance of knowing who I really am, just happens to be the captain of this border guard encampment. She has me to rights, so there is no use trying to lie to her. The question here is, do you both wish to stick to your tales, or do we lay it all out for her?"

I took a long moment before I answered. "I think since I am entering a new country, I would like to do so as myself. I would hope once we explain the circumstances of why I left home, that Captain Shala would keep what we tell her private. I think we can ask Wright, on his honor, to hold what he hears in this room to himself. Once we leave this room, until we part from the second rover family, we should continue with the names and tale we have given them."

"I would concur," stated Rosilda. "I have come to trust Wright. The captain, I think, is a woman of honor."

"We are agreed then?" questioned Arnar. Rosilda and I both nodded our heads in agreement. Kipp just stretched and yawned.

Captain Shala knocked lightly on the office door, alerting us to her presence. She then entered carrying a tray, followed by Wright carrying another one. Once tea was poured into thick mugs, and we each had grabbed a meat pie, clearing the second platter much to the annoyance of the cats in the room, Arnar began to speak.

"It is I who owe you a debt, for if it were not for you and the kindness of your fellow guards, I would probably not have survived that day. You are correct, I am Arnar. Why I have arrived on your side of the border is not my tale to tell."

Before the captain could speak, I entered the conversation.

"I would ask, on your honor, that what is said in this room next stays in this room. My life, and the lives of my loyal companions, depends upon your discretion."

Wright did not hesitate to say, on his honor, he would not mention, without our leave, what he heard here this day. He did suggest that he was reluctant to not discuss this conversation with his wife. I suggested that when we met up with the rest of his family, we could discuss that. Captain Shala swore on her honor that she would not discuss what we revealed unless she felt our revelations threatened Sommerhjem. I could not fault her for that.

Taking a deep breath, I began. "I am Lady Perrin, daughter of Laird Leifur, heir to the landholding Nytt Heimili of Bortfjell. As you are already aware, Prince Mallus has decreed that no one who is of foreign birth, or has one or more parent of foreign birth, can hold any significant position of rule in Bortfjell. He did so to prevent some of his half siblings from ever ruling. It also meant, because my mother was not from Bortfjell, that my eventually becoming laird of Nytt Heimili would no longer be possible, unless a new ruler of our land rose to power and changed Prince Mallus' edict.

"I would have stayed, hoping for that chance, for I have been raised to become the next leader of our clan. Unfortunately, I discovered that my father's new wife and her brother were also aware of that possibility. They did not wish for my baby half-brother's chance to be the next laird to be diminished should Prince Mallus' proclamation be overturned. They plotted to do away with me after my father and his party left for the capital. Obviously, I did not wait around to help them carry out their plan. Fortunately, Arnar and my long-time friend, Rosilda, held loyalty to clan over loyalty to the new ruler. They have aided in my escape, at great risk to themselves."

"And so, you chose to head into Sommerhjem?"

"Yes. As I have stated, my mother came from beyond the border of Bortfjell. Having no destination in mind when the three of us decided that my staying on our landholding was going to be detrimental to my health, Arnar suggested we try to reach Sommerhjem."

"Rosilda?" Captain Shala turned her attention to my childhood friend.

"What I told you when we first sat down in your office was the truth, except for my name."

"What you have just told me begins to explain why you would risk crossing the pass in a raging snowstorm. What are your intentions now?"

"We hope to travel farther into Sommerhjem, perhaps to find my mother's folk. I do not have much hope for that, for I have so little to go on. We each have some skills, so perhaps we could be guards for hire, or find some other kind of work. For now, we have supplies and funds so as not to be a burden on anyone. Wright has said we could continue to travel with him and his family, which would be helpful. It would give us a better grasp of customs and the lay of the land. On my honor, we mean no harm and have no nefarious plans or intent."

"Thank you for telling me who you all are, and why you have crossed the border. I have only a few more questions, and then I will let you go settle in to wait out the storm. Lady Perrin, you say you do not know where in Sommerhjem your mother came from. Is that correct?"

"Just call me Perrin, please. To answer your question, yes, that is correct. I do not know where in Sommerhjem my mother came from."

"What was her name?"

"My father called her Helka. He never mentioned a last name, nor a place name. I have been told that my father adored her. My mother, you see, died when I was thirteen years of age. My father was devastated by her death and filled with grief. His way, I guess, of dealing with his loss was to not speak of her."

"Helka, you say?" remarked Captain Shala.

89

"Yes."

"That is an uncommon name in Sommerhjem. Wright, you look like you might know something."

"I have heard that name only once before. We were traveling to the mountain town of Mellomdaler located in the Ryggard mountains for a commission several years back. We were following a lane along a long line of cliffs northwest of Mellomdaler when what looked to be a potentially bad storm was coming in from the west, and we were feeling quite exposed. We turned down a lane that turned east away from the cliffs, hoping we might find some shelter. What we found was a small community nestled in a tucked away valley that I had not known about. The folks there were truly kind but very secretive. It turned out that they were a community of makers of fine porcelain. They had discovered a good source of kaolin, a soft earthy whiteish clay, which contains something needed to make porcelain. They also had found, in the nearby mountains, other minerals they had need of. Like many who are occupied with crafting very specialized goods, these folks had settled in a place where the secrets of how they made their goods could be guarded. So, their settlement not only provided them with the materials they need, but also allowed them to do their craft away from prying eyes.

"Sorry, this is a long explanation to get to the answer to your question. We were at this settlement for several days due to the severity of the storm, and I met an elder there who was named Helka. In my conversation with her, I had exclaimed that I had never run into anyone in my travels who was called by that name. She explained to me that it was an old family name, and usually there was only one named Helka each generation. She did not say anything about having a daughter or other relatives that currently had that name."

"Thank you for that information," I told Wright. "It would be as good a place to head for as any. Captain, you said you had several more questions."

"My next question is certainly not as serious as the others I have asked this day. Actually I have two questions. First, how did you come to have an elusive wild hill cat traveling with you?"

"I truly do not know. Kipp here seems to have found me, I think, rather than the other way around. I began to really notice him when my stepmother essentially banished me to the women's workroom."

When the captain raised a questioning eyebrow, I suggested that that was a tale for another time.

"I began to see him everywhere I went. He would show up in places when and where I least expected him, nor could I figure out how he got there. On the night I left, he became my guide through places in the keep I never knew about, and he and the other manor cats helped me to eventually meet up at the old mill ruin where I rendezvoused with Arnar and Rosilda."

"And after that?"

"Well, he just settled himself on the back of my horse, snuggled himself right up against the small of my back under my cloak, and has tagged along for the ride ever since."

I chose not to mention the time Kipp had launched himself off the hollow tree trunk, thus running off the two men who were about to discover Lakyle and me hiding within. I thought I would keep that little tidbit of information to myself. Never know when it might come in handy.

"As for my second question, have he, or you, or the both of you combined gathered a clowder of cats around you before?"

"Yes, upon occasion. And no, I do not have any more of an explanation for the cats gathering around us than I have an explanation for why Kipp chooses to continue to travel with me."

Captain Shala sat forward in her chair and moved a cat aside so she could place her elbows on her desk. She then steepled her fingers together, placing them under her chin. She was silent for a time. Finally, she spoke.

"Those are all the questions I have for now. When the weather clears, I can see no reason why the three of you cannot travel on into Sommerhjem. Excuse me, Kipp, the four of you. Know I will keep what you have told me here quiet. While we can watch your back trail for any leaving Bortfjell through the pass and try to determine if they might be those you fear have not stopped looking for you, we cannot always stop the traffic that finds its way through the mountains by ways other than this pass. I hope you have covered your back trail sufficiently."

As did I.

CHAPTER FIFTEEN

I left the border guard captain's office with mixed feelings. I was, of course, relieved that we were going to be allowed to continue our journey into Sommerhjem. I was nervous that others now knew who Arnar, Rosilda, and I really were. I knew the old adage was true: more folks knowing a secret creates more chances for the secret to be revealed. In addition, now that we had achieved our first goal, that of reaching Sommerhjem safely, I realized none of us had planned what we would do once we crossed the border.

We had declined the offer to sleep in the barracks, choosing rather the option of the hayloft. We did, however, welcome the invitation to eat in the dining hall. Captain Shala had also invited the rover families to join us. Since it was several hours before the evening mealtime, Arnar, Rosilda, and I headed to the barn that housed our horses and packs. We thought we would gather our blanket rolls and whatever else we would need to set up a comfortable place to sleep in the loft.

Upon arrival inside the barn, we were greeted with a strange, confusing sight. Lakyle had his back pressed against a stall door and looked terrified. A guard was laying at his feet. Three other guards were standing a ways off, doubled over with laughter.

As I approached, the man on the floor opened his eyes and moaned. The other three guards tried to stifle their laughter, straightened up, and one was wiping tears off his cheek. Lakyle remained frozen in place.

I directed my question to one of the border guards who seemed to have gained the most control of her mirth. "Is the fellow on the floor all right?"

"Ah, yes ma'am. Just had the wind knocked out of him."

I turned back and addressed Lakyle. "Are you all right?"

My voice seemed to have penetrated Lakyle's fear, and he indicated he was.

I turned back to the three border guards. "Just what happened here?"

"It was just a friendly prank, you see," the female guard answered. "The young lad was so intent on grooming his horse, that he was paying no attention to us. Zan, the man who is flat on his back on the ground, decided he would stealthily sneak up on the lad, grab him, and pick him up."

I was beginning to get a glimmer of what had happened.

"All went well. Zan got to the lad without the lad noticing him. He reached around the lad, and then in a move no one was expecting, the lad did something. It was so fast I am not quite sure at this moment just what he did. All of a sudden Zan was on the ground. It stuck me funny, I am sorry to say, and I started laughing. My laughter caught the others, and then they started laughing, and then we could not stop. You see, Zan is a big prankster, and the prank was on him. I apologize, we should have seen to the lad."

By the time I had finished talking with the three guards, I turned to find Arnar and Rosilda were standing with Lakyle. He had a rather pleased look on his face. I could imagine that my two companions had heard his side and had praised him on his quick thinking and using one of the kazan moves Arnar had been teaching him. My thoughts were interrupted when the border guard I had been talking to asked a question.

"Ma'am?"

"Please call me Milva."

"Ah, Milva, can you tell me just how that young lad managed to drop Zan to the ground?"

"It is a kazan move that Raxit has been teaching Lakyle so he can defend himself if someone tries to harm him."

"Kazan?"

"It is an ancient discipline of meditation and self-defense. It helps calm the mind and strengthen the body. It also helps keep one's body flexible."

"It is a new way of fighting then?"

"No, it is an old way of defending oneself. When not traveling, it is a discipline I practice each day, usually at dawn."

"Can you teach it to me?"

"It is a discipline that takes many long years to learn. Raxit is a master of kazan, and Brina is close. I am not at their level yet. What Raxit taught Lakyle were some simple moves. He has been practicing them as we have traveled. Much as I am sure any one of us would be glad to show you some of the moves, I fear we will not be here long enough to do so, for we will leave as soon as the road down the mountain is once again open."

When the border guard looked crestfallen, I made a suggestion. "With the edict from Prince Mallus aimed at those of foreign birth, you might see others who have grown up in Bortfjell, but were not born there, or one of their parents was not born there, who are now fleeing into Sommerhjem. Prince Mallus' edict was to prevent any type of ruling power being in the hands of those he did not see as true Bortfjellians. Unfortunately, it has given rise to an anti-foreigner movement. Perhaps, someone crossing your border into Sommerhjem might come with the skills to teach you kazan. Might be something to mention to your captain."

Though disappointed with my answer, but thoughtful about my suggestion, the female guard joined her fellow guards and walked away teasing Zan for being bested by a lad half his size and a great deal younger.

Once the border guard group had returned to their chores, I joined Arnar, Rosilda, and Lakyle. The lad still looked a bit shaken by his encounter with the would-be prankster. He also was beginning to look a slight bit proud.

"The lad handled himself well," Arnar stated. "I have suggested to him that in other circumstances, freezing in terror after felling an opponent might not be the best choice. Running swiftly away to a safer environment might be better. Under these circumstances, holding his ground was a good choice, once he chanced to notice the other three guards were doubled over in laughter rather that charging at him."

"The woman border guard told me that your move was so fast that she could not even explain just what had happened, other than that Zan tried to grab you, and then he was on the ground with the wind knocked right out of him. Now let me give you a piece of advice that Raxit gave me after my first major success. He told me I had done fine. He then told me to wipe the whole episode right out of my mind and not think on it again. The next opponent might not go down so easy, and I had a lot to learn.

Getting all puffed up on my success would make me more vulnerable to the next attack, for I would be overconfident. He had been right. I took a good trouncing when I faced my next practice partner. I think that might have been you, Brina."

After we helped Lakyle finish up his chores, Arnar walked him back to his homewagon to explain to Wright what had happened in the barn with Lakyle and the border guards. The rest of the day was uneventful. Morning brought disappointment.

What was supposed to be a quick late spring storm turned into a three-day blowing and drifting snowstorm producing heavy snow. As quickly as it had come, it ended. Just as quickly, the temperature rose as the sun shone brightly, causing the snow to begin to melt rapidly, leaving the ground full of muddy puddles.

Even though anyone who might have picked up our trail would also be delayed at crossing though the pass, the weather might have been better on the Bortfjell side of the mountains. If that had been the case, they could have closed the gap between us while we were stuck at the border guard encampment.

Finally, it was reported that while the pass was still closed, the way down the mountain from the border guard encampment was clear. We were told that the farther down the mountain we traveled, the dryer and clearer the road would become. I know Arnar, Rosilda, and I were anxious to head out. Wright was even more anxious, for he was worried about his family who were waiting for him, and what they might be thinking because of our delay.

As I got ready to mount up, I looked around for Kipp. He had been about his own business these last few days. I would see him as I tucked in for bed and would leave him napping on my blanket roll when I rose. I do not think he spent the night with me. I worried that since we were in the mountains, he might choose to stay. The idea left me sad and feeling lonely. Besides Arnar and Rosilda, he had been my constant companion since before I had left home.

The rover homewagons and carts were hitched up and began to move out. Arnar and Rosilda had mounted and looked back toward me.

"You go ahead, I just want to check to make sure my backpack and satchel are really tied on tightly. I'll be right along."

"We'll wait," said Arnar in a voice that brooked no argument, "though you might want to move aside so your furry friend who is waiting patiently at your feet might have room to jump up on your horse."

I ducked my head partly to look down and see Kipp at my feet and partly to hide my face, which I was sure had a myriad of emotions crossing it.

"So sorry, Kipp. Hop on up." I stepped away from the horse, fussed with the reins, and finally mounted. "So, you two, what are you waiting for? Sommerhjem awaits."

As Arnar and Rosilda urged their horses forward to catch up with the rover homewagons, I thought I heard muffled laughter floating back to me on the breeze.

The road leading down the mountain was in fair shape. Captain Shala had explained that the snowstorm had set back the road workers who lived at the bottom of the mountain road, so the road might be a little rough. I was glad I was on horseback, for it turned out the spring rains and recent snow had indeed left the road a bit rugged. I imagined the rovers were getting jostled about in their homewagons.

It took us most of the day to get down to the forested hills where travel was easier. Before we had left, Wright had told us that the other rover family was going to head toward the coast once they cleared the hill country. Wright intended to head south. Since we had no plan other than to seek out the community of porcelain makers on the slim chance that my mother Helka might have come from there, which was south and eventually east, we were going to travel south with Wright and his family for a while. We knew they would be stopping at some of the early spring fairs. Once they started to do that, we would have to figure out if we wanted to spend several days in any one place or begin traveling on our own.

While we traveled with the rovers, they told us about their life on the road. With the beginning of spring, they traveled to the early spring markets and worked for coin or barter. Wright, being a wood smith, had items he made for sale or barter, and he would take on small jobs. Since he often traveled with his sister's family, sometimes the two of them would take on bigger jobs together. His wife was a leather smith. He had told me she crafted beautiful items which sold well at the large summer fairs. His brother-in-law was a farrier. At the large summer fairs, they would set up a booth and try to earn a living selling the items they had made in their spare time during the cold months. Fall harvest festivals followed, and they had ones they traveled to annually. The cold months were the hardest, for if they did not make enough in the spring, summer, or fall in either coin or barter, it became pretty subsistence living, unless they could get a commission such as they had had these last cold months.

With all this traveling across the land and back, the rovers often stopped at farms and asked if they could camp on the farmer's land. In return, the custom was to offer whatever help they could in exchange for a place to stay for a night or longer. The system seemed to be mutually beneficial for all parties. Because we were with the rovers, there was no question that we were included in both the work and the place to stay. Wright had also explained it was a custom for folks who were on a walkabout, something that young folks often did for a season or a year, to stay at farms and offer work in exchange for a meal and a dry place to sleep.

We traveled through the day without stopping for any length of time, just long enough to stretch our legs and give the horses a chance to graze and drink. Now that Wright was in Sommerhjem, he was anxious to get to where he hoped his family was still camped.

When it was about an hour before dusk, Wright pulled his homewagon down a lane leading to a small farm. The byre-longhouse and outbuildings were all made of stone. Though the holding was not a large one, it was well maintained and well laid out. As we rode down the lane, I could see that the folks who had this holding had tapped the trees for the sweet spring sap. This high up, I could see by the number of buckets still hanging off the trees that they were still gathering the sap. Lower down, out of the hills, the sap had probably stopped running.

When we pulled into the clearing a short way from the thatched roof byre-longhouse, several barking dogs came tearing around the corner and halted about ten feet from Wright's homewagon. I pulled up short behind the second homewagon, a bit worried about the charged atmosphere created by the dogs and the fact that I had a wild hill cat just behind me on my horse.

An aproned woman dusting flour off her hands stepped out of the byre-longhouse and called to the dogs. They immediately moved to her side. She was followed out the door by a small girl child who clung to her mother's leg, half hiding behind her.

"Well met, rovers. How might I help you?"

"We have traveled down the mountain this day and would ask if we might camp here. We would be happy to do chores or help with anything that needs helping in return," stated Wright.

"You and your companions are welcome to camp here this night. In return, we could use some help cutting and splitting some wood and feeding the animals. I see by your sign that you are a worker in wood. I think good fortune has sent you this way. Seems my two large, rambunctious sons thought it was quite all right to wrestle with the dogs and each other inside. As a result, they broke the end legs off my baking table. Would you be able to fix it?"

Wright replied that he would be happy to take a look.

After taking care of my horse and watching Kipp begin to stalk a mouse near the grain bin, I headed off for my assignment. My job that evening was to haul wood to the sap house, which was in a small clearing beyond the barn section of the byre-longhouse. There I met the two rambunctious sons and their father who were busy boiling down the sweet sap into syrup. They were glad for the help. These hardworking folks were very much like the crofters and larger farmers on Nytt Heimili's land. Seeing them made me homesick.

I was shaken out of my reverie when Arnar suggested I get a move on, for there was another pile of wood waiting to be hauled. When we finished with our chores, the farm family invited us in to share a meal. We contributed what we could spare, and all of us sat down at the long kitchen table to eat. It was the most pleasant time I had had in a long time. I just needed to make sure I did not get too used to this temporary peace.

CHAPTER SIXTEEN

Grimur was pacing the sitting room of the suite of rooms his sister had assigned him in the manor of Nytt Heimili. Scattered about the floor were bags and half-packed trunks. Clothing and other possessions were flung or stacked on every available piece of furniture. He snapped out the command for someone to enter when he heard a knock on the door. A rawboned woman dressed in traveling clothes stepped into the room.

"Donnola, shut the door. Report. You had better have brought me some good news."

Donnola, a fit woman of medium height with long blond braids falling down her back, upon looking around the sitting room, exclaimed, "Are you redecorating? Or are you moving?"

"I'll explain the mess later. Tell me what you know."

"Timir …." Donnola shivered when she said the name. Clearing her throat, she went on. "Timir has begun piecing together what he thinks happened."

"Has he found her?"

"Not yet. He thinks he has picked up her trail. He thinks she is not traveling alone as we first surmised. She is quite possibly traveling with two others."

"Who?"

"There are two folks from here who have not been seen since around the time Perrin disappeared. Mind you, that could just be a coincidence. I have never liked coincidences, however. One was the woman who had just finished her border guard service, called Rosilda. She is the one who had been accompanying Perrin on her rides about the landholding. Seems she was just here visiting her family for a while and left for an unspecified destination."

"And the other?"

"It is an old man named Arnar who, until recently, was the one who instructed Perrin in weapons and kazan. He had been dismissed from the manor barracks and was camped in the hills with other old and redundant folks. Seems Perrin and Rosilda visited Arnar. After they visited, he stalked off in a fit of anger, taking his gear with him. I guess it was not unknown for him to take off from the encampment for days at a time. However, we found out he had several horses pastured at the cottage of a woman known as Elder Nambi, and those horses are no longer there."

"I see. You both suspect that these two folks are traveling with Perrin?"

"Yes, sire. As you know, we were the two of your trackers traveling toward the southern border, suspecting Perrin might head to her mother's land. Unfortunately, as you know, we could not leave here right away since we took the time to try to discretely find her on the landholding ...."

"And you were dragooned into another more open search for her after the Laird returned unexpectedly early."

"The delay and the heavy rains on the night Perrin disappeared made it hard to pick up any trace of her. What has helped was knowing that she might be traveling with two others and on horseback."

"Have you found them?"

"Not yet. I think we are on the right track. Along the way, we heard tell by folks coming toward us that they had been passed by three border guards. Two women and an older man. Then one evening we happened to stop at an inn and ran into four men who, shall we say, had very loose tongues, and told the tale about how they were trying to harm some rovers. They were going to tip the rover's homewagon over to create a great deal of hardship for the rovers. They told us a woman on horseback charged one of them, jumped off her horse, and made some lightning-fast move causing the man to end up on the ground. The other two with her made swift work of the others in the bunch."

"That move sounds like someone trained in kazan. A discipline that we know Perrin is very skilled at."

"That was our thinking. We also think that the folks we are looking for began to travel with the rovers. Our luck was good when we reached

Høyhauger and stopped in at the pub frequented by folks from this area. Seems a man who might have been Arnar spent several hours talking with a young border guard, so might be aware as to what has happened here. We also talked to several folks who, let us just say, were eager to sell information. Seems that the man we thought was Arnar spent the day gathering supplies and a pack horse. No one else was with him. He did not cross the border that day."

"How unfortunate that he was not caught before he was able to gather supplies. If he is traveling with Perrin, that means they are much less vulnerable and weak, for they now have equipment and probably have more food."

"Several days later, two rover homewagons and three riders, one man and two women crossed the pass. Unfortunately, when we arrived in Høyhauger, the pass was closed due to a rare, very heavy spring snowstorm. Equally unfortunate was the fact that the trio we had been following were the very last to cross the pass before it was closed. When I left to come back here to report, the pass was still closed. One of the folks we talked to thought the rovers and those with them took a high risk to leave when they did. Obviously, there has been no word whether they have made it to the Sommerhjem side of the pass or perished in the attempt."

"Why do I think, considering how lucky they have been leaving Nytt Heimili and eluding detection, that while nature was unkind concerning the storm, that the trio and the rovers survived?"

"Quite possible, I am afraid. What do you wish for me to do next?"

"Go and get some rest. Resupply. I, in the meantime, will get the servants back in here to pack up my belongings. It has been strongly suggested by Laird Leifur that my visit here is over. My sister and I greatly miscalculated concerning the Laird. We had managed to keep him so isolated that we thought he was unaware as to what was really happening on the landholding and at the manor. Since he has been back, he has sent more than me packing, and my sister is going to be quite surprised and very disappointed when she returns from the capital to discover she has lost considerable power and standing here. That does not mean that the end result will not be the same. As long as Prince Mallus remains our ruler, my nephew will be raised to become the next laird of Nytt Heimili."

"The problem is that a change in rule could place Perrin back in line to become the next laird."

"You speak the truth. On the morrow, shortly after dawn, I will meet you on the road heading to Høyhauger. Will Timir have waited for you to return?"

"No, he said he was going to cross the border as soon as the pass was once again open. He planned to send a messenger bird to the general Høyhauger roost in my name to indicate where he was heading and if he had had any luck."

As promised, Grimur met up with Donnola at dawn, and they set a swift pace heading toward Høyhauger. On fast horses, and with good weather and good roads, they reached the border town in half the time it took most who traveled that road. They arrived and stabled their horses at the Copper Kettle Inn. Once settled in their rooms, Grimur and Donnola went down to the connected pub to get a hot meal.

To their immense surprise, they found Timir sitting with his back to the wall at a table tucked away in a corner. It was not surprising that the other patrons of the pub had chosen not to sit near him. Timir was of average height but not average build. Muscles rippled under his tunic, which was stretched across his overly broad shoulders. It was not his look of strength which kept folks away, however. It was the look in his dead dark eyes. Anyone with any sense knew it would be prudent to stay as far away from this man as possible. He was the type of folk that sent shivers of fear down one's back just looking at him.

Once Grimur and Donnola had pulled up chairs, joined Timir, and requested a meal, Grimur addressed him.

"I did not think we would find you still here."

"Luck turned," Timir told Grimur in a gravelly voice.

"And just how did luck turn?" Grimur responded impatiently.

"The snowstorm closed the pass. Once the snow had melted, the pass was still closed due to a rock fall that has taken days to move off the road. The road will be opened on the morrow."

"Are you convinced that those we seek are across the border in Sommerhjem?"

"Yes. Each time we have run across the trail of two women and one older man traveling together, while some things change, many things stay the same. The man, despite having a beard or just having a mustache, being a border guard, a traveler of little means or a traveler of means, has a slight limp and a hand that has been damaged. As for the women, again despite what they are wearing and purporting to be, they also fit the general description. The rover homewagons, which are hard to miss because they are never plain, fit the descriptions of rover homewagons that were accompanied by three riders."

"About the rock fall. Could we have been so lucky that it fell on those we hope we are following?"

"Sadly, no."

"Was there any indication that the snowstorm did them in?"

"No."

"How far do you think we are behind them?"

"At least a week."

"Do you have any good news at all?"

"Perhaps. It is my understanding that when some rovers, traders, and other travelers from Sommerhjem return from Bortfjell, they often stop in Klippebyen to resupply before heading off to spring markets and then on to summer markets. I suggest we head there on the morrow. Oh, and one other thing. There was some rumor about one of the women having a cat riding with her on the back of her horse. A brown-striped cat, the informant thought. Odd."

CHAPTER SEVENTEEN

The day after we had stayed overnight at the farm, the other rover family we had been traveling with bid us farewell and headed west. By midafternoon, we pulled into a campsite just off the road where Wright was to meet the rest of his family. The campsite was occupied by just one rover homewagon. Wright had hardly halted the horses before he jumped down, swept up a wee little girl, and pulled a tall, redheaded woman into his arms. A man and a woman came rushing out of the homewagon, and there commenced a loud, joyous reunion with everyone talking at the same time. Once the commotion settled down, Wright introduced us to his family.

"This is my wife, Brodie, and my youngest, Keitha. She is a little shy. This is my sister, Sawyer, and her husband, Stodd. Family, these three folks traveling with us are the reason we have arrived safely. A sudden snowstorm at the pass is the reason we are late."

We had decided that once we were with Wright's family, we would go by our given names. Wright introduced us as Perrin, Arnar, and Rosilda. When he had finished with the introductions, Lakyle piped up.

"You forgot about Kipp, Father."

"You are right, lad. I did indeed. The cat sitting on Perrin's horse is a wild hill cat from Bortfjell who has been traveling with us. He is also responsible for creating a diversion, so Lakyle and Perrin were not harmed by the bullies who had taken a disliking to anyone they deemed foreigners."

"Yes, we faced a little of that ourselves," stated Brodie. "It does help to have someone of Stodd's size along to discourage the bullies, who I find are not very brave when faced with some real opposition."

I could certainly see why. Stodd was not only tall, but he was solid muscle. I could tell that he probably had no trouble handling large horses as a farrier.

Brodie suggested that we all dismount and get settled, and as it was too late in the day to move on, we might as well stoke up the campfire and put the kettle on. The rest of the afternoon passed swiftly by. We cooked and ate dinner together, and once Lakyle and Keitha had settled into bed, the rest of us gathered around the campfire to talk softly amongst ourselves.

"I imagine Wright has had an opportunity to fill you in on who we are and why we have come to Sommerhjem. We all agreed before we left the border guard encampment that it would not be fair to all of you, if we continued to travel together, and you did not know the danger that might be following me."

"Our family owes you a great debt for helping discourage those who intended harm to my mother, my brother, and my nephew," stated Sawyer. "We have agreed that you are welcome to travel with us as long as you wish. I do have a few suggestions to make that might make you harder to find, should someone have picked up your trail."

"Go on," suggested Arnar.

"While we have been waiting this last fortnight, we have shared this campsite with other travelers. Some were from Sommerhjem, and some have been from Bortfjell. While folks from our two countries look physically very much the same, their clothing, saddles, and tack are different. Also, your horses are of a slightly different breed, except for your pack horse."

I had not given much thought to our clothing, horses, saddles, or tack. Since we had been spending our time with either rovers whose clothing is distinctive, or the border guards who wear uniforms, I had not really thought about how we might look different or stand out to anyone paying attention to us.

I turned my attention back to the conversation when Stodd spoke up. "While I was helping settle Wright's horses, I took a look at what the three of you are riding. I noticed that Arnar's and Perrin's horses are a little long in the tooth. Rosilda's horse is younger but showing some signs of fatigue from what must have been quite a journey for all of you. I don't mean to be personal, but do you have the means to purchase horses that might be a bit less travel worn?"

I answered in the affirmative. With what my father had left me in the wishing tree, I could cover the expenses.

"I am sure Wright told you I am a leather smith," said Brodie. "I think when we get to the next big town, which is Klippebyen, you might want to trade out your saddles and tack. If you will allow me to help, I know folks there who make fine leather goods, and I think I could help you find some used gear that, with a little hard work, would clean up quite nicely."

"Might I also suggest that you purchase different clothing," Wright suggested, joining the conversation. "Actually, knowing what little you have told me that you were able to leave Bortfjell with, you have already thought of that. I have been thinking about how you might want to present yourselves to draw as little attention as possible. Perhaps your clothing should be of good quality, but a little bit worn. You would look like you come maybe from a merchant family who is temporarily a little down on their luck."

All of Wright's family had given us well-thought-out suggestions. After the rovers had gone to their homewagons to settle in for the night, the three of us sat a little longer and discussed what they had said.

"I feel quite foolish and very unprepared for this forced adventure I find us on," I told the others. "In my defense, it is not like I had weeks to plot or plan my escape from a possible attempt on my life and being forced to flee in the middle of the night. I have just been putting one mile after another behind me with little or no thought as to what is ahead. The suggestions Wright's family gave us this night are good ones."

"They are good. However, we will also need some serious coin," suggested Rosilda.

"That brings me to an issue I have meant to talk to you and Arnar about. Before I left home, my father, anticipating that I might need to flee, left me considerable funds. I had hoped to have some time over the next few days to distribute the funds among us. I have been concerned that if something happened, if I were captured or killed, and you all got away, that would put the funds in the hands of those who would do me harm, and those funds would be lost to you. I think it will be better to divide the funds up among the three of us for safety. I will not hear any objection to that plan. Neither of you had to leave Bortfjell with me, yet you have chosen to leave home and hearth ..."

"Such as they were," stated Arnar.

"… such as they were, to travel with me. You have shown no inclination to abandon me and turn back. I think, by whatever means, we should follow the suggestions we were given this night. Are we agreed?"

My companions reluctantly agreed on the distribution of the funds my father had left me. I took some out of each place where I had hidden the gold, silver, jewels, and coins. Arnar and Rosilda then squirreled their portions away in hiding places that others might not find immediately. I was thankful that my cloak was a plain one and would not give me away as being from Bortfjell, so I did not have to remove all that I had sewn into it. I had checked with Brodie concerning my satchel, backpack, and blanket roll. She assured me that they would pass here in Sommerhjem because of their plainness and well-worn look.

We also discussed what Wright had suggested as to stopping in Klippebyen to purchase clothing, horses, and gear. Rosilda and Arnar agreed that we should follow their suggestions. I think they reluctantly agreed about who might be paying. With the plan in mind, the next day we continued to head south with the rovers.

We arrived late in the afternoon about a quarter day's ride from Klippebyen. We pulled off the main road and down a side lane, finding a camping spot next to a small spring. In the morning, as we broke our fast, we told Wright and his family that all their suggestions concerning our transformation were good ones. It seems that they had been thinking more about the discussion we had had earlier in the week and had some suggestions on how we could accomplish our transformation from looking like we were from Bortfjell to looking like we might be native to Sommerhjem.

"You all speak our language fairly well and have improved with Lakyle's help," Wright suggested. "However, might I suggest that the three of you do not enter the town and stay here with the homewagons, our daughter Keitha, and my mother Burle. The rest of us will go into town. If you will trust us to make good decisions for you, here is our plan. Stodd will trade your horses for good mounts."

"Nothing fancy mind you, simply good sturdy horses," suggested Stodd. "I will find ones that are good for traveling long distances. In case you need some speed, they will perform a bit better than the ones you have now."

Arnar, Rosilda, and I agreed that Stodd, as a farrier, was sure to know a good horse when he saw one, if the ones pulling the homewagons were any indication. We also acknowledged that he would know what kind of horse would be most suitable for the type of traveling we would be doing.

"Meanwhile," said Brodie, "I will take your saddles and tack into a leather smith I know. I had intended to stop there on our way south, for he always has some fine leather for me to bargain or barter for when we are up this way. I will try to barter your saddles and tack for leather. I will tell him some reasonable tale as to how I acquired them. Once that transaction is done, I will wander the market and see what I can pick up to replace your gear. It would not be unusual for me to do that. I have a good eye, if I do say so myself, for leather goods that might not look good to a less discriminating eye. Sometimes something that looks neglected or very dirty is a hidden jewel under the dirt and grime."

"What about our boots?" Arnar asked.

"They should be fine. They are similar in design to what is worn here near the border."

"Now, as for your clothing," stated Sawyer, "Wright and I will wander the market and try to pick up the type of clothing we talked about, a genteel worn look for the three of you. We will try to pick clothing that is as close as we can get to your sizes. Burle is an excellent seamstress. She has offered to do any needed mending and alterations. Once the three of you look more like someone from Sommerhjem rather than Bortfjell, you can pick up more clothing along the way."

I was humbled by the effort the rover family was making to be sure we would be less traceable by those who might be following us and wished me harm. They brushed off my profound thanks, stating they owed us a debt. I think at this point, what little we had done had already been repaid many times over.

It was hard to wait for Wright and the others to return from Klippebyen. The hours passed way too slowly for me. Wright had assured me that we were safe from folks trying to cause harm to their families and their homewagons. Rovers were generally respected in Sommerhjem. While they traveled the land and were itinerant folk, rovers had the reputation of being honest, hardworking folk who held to a strict code of honor.

While Wright's assurance that folks from Sommerhjem might not cause harm was comforting, I was worried that folks from Bortfjell who were looking for me might cause harm if they discovered us here. With our horses gone, we would be left on foot to try to escape. We would have to leave the pack horse behind with most of our possessions. When that thought occurred to me, I called Rosilda and Arnar over.

"I think each of us should put together a pack of what we might need if we have to take off on foot. Mind you, I trust Wright and his family with our secrets and our continued safety."

"I hear a however coming," suggested Arnar.

"You are correct. I just want to be prepared if we suddenly have to leave on foot. I do not want to put Wright's family in danger, should folks who are looking for us come upon this campsite. Without our horses, we would have to run into the surrounding forest and try to elude pursuit."

"We also need a plan of where to meet up should we become separated," advised Rosilda.

"I would suggest that if we were to become separated, we try to make it to the valley of the porcelain craft folk. If, after a time, you need to move on from there, leave a sign of the direction you have gone. Remember, Arnar, you used to leave symbols for us to see if we could find where you had left instructions of where we were to go next when you were training us. Is that your own code or would others like those trying to track us know it?"

"Ah, good thought, Perrin. The symbols I taught you were of my own making. I only used them with the patrol I led when I was with the border guard, and just you two when I was training folks at Nytt Heimili. If I remember, you were both quick studies. Let's get those packs assembled, and then take some time today to refresh our minds by going over the symbols."

With something constructive to do instead of pace and worry, the time passed much more quickly. We took a break and fixed something to eat near noon. After the meal, we spent some time with Burle and Keitha doing chores. When the young girl began to yawn and rub her eyes, her

Amma took her into the homewagon and tucked her in for a nap. When Burle came back out of the homewagon, she joined us at the cookfire.

"Wee lass is plumb tuckered out. Too much excitement and joy having her father and brother back. Now I know you folks really want to be up pacing around the campsite, or chopping wood, or doing anything else to pass the hours. I would ask you to settle back and have another cup of tea. Let us spend some of this quiet time while Keitha is asleep to talk. It will give me a chance to let you know the lay of the land."

We settled in as Burle had asked. Kipp jumped up on my lap, turned around several times, and made himself comfortable. He did not nap. He was attentive, as if he were listening to all Burle had to tell us.

Over the next hour or so, Burle gave us a very condensed lesson on how Sommerhjem was ruled, how the work of the land was broken down, and the customs that varied from region to region. She talked about the role of the rovers, the foresters, the traders, the merchants, the craft guilds, the farmers, the fishers, the large landholders, and others. I was not sure I could begin to remember all that she told us and wished I had had a journal in which to write it all down. Our lesson ended when a very sleepy little lass climbed down out of the homewagon and wanted her Amma's attention.

Finally, midafternoon, Wright and the others rode in. It took us some time to look over the horses and the riding gear. The horses were a solid reddish brown in color and somewhat smaller than the horses we had been riding. They were well muscled and looked well cared for. The same could not be said for the saddles and tack.

"I see you eyeing that saddle, Perrin, and the look on your face suggests that you do not see much beauty in it. I am going to make a believer of you yet. Give me a short time. You'll see," stated Brodie firmly.

"If you say so."

"I say so."

After Arnar left Sawyer's homewagon with his new clothes, I left Brodie to her task. Rosilda and I went with Sawyer into her homewagon to sort out the clothing she had brought back for us. Since I had not entered either of the homewagons before this time, I was surprised at what I found inside. It truly was a home on wheels with beds, storage, table and seating, a small wood stove, and a place to wash up. It was all very compact, neat, and organized. It was a wonder of ingenuity, and I thought it might be grand to travel in a homewagon. It sure would be much better than sleeping on the ground in a tent or under a lean-to.

When I walked out of the homewagon carrying a bundle of clothes under my arm, I had a chance to look over my two companions. To my untrained eye, we now looked very much like those we had seen on the road. I hoped this ruse would help us blend in.

Once we had packed our new items in our saddlebags and in bags to go on the pack horse, I returned to the cookfire where Brodie was sitting. As I approached, she set aside the rag she had been using to polish the leather on a beautiful saddle.

"That cannot be the saddle I saw just a short while ago."

"Yup. All it took was a little elbow grease and a bit of time. I also need to tell you that I got a really good trade for your saddles. Seems my fellow leather smith was more than happy to get his hands on all your Bortfjellian saddles. He has always wanted to study how they were crafted. I got more leather than I had hoped for from him, and he got what he had wanted for some time in return. If anyone were to come into his shop, he would probably not let them look too closely at the saddles. He is going to guard those saddles and keep them secret, because he will probably discover a new technique or design and will not want other leather smiths to find out his secrets."

That was good news. Now I could only hope that our horses would not be noticeable where they had been traded. Stodd had informed us that he had traded the horses at the animal pens where he had the good luck to run into a horse trader he knew.

"I had made up a plausible tale about how I had acquired several horses during my cold months commission. I then told him that just over the border, I had met three riders who needed better mounts and were willing to pay in coin and barter. The barter was their three horses for the ones I had, plus a fair amount in coin. My wife had a good haggle with them over the tack on their horses for some she had. They seemed extraordinarily eager to exchange their Bortfjellian horses and tack for ours." Stodd informed us. "In my discussion …"

"In your spinning of a tall tale, you mean," Sawyer remarked.

"… with the horse trader, I told him that we had lucked out with a grand commission this month in the high hills. However, we were going to need some riding stock, for we did not want to have to hitch up the homewagons every time we wanted to make the hour and a half trek into the nearest village. The ones I had with me were not suitable for the tracks we would be traveling in the high hills. So, we then settled into haggling for a good price on the horses we brought back. Of course, part of my bargain was that he ended up with your horses. Worked pretty well, if I do say so myself."

"We also subtly let the horse trader and the leather smith know that the three we had met and traded with were heading down the royal road in the direction of the capital. We didn't know much about them, just that they seemed in a hurry," stated Brodie.

I was impressed as to how carefully our rover friends had tried to cover our tracks. I could only hope it worked.

Chapter Eighteen

Just before we all turned in for the night, Wright and Sawyer approached us. They invited us to join them in Sawyer's homewagon, for they wanted to discuss the route that they intended to take starting the next day. Once we were all seated at the table, Sawyer unrolled a map.

I was amazed at the detail of the map and wished I had a way of copying it. Not only did it have the main roads including the royal road marked, it also had smaller lanes marked, and what I suspected were mere paths. In addition, in writing almost too small to read, there were notes and symbols.

"We are camped here," stated Sawyer, pointing to a spot on the map with her finger. "I would suggest that the three of you take this lane here and head east. We will head back through Klippebyen and continue down the royal road, heading south. When you reach this crossroad, you need to head south. In a day's time, if we turn east here, we will meet up with you here near this small falls."

I thought of the idea of riding hidden in the homewagons, but I dismissed it fairly quickly. I could see what Sawyer intended made more sense. "You are thinking if anyone has connected the three of us with you, if they surmised we have come to Klippebyen, and even if they discover our horses or gear have been left behind, they might be thrown off our trail by trying to find a trace of all of us together on the main road. Good idea."

"We were always headed south and east, for our clan gathers here about this time each spring," Wright said, pointing to a spot on the map. "It gives us time to meet up with family, exchange news and information, and generally take some time to get ready for the summer fairs, if that is

113

one's normal plan. After that, Sawyer and I have a commission to do the carvings on the trim and shutters of Lady Jegerinne's hunting lodge, which is in the direction you wish to go. This is a good project for us, since our skills are more suited to larger carving projects than to smaller woodcraft items. We do go to some of the summer fairs to display our carving skills. We get a few commissions at the fairs, but most of the time, our commissions come by word of mouth. We have gained a good reputation over the years."

I had noticed that even the farmhouses, barns, and outbuildings had beautifully carved trim and shutters. Wright had also carved and painted similar designs on his homewagon. The designs were intricate, beautiful, and unlike anything I had ever seen in Bortfjell. When I had asked Wright about them, he had explained the designs were as old as time, took a long time to learn, and required a great deal of attention to craft and carve.

My attention was drawn back to the conversation as Wright continued. "While you might think it would be too risky for you to meet back up with us and camp with us at the clan gathering, I think it might be a good choice. Your trail would certainly be muddied when all the gathered homewagons and horses leave the gathering. Anyone following you would not know which homewagon or homewagons to continue to track."

I was beginning to really appreciate both Wright's and Sawyer's clever thinking. They certainly did not need to continue to help us or ask us to continue to travel with them. I knew that when we reached the parting of the way for good, I would miss them.

After we left the homewagon, I noticed that Brodie was still sitting out by the campfire working on something. She looked up when I asked if I could join her.

"Ah, good, it's you. I have been thinking about how we have done a lot this day to change you and your companions' appearance. There are two areas where you are still quite identifiable."

"Arnar is one."

"Yes. A simple fix would be for him to always wear riding gloves. On horseback, his limp is of course not noticeable, but his hand is."

"An easy fix, since I saw among the items you all brought back were several pairs of gloves. I imagine he may have already thought of that. What is the other problem that might give us away?"

"Kipp riding behind you on your horse."

I must have looked highly concerned. The idea of leaving Kipp behind was not acceptable to me.

"I am not suggesting you not travel with Kipp, if he chooses to continue with you. I have just finished working on something that I think might solve the problem of him being noticed. Come, follow me to that downed tree where your new saddle is resting."

When we arrived at the downed tree, Brodie placed what she had been working on behind the saddle. It looked like a modified pack that would fit on the horse's rump and attach to the two saddlebags.

"How would Kipp look anymore hidden riding on top of that than he looked riding on top of my backpack and satchel?"

"Because it is open to your back and has a flap that will quickly flip forward to cover even that opening. Kipp can crawl in and curl up on the padding of sheepskin I have put inside. It would keep him warm and dry on rainy days. Now mind you, he may not want to go inside. If he does not like it, you can just tuck it in your gear on your pack horse."

"Thank you, we'll have to see …."

I stopped talking when I saw Kipp jump up on the fallen tree, navigate across the saddle, stop, poke his head in the pack, crawl in, turn around once, and settle in.

"I guess that answers the question as to whether he might like it," I told Brodie. "Thank you. I will never be able to thank your family enough for all that you have done for us. You all have been so kind."

"It's just the rover way, I guess. Folks here in Sommerhjem, for the most part, help one another, especially those of us who travel this land."

I wondered if that were true in Bortfjell. If I traveled my homeland, would the farmers and crofters welcome me to camp on their land? If I chanced upon a campsite where others had chosen to camp for a night, would they invite me to gather at their cookfire? I did not know, and that thought made me realize how very narrow my understanding of Bortfjell really was, even though I had been more educated and trained than most. It saddened me that I might now have more understanding of the everyday, commonplace ways and customs of Sommerhjem than I did of the land of my birth.

It seemed strange the next day not to be traveling with the rover families. We did not hurry, for we needed to get used to our new horses. I found the one I had chosen had a smooth gait, and the new saddle was comfortable. Kipp spent his time either on top of the new pack or snuggled inside. I had had a conversation with Kipp before we started off. Although I felt a wee bit foolish talking to him, I had suggested to him that if someone approached us, he might want to make himself scarce.

Our first occasion to see if my talk had had any effect was about an hour into our ride. Coming toward us down the lane was a wagon. There was a driver and someone sitting next to him. I saw Rosilda urge her horse forward and pull alongside Arnar. I was far enough back that I could not hear what she said. I did see her reach into her cloak and put on gloves. Arnar did the same. I did not need to, for I was already wearing mine. We had decided if we all wore gloves while riding, a fairly common practice, that Arnar would not stand out. It would take some practice for us to do this as a routine.

I looked back over my shoulder to see if Kipp was sitting on or in the pack. He was inside.

"Kipp, folks are coming so could you stay inside the pack?" He of course did not answer. He did, however, pull himself farther inside.

As we passed the oncoming wagon, we tipped our hats in greeting and passed on by without incident. Off and on throughout the day we met others on the lane. Gloves remained on, Kipp remained hidden, and it seemed no one paid us very much attention.

The weather was mild during the day, but still chilly at night. We got good at setting up camp each evening and packing up each morning. We had learned that not just rovers stopped at farmsteads and exchanged a place to camp for offers to help.

I was glad I had not been raised by my stepmother from early childhood on, for I would never have made it this far. I would have been appalled at being asked to muck out a barn, chop wood, catch a piglet, sleep on the ground, or bathe in a creek. My hands would have been full of blisters, and my skin burnt to a crisp. I sent a silent thanks to those who had trained me.

We met back up with the two rover families just where we had arranged to meet. Later that day, we found ourselves in a large clearing filled with more than a dozen homewagons of all sizes, colors, and painted designs. The sight was almost overwhelming, for as Wright had explained to us when we had first seen his colorful homewagon with its intricately carved and painted designs, a rover would never drive a plain homewagon.

I had worried how Wright and his family would explain the three of us, and if we would feel welcome. He just introduced us as friends who had helped him and his family along the way. He did not go into any elaborate explanation, and no one asked him to explain further. I was surprised by that.

That evening after the dinner chores were done, folks gathered around a central fire ring. Some of the rovers brought out fiddles, drums, mountain flutes, and other instruments, and filled the night air with lively tunes. Every once in a while, when the musicians would take a break, one of the elders would tell a tale. Some of the tales were filled with humor, others were tall tales. As the evening drew late, the music became softer, children were taken off to their respective homewagons for bed, and the fire burned down to embers.

When we had first arrived, Kipp had vanished into the surrounding woods, and I had feared that he would not come back due to the large number of folks, dogs, cats, and children. When the fire was just coals, I felt him climb onto my lap and settle in. I know I breathed a sigh of relief.

Midafternoon the next day I was sitting alone on a log out away from the encampment because I had wanted to spend some quiet time away from folks, even though the only remaining rovers were Wright's and Sawyer families and a rover elder. The other rovers had been packing up and leaving all day. I had enjoyed meeting the other rovers and learning about how they worked and traveled the land. I had enjoyed the music and comradery of the evening. I was sorry to see them all go. I was especially sorry that the two rover families we had traveled with had delayed their meeting up with their friends and relations because of helping us, and so had had so little time with them. They had just shrugged off my apologies, saying gatherings were always everchanging due to weather, commissions, road conditions, and other delays.

I was so lost in my thoughts that if not for the sound of the snap of a twig underfoot, I would not have I looked up to see an elder rover approach.

"Might I share your log?"

"I would be honored."

"Your friend will not mind?"

I looked around to see what who she was talking about. I had thought I was here alone.

Seeing the look of puzzlement on my face the elder pointed upward. I looked up and saw that Kipp was resting on the wide tree branch above me that was providing shade. I had not realized he was there. I was surprised that this woman had spotted him, since I had a hard time finding him at first.

"I have not seen his kind this far south in quite a number of years. A wild hill cat, is he not?"

"Yes."

"More commonly found in the high hills of Bortfjell."

This was not a question on the part of this elder, rather a statement. I did not know what to say.

"Please relax. Your secrets are your own. Now, I have been quite rude and not introduced myself. I am Wright's and Sawyer's great aunt. I am named Iona and am a gem smith by trade. I would speak to you about something you are carrying."

At that moment Kipp scrambled down the tree he had been resting on, placed himself in front of me, and looked to have puffed up to twice his size. I did not know what had caused his stance, until I looked up to see a silver-coated cat the size of a herding dog silently slipping out from behind a tree opposite me. I quickly glanced at Elder Iona to see if she was as alarmed as I was. She was not. Elder Iona sat next to me with her hands resting on her knees, alert and watching. I was afraid to speak.

As I watched, the large cat stopped about halfway between us and the tree he had been behind. He proceeded to sit down and calmly began to clean an ear. I looked at Kipp, whose fur was no longer standing on end, and to my amazement and alarm, he began to walk toward the silver-coated cat. When I would have leapt up, Elder Iona put a calming hand on my arm.

"Your hill cat will not be harmed by my hunting cat. It will be all right. Watch."

Kipp headed straight toward the hunting cat, stopped a foot away, and sat down. The two cats spent a long moment or two taking each other's measure. It looked to me as if they both nodded their heads, then stood up and approached each other. I held my breath. After the cats touched noses, both headed our way. Kipp settled himself at my feet, and the hunting cat settled himself at Elder Iona's feet. I took a breath.

"The hunting cat at my feet is called Lorcan. Does your hill cat have a name?"

"He is called Kipp."

"It looks as if they have greeted each other. Your Kipp is quite a protector."

"Why have I not seen Lorcan around the encampment?"

"He makes himself scarce in large gatherings. He often does not return to my homewagon until long after dark. Now then, now that we have that settled, we can get back to why I sought you out."

CHAPTER NINETEEN

Elder Iona had to wait a while longer, because after Kipp and Lorcan had settled, we heard rustling in the undergrowth. We paused to find out who might be either approaching or lurking. Both the cats appeared relaxed and did not stir. Just as we were about to continue our conversation, a small calico cat slipped into the clearing, followed by a black and white patchy cat, a gray striped cat, and a large yellow cat. They too settled down near us.

"Just out of curiosity, Perrin, does this happen often, this gathering of cats?"

"Upon occasion. More frequently of late. I do not know if it is Kipp that somehow attracts them, or if it is me. Maybe the two of us together. I just do not know. I wonder where these cats came from. Perhaps a nearby farm?"

"Hum-m-m. I will have to think on this. Meanwhile, I wish to get back to why I sought you out. In your country, do you know of folks who are sensitive to objects of power?"

"Yes, I have heard of such."

"I am one such among the rovers. It is not something that is widely known. I would ask that you keep what we are about to discuss just between us two. Perhaps I should suggest we keep this among the four of us and the gathered cats."

I was beginning to like this elder who had eyes that twinkled and a hint of mischief in her demeanor. I asked her the same boon, that what we discussed would stay in this glen for now. She agreed.

"When I sat near you last night as we listened to the music, and again now, I sense you are carrying on your body several items of power."

To say that I was surprised by what Elder Iona just said would be an understatement. Thinking back on what I had tucked into my boots, sewn into my cloak and blanket roll, hidden in my pack, and carried in a pouch secreted away in an inner pocket, I could not imagine what I might have that would be an item of power, much less two items.

The only other item I had on my body was my mother's medallion. I realized at that moment I knew almost nothing about the medallion. My father had told me my mother never took it off. He did not know the history of the medallion, or why it was so important to my mother. I was a bit reluctant to show it to Elder Iona. Suddenly, Kipp jumped up on my lap, stretched a paw up, hooked the medallion's chain with a claw, and tugged.

"Thanks, Kipp, I can take it from here." I reached in under my shirt and pulled the chain all the way out. I lifted the chain over my head and held the medallion in my hand in such a way that Elder Iona could see what I had. She did not reach out to take it from me. Rather, she leaned forward to take a closer look.

"Might I ask you the history behind this medallion?"

"I know very little. It belonged to my mother who always wore it and never took it off. My father gave it to me just before I left home. I was told my mother came from beyond, which is to say she came from beyond the border of Bortfjell. It was surmised that she came from Sommerhjem. Her name was Helka, and Wright has suggested she might have come from a small valley south and east of here where porcelain crafters live. We intend to head that way."

"An entirely possible conjecture that your mother came from there. What is interesting is that the medallion is both unique and incomplete," stated Elder Iona, staring off into the distance.

"Because?" I asked after several moments.

"Oh, my apologies, Perrin. The medallion is neither metal nor wood. It is made of something quite rare, and few of us are left that know the secrets of working with the material. In addition, there should be a gem in the middle of the medallion. Do you by chance have a polished black stone that has flashes of color within?"

121

I thought back to the gems that I had dumped out of the pouch my father had left for me in the hollow of the wishing tree. There had been a beautiful polished black stone like the one Elder Iona had just described. I had been drawn to it and remembered I had tucked it away in a hiding place in my left boot.

"I think I have what you just described. If you do not mind, I will step away from here for a moment to retrieve it. Or not," I said, since Kipp was blocking my way from moving off the log. "Apparently Kipp has another idea."

"So it would seem. Interesting."

I took my left boot off, retrieved the black polished stone, and put my boot back on.

"If it is all right with you, Kipp, I will show the stone to Elder Iona." As I held out my hand, a light arced from the stone in my hand to a stone in a ring on Elder Iona's finger. I almost dropped the stone. When I could see again, I looked at Elder Iona questioningly.

"What you hold in your hand is a firestar gem. Firestar gems are exceedingly rare. One of the interesting properties of firestar gems is that when one firestar gem is near another firestar gem, and it is in the possession of someone with good intent, it will arc, of like to like. Also, when a firestar gem is near an object that is more than what it seems by its outward appearance, it grows warm. Perhaps the most interesting property of firestar gems is that they seem to choose who will wear them."

"What do you mean that firestar gems choose who will wear them?"

"I wear a firestar gem in the ring on my finger. It was not handed down in my family from generation to generation. It was a gift from a Günnary elder, a master gem cutter, and a mentor to me for a time. It was a stone that he had on his work bench, and I kept getting drawn to it, day after day. Mind you, he had a number of gems on his workbench that were cut to dazzle the eye and catch the light. However, it was the dark black stone that kept drawing me back. Forgive me, I have allowed us to get a bit sidetracked. Let us get back to the medallion."

"I know the medallion belonged to my mother. I do not remember if it had a firestar gem in the center of it. I cannot recall if I ever saw it more than once or twice."

"It could be that there was another gem in the medallion when your mother wore it. I think in your case, the two items belong together. Will you trust me with both the stone and the medallion for a short time? As I said before, that medallion is made of a material that few can make or handle. It of itself holds some power. That you are also in possession of a firestar gem that reacts to you suggests that in this time, the two items belong together."

I do not know why I thought what Elder Iona was suggesting sounded reasonable, yet for some reason, I did. Kipp apparently thought so too, since he leapt onto my lap and used his head to move my somewhat hesitant hands toward Elder Iona's outstretched hands.

"Will you wait here for me? My tools are back at my homewagon, and I need them, a bit of fire, and some water to set the firestar gem."

"Ah, Elder Iona …." I started hesitantly. I had become alarmed when Elder Iona mentioned fire.

"I promise, no harm will come to either the medallion or the firestar gem, Perrin. I promise on my honor."

Knowing what pledging on one's honor meant to a rover, I handed Elder Iona the medallion and the firestar gem. She had me place the two items in a silk-like cloth that she had draped over her hands.

"The cloth is golden pine spider silk. Besides being beautiful, if an item of power is wrapped in golden pine spider silk, it can prevent most from detecting it."

When Elder Iona left, all of the cats chose to stay with me. Kipp settled on my lap, and Lorcan shifted over to stretch out in front of my feet. I did not know what to think of what had just occurred. I wondered if my father had known what mother's medallion was made of. Also, had the firestar gem been my mother's, or was it just something from my father's treasury?

Suddenly, an unrelated question occurred to me. Were hunting cats common companions of folks in Sommerhjem? I knew there were hunting cats in the eastern mountains of Bortfjell. I had never heard of any of them companioning with folks. I had not ever heard of a hunting cat being seen even in the high hills, much less traveling with anyone. It then occurred to me that I had not ever heard of anyone in Bortfjell traveling with a wild hill cat. It was with that thought I realized once again that Kipp was certainly not a pet as the cats of the manor were to some folk. He was wild after all. He felt more like a companion, and I found great comfort in that thought.

Elder Iona returned about a half hour later and sat once again next to me on the log. She then handed me my mother's medallion. As I looked at it, not only could I see how beautiful the firestar gem looked placed in the medallion, but I could also feel the rightness of it. There was a feeling of great age about the medallion, though I could not explain why I thought that. My thoughts were interrupted when Elder Iona spoke.

"There is a feeling of rightness of the firestar gem being in the center of the medallion. I also felt as though both the medallion and the firestar were quite old."

For a brief moment, I wondered if Elder Iona was able to read my mind. I shook that thought off as fanciful. I had a few questions to ask her before my friends became worried by my long absence.

"I wonder if I could ask you a few questions?"

"Of course, and if I can answer them, I will."

"Is it common for hunting cats to accompany folks in Sommerhjem?"

"It has been known to happen occasionally. It is an extremely rare occurrence. Lorcan is by no means tame or a pet. I am honored that he chooses to travel with me. Do wild hill cats often travel with folks in Bortfjell?"

"To be honest, I did not even know he was a wild hill cat, since I had never had the occasion to see one before Kipp. I just thought he was a larger than average cat like those cats who lived in the manor, or on the farms and crofts, or in the village. And no, to answer your question, I have never heard of one traveling with a folk."

I almost did not catch what Elder Iona said next, for she said it so quietly, as if she were saying something mostly to herself.

"I wonder if the Neebing blessed are beginning to walk the land."

I did not have the opportunity to ask her what that meant because we were interrupted by Lakyle running down the path toward us.

"You have to come back to the campsite, you have to come now," Lakyle said with great urgency. "Hurry."

CHAPTER TWENTY

In a back corner of the main room of the Horse and Coach Tavern, Grimur waited impatiently for his traveling companions to return. It had been a frustrating ride to Klippebyen. They had found no trace of Perrin or her supposed companions along the way. The delay in crossing the pass from Bortfjell into Sommerhjem had made finding his quarry nearly impossible. With funds beginning to run low, they would have to find Perrin soon, or they would be forced to return to Bortfjell. Grimur was roused from his thoughts when the serving lass set his meal before him. Looking up, he noted that both Timir and Donnola were heading toward his table.

"Well?" he said to the two as they sat down.

"And a fair greeting to you too," Donnola shot back. "Perhaps we might call for a meal and a drink before we share what we have found out. It has been a long day already."

Grimur snapped his mouth closed on the biting remark he wanted to make to Donnola. She did not give him the deference he felt he was due. At this point in the search, he needed to put up with her. Once back home, that was going to be a different matter. Timir said nothing, sitting in stony silence as usual.

After the meal was consumed, Grimur addressed the two at his table. He did not leave the impatience out of his voice. "Now that you have eaten, have you found out anything?"

"It appears we are about a day behind those that we think we are following. We talked to a number of stable owners and horse traders, in case Perrin decided to change horses. We finally found a horse trader at the animal pens who had recently done business with a rover farrier. It seems that the rover farrier, one that the horse trader has dealt with in the past, traded three horses, two older horses and one of middle years, that were Bortfjell bred. Said the rover sounded like he had made himself a good profit by trading three folk for good horses he had acquired over the cold months. Met these folks at a campsite about a two days' ride from the pass. These folks traveled a ways with them rovers, and then headed south down the royal road. Said the folks were heading toward the capital," said Donnola.

"Then we need to go toward the capital?"

"No," said Timir, speaking for the first time. "As you know, I have served the prince for a number of years. Part of my service was here in Sommerhjem. I still have a network of informants here. I connected with one of my old informants who told me another rover, a leather smith, traded three saddles and tack, that were of Bortfjell origin, for leather. Later, this same rover woman was seen bartering for used saddles and tack. My informant said he was following the woman because he thought she had more coin than is usual for a rover. He also noticed she had a good eye for used merchandise. Got herself some good bargains."

"What we have suspected since the pass is our quarry left Bortfjell traveling with two rover homewagons. Now we find that a rover farrier has traded three horses bred in Bortfjell for three horses bred in Sommerhjem, and at the same time, another rover is trading three saddles and tack that are of Bortfjell making. However, the farrier's tale could be true."

"It could be. The rover's tale of needing horses better suited for the high hills, where the rovers have their next commission, has a ring of truth to it. It could also be full of fog. What I know is," stated Timir, "if the three we are trying to find have headed down the royal road, they are long gone and would be almost impossible to follow. If on the other hand, the horses the farrier acquired this day are indeed for those we wish to find, then our last chance to do so would be to find the rovers."

"And just how do you propose we do that?" Grimur growled. He was fast losing patience with the whole search.

"I had a chat with the leather smith who had acquired the saddles. At first, he denied he had any Bortfjellian saddles. With a little cajoling, I got him talking. He remarked that he was surprised that the rover woman, her name was Brodie, had not kept at least one of the saddles to take apart and learn from. Said she was an extremely talented leather smith. Said the saddle bags and other leather goods she made were beautiful and in high demand," said Donnola. "So I asked him if she was still in town, pretending that it sounded like I should check out her goods too. He told me to his knowledge she had left town, but she occasionally sold her wares at the midsummer fairs, and I might run into her there. I asked if we were very far behind this rover leather smith. He said, 'Why no, as a matter of fact, they are not too far away at a gathering of rovers.' Even gave me the directions on how to find where the rovers are camped." Donnola had a slightly smug look on her face when she finished telling the others what she had found out.

"How far is this rover encampment?"

"About a full day and a half day's ride by wagon. We could make it in less time. It seems the rovers are gathered there for about half a fortnight, so they might still be there. If we left early in the morning, we would arrive just about in time for the evening meal tomorrow. These Sommerhjem folks have a tradition of inviting other travelers to share a campground and a meal. They are a weak folk," Timir stated in disgust.

"We will leave at first light. If the three we are looking for are with the rovers, we will figure out some way of separating them from the rovers and take care of matters so we can go home."

"Best we leave a bit later. If we arrive too early in the afternoon, the rovers will wonder why we are stopping so early rather than traveling on to the next village and finding a comfortable inn. By arriving at the time of the evening meal, we have a better excuse to stay," Timir countered.

Fortunately, good sense overrode impatience, and Grimur agreed to follow Timir's recommendation. Early the next morning Grimur settled up with the innkeeper and with the stable where they had left their horses. Since they were traveling light, it did not take long to be ready to ride, and they were soon heading out of Klippebyen. Once through town, they traveled at a steady pace, stopping only for short periods of time to rest and water the horses.

Chapter Twenty-One

Kipp jumped off my lap before I could stand up. He and the hunting cat Lorcan raced down the path after Lakyle. Elder Iona signaled that I should follow them, and she would be right behind. I ran after Lakyle and the cats. Once I reached the campsite, Arnar was waving me over to where the horses were.

"Quick, help saddle up our horses. While we are working, I will explain what is happening."

I did as Arnar asked. I noticed that Rosilda's horse was already saddled. When I looked around, I saw that she had taken our lean-to down and was rolling it up. All our gear which had been inside of the lean-to, or was carried on the pack horse, was in a pile. My attention was drawn back to the task at hand when Arnar urged me to get busy.

"What is going on?"

"Seems the horse trader, Revan, that Stodd traded with, is an old friend. Revan became a bit alarmed when a man came to the animal pens. The man was overly interested in our former horses and where they had come from. The horse trader gave them the tale Stodd had told him. Normally, Revan would not have thought further on the conversation. However, another of the horse traders made a remark to him after the man who was doing the inquiring had left."

"What was that about?"

"Seems this other horse trader had had a run in with the man a number of years back. Called him Timir. He suggested that this man, Timir, was not one you would like to have an interest in your affairs. Timir is the kind of man who sends shivers down your back. Rumor had it that back then

Timir was from Bortfjell and was up to no good in Sommerhjem. Then Revan became more concerned after his son told him of a conversation he had overheard at the Horse and Carriage pub last night. Seems this Timir, who was so interested in our horses, and a woman entered the pub together and met with another man over a meal. Revan's son overheard them talking about trying to track folks from Bortfjell and suspected these folks they were trying to find might be traveling with the rover who sold the horses. Before dawn broke, Revan sent his son off to give a warning to Stodd that trouble might be headed this way. Revan's son, who knows this area well, took a shortcut to get here. He suspects that Timir and his fellow travelers are not far behind."

"Are we leaving then?"

"No. We are saddling the horses so that should this Timir and his companions arrive, our rover friends can look like they have been out on the horses and are now removing their gear. When you are done saddling up your horse, we need to move all our gear into Wright's cart. Also, we need to make sure the place where our lean-to has been looks less used as an area where there was a lean-to.

"I understand the plan is to make it look like the Wright and Sawyer are truly the owners and users of the horses. What then of us? And what of the Elder Iona, who is also camped here? Are we not putting them into more danger than we have before?"

"Wright and Elder Iona are speaking to each other now. From what I could gather, the rover elder is more than aware of this man named Timir. She knew of him and his reputation. We do not have time to go into that now. Just know that these kind rovers intend to hide us away, and apparently this is not the first time they have done something like this. That is perhaps a tale for another time. All I can tell you now is Wright assures me not one of his family, including the children, will give us away."

When we finished saddling the horses, Arnar and I helped Rosilda pick up our gear and move it into the cart that Wright pulled behind his homewagon. Our personal gear, such as our blanket rolls and packs, we put into Elder Iona's homewagon. After a quick perusal of the area where we had camped to make sure we had not left anything out, Arnar, Rosilda, and I climbed up the short stairs of Elder Iona's homewagon, entered, closed the bottom door behind us, and settled in to wait.

I looked out the top door of the homewagon to see the rovers busy at many tasks. Wright and Sawyer were raking the areas around where the other homewagons had been. Lakyle was raking where our lean-to had been set up. Stodd was sawing, splitting, and stacking firewood. Burle was stirring something in a cook pot over the fire and chatting with Elder Iona. Brodie was off in the forest with Keitha looking for early spring edibles.

It was such a peaceful everyday scene. Just folks going about their everyday chores. I had an urge to leap up, grab my saddle bags, fling the homewagon door open, charge down the steps, and leap on my horse in order to ride away from here as fast as I could. Just as I was about to jump up, Elder Iona entered the homewagon.

"Steady lass. All will be well. Before Revan's son left, he mentioned that his Da was going to speak with someone in the royal guard that is stationed in Klippebyen. While Revan had never met Timir before, he had heard of a man named Timir from his father. When he described Timir to his father, he suggested Revan take the information to the royal guard. Seems that this Timir fellow is a wanted man in Sommerhjem. Perhaps Timir thought enough time had passed, and folks might have forgotten. Revan's son might be the first of many visitors we might be having this day. You just need to be patient."

An hour passed, then two. All was quiet in the homewagon, except for the soft snores coming from Kipp. Lorcan was curled up on Elder Iona's bed, alert and not sleeping. I could hear the quiet murmur of the folks sitting around the cookfire. The quiet was broken by the sound of running feet.

"What is it Lakyle?"

"Three riders approaching. Two men, one woman."

"Time to follow the plan, family," Wright told the others.

Before I closed the homewagon top door all but a crack, I took a quick look out and saw Lakyle moving toward the pack horse with a brush in his hand. Brodie was carrying Keitha up into her homewagon. Sawyer, Wright, and Stodd had moved to the horses and were beginning to remove the saddles. Burle remained at the cookfire, having a cup of tea.

As Elder Iona left the homewagon, she reminded us to leave the door open a crack so we could hear what was going on. She also admonished us that under no circumstances should we leave the homewagon. I watched until she settled in at the cookfire next to Burle.

I had discovered that I had a clear if limited view through the crack in the door. When I turned around to tell Rosilda and Arnar what was happening outside the homewagon, I noticed that both Kipp and Lorcan were no longer with us, for they had slipped out the half door in the front of the homewagon that allowed one to climb out to the driver's seat. Their leaving caused me some concern, since I could not know if those who might be coming knew I was traveling with a wild hill cat. Also, they might recognize a wild hill cat if they saw one. Kipp could put all the planning in jeopardy should he be spotted. I wished I had thought of that earlier. It was not as if I could leave the homewagon now, try to locate him, and bring him back inside. I had no time to worry about that now, since I could hear horses approaching.

Once the horses had been brought to a stop, a male voice called out, "Well met, rovers. May we camp here with you?"

Unfortunately, I knew that voice. I turned to my companions and whispered, "Grimur." They nodded that they understood.

I heard Burle say that they had a rabbit stew cooking that would be ready about the time they had all taken care of their horses. She suggested that the new arrivals set up a shelter, for it looked as if it might rain. She also suggested that it was custom to share any supplies, if they had a mind to.

Rain is going to make an uncomfortable night for them, I thought. *They do not seem to have much gear. Probably staying at inns along the way.*

I saw the man I assumed was Timir give Burle a quick look of disgust. He seemed to hold the rovers, or maybe rover customs, in contempt. I did not know if sharing campsites and food was a common custom in Bortfjell since I had rarely camped there. I once again realized that my training had been extremely limited, as was my knowledge of the customs of those folks who did not live on a landholding. I, for one, felt if this courtesy of sharing a fire and a meal with fellow travelers was not our custom, it should be.

As I watched, Grimur handed his horse off to the woman who had ridden in with him and swaggered over to where the rovers were working with the riding horses.

"Fine looking horses," he said to Stodd. "Didn't know you rovers had riding horses, only fine horses to pull your homewagons."

"It is not unusual for us to have riding horses in addition to the horses we have to pull our homewagons. Depends on need. We have taken a commission in the high hills far enough from the closest village to make walking to that village a quarter day's journey. The horses that pull our homewagons are not very comfortable to ride and not well-suited for the high hills trails."

"We were talking to a horse trader in Klippebyen. What was his name, Donnola?"

"Revan."

"Yes, that's right. Anyway, this Revan fella had some Bortfjell bred horses. Said he traded for them with you folks. Said you had traded some horses to some folks a while back for the Bortfjell horses."

"Did," replied Stodd.

"Well, you see, we have been trying to find a man and two women who might be the folks you traded horses with. They left, um, in a hurry and forgot some, um, items of value. We just want to find them to give them what is their due."

Sounds all very lovely, that 'give them what is their due' statement. All Grimur thinks is my due is my sudden demise, I thought glumly.

"Sorry, we cannot help you," suggested Stodd. "We parted ways with them about two days south of the Høyhauger pass. Said they were heading toward the capital down the royal road."

Donnola spoke up for the first time. "It was my understanding that this campsite was a gathering of many rovers this time of year. Why are there so few of you?"

"This gathering always happens about this time in the spring. All who are in the area come together here. The other rovers started gathering about a fortnight ago. We were delayed along our route and arrived near the end of the gathering. Most of the others left yesterday or this day. We intend to leave on the morrow. Just taking the day to tidy up, restock the woodpile, and make sure we leave the place better for those who come after us. Is that not a custom in your country?" Wright questioned.

He did not receive an answer. Instead Donnola continued on the subject of what she had learned in the marketplace of Klippebyen.

"When I was wandering the market, I ran across a leather smith who had three Bortfjellian saddles. Said he traded them for some leather. I see by the sign on your cart that one of you is a leather smith. I wondered why you folks didn't keep the saddles for yourselves."

"My wife Brodie is the leather smith. She had no use for Bortfjell saddles, for they do not trade well the closer to the capital one is. Not something we could sell at the summer fairs. The ones we are using now she picked up in the Klippebyen market. To most looking at them in the used saddle heap where she found them, they would have passed them by. She has a good eye, and as you can see, this one I am holding is a fine saddle now that she has cleaned it up."

"Grimur, I donna believe a word these folks are weaving. Their answers are too slick, and I should know how to spin a tale. This polite conversation grows wearisome."

"Now Timir, let us not be rash. I am sure if we were to, say, offer these fine folks a bit of coin, they might be willing to tell us where the folks we want to find might be located."

"I tire of this chase. Coin will not persuade these rovers to tell you anything. It is not in their code. I have a better way of getting the information that we want."

With that said, Timir snatched Lakyle off his feet and held a knife to his throat.

"Now folks, I suggest you start talking. Make it fast for my arms could grow weary quickly. Oh, and while we are waiting the very short time it is going to take for these weakling rovers to give us what we want to know, you, old woman, the gem smith, you can go get us your stash of gems. Might as well make this tedious trip worthwhile."

CHAPTER TWENTY-TWO

I quickly turned back to Arnar and Rosilda. In a whisper, I told them what had just happened outside. When both started to move toward the front of the homewagon, I motioned them back.

"Wait. No sense in all of us rushing out there. It is me they want. I am going to step out of the homewagon. Why don't the two of you slip out the other door? Wait for any chance to help. Let me try to talk to them and get Timir to release Lakyle."

I knew the others wanted to argue with me. We did not have time for that, for Timir made his threat once again, which could be heard quite clearly as Elder Iona eased the homewagon door open.

"If you slip out the other door, you might be able to …."

"We are not going to abandon you folks. I am going to go out now. Arnar and Rosilda are going to slip out the other door. Take your time getting your gems."

I moved past Elder Iona and walked down the stairs of the homewagon. I saw that Timir had set Lakyle on his feet, but still had a hard grip on the lad's arm and still had his knife close to Lakyle's neck. I noticed Lakyle looked scared, which was to be expected. He was also holding still and steady. I gave him a hand signal we had taught him while practicing kazan, for him to hold and be ready. I moved to position myself equidistant from Timir and the woman who stood between him and Grimur.

"Where are the others?" demanded Timir.

"What others?"

"The ones you have been traveling with from before you left Bortfjell."

"You mean those two who left with the other rover family after we crossed the border?"

"What do you mean left? Were they not folks you knew?"

"No, they were just two folks I ran into who needed to muddy their trail just like I did. Was a rather serendipitous meeting with them my second day on the run from Nytt Heimili. A good bit of luck you might say." I then turned and addressed Grimur.

"So, Grimur, you were not satisfied that I had left Nytt Heimili, or Bortfjell for that matter. Am I that much a threat to you and your sister's plans for your nephew? Has your fortune in life stooped so low that you now hang out with thieves and folks who would hurt younglings? You do not seem to be in charge here."

I hoped that by insulting Grimur, I might cause a rift between him and his companions. I knew that Grimur was not in charge any longer. I just hoped Grimur still felt he was. If I could cause a distraction, it might allow others to do something to get Lakyle free from Timir. The look Timir was directing at me helped me understand that anyone of any sense would know it would be prudent to stay as far away from this man as possible and not cross him.

"Now, um, Perrin, we just want to talk to you, straighten things out, um, get your solemn promise that you will not return to Bortfjell to claim your position as the heir of Nytt Heimili. We could just ride into Klippebyen and find a, ah, magistrate to draw up papers to that effect. Then you would be free to go on your merry way."

"I see. You just want me to blithely leave here with you and your two companions and ride off to town?"

"Why, yes. Get everything settled."

"I can see a number of things wrong with your solution to what you view as a problem. First, I am not sure the courts of Bortfjell would recognize a promise sworn before a magistrate of Sommerhjem. I am also sure I do not trust you to keep your part of such a bargain, for you would never be sure I would keep my part. In addition, the way change happens so fast in Bortfjell between the princes, I could be welcomed back with open arms at home, thus ruining all your plans for my half-brother. I do not think you and my stepmother are comfortable with that possibility. We seem to be at an impasse."

"No, no, you can trust me."

Oh sure, I can trust you about as much as I can trust a mother grevling to not protect her cubs.

"And what of your companion's demand of the gem smith's gems?" I asked, trying to keep the conversation going. While I had not noticed any movement from behind Elder Iona's homewagon, I hoped Arnar and Rosilda were able to move away from it and might be of some help soon. Meanwhile, I saw that the rovers had begun to inch closer to where Lakyle was being held. Unfortunately, Timir had noticed also.

"Step back, or the lad gets hurt," Timir barked gruffly. Turning to Grimur, he said, "We are wasting time. You have found your quarry. Everyone here knows what is going to happen next. You need to take care of her. Donnola and I are not going to do your dirty work."

I saw Grimur go a little paler than he normally was. My guess is he never expected to be the one to have to dispose of me. His kind always had someone else take care of the dirty tasks.

"Once that is done, we'll tie the rovers up, grab the gems, and head home. By the time the rovers get loose, get to some type of authority, we will be long gone."

"But, but, they will know at the pass," stammered Grimur. "They could send a messenger bird that would arrive before we would."

"Hah, you think we don't know how to slip into Bortfjell undetected?" scoffed Donnola. "I grow tired of all this talk, Timir. You knew all along that Grimur has expected us to take care of everything. We do not need him. After all, his sister is the one who is really paying us, not him. We will just tell her when we get back that he met with an unfortunate fate in Sommerhjem."

With that said, Donnola grabbed Grimur, kicked his legs out from under him, knocking him to the ground. In one swift movement, she turned him over and tied his hands behind his back. Before he could even begin to protest, Donnola had searched through his pockets, looking for and taking everything of value. She then tied his ankles together and pushed him away. Standing up, brushing her hands together, she directed Wright to bring her Grimur's saddlebags.

Once Wright dropped Grimur's saddlebags at Donnola's feet, she ordered him to fetch some rope from his and other rovers' homewagons and carts. "And do not think of trying anything clever. Move quickly. Timir is not a patient man, and he has the lad. The lad is your son, isn't he?"

"I'll do as you ask. Please don't hurt Lakyle," Wright pleaded as he moved swiftly to his cart.

Meanwhile, Timir hollered at Elder Iona. "Old woman, you had best get out of that wagon with the gems right now, or the lad here is going to be hurting."

Elder Iona quickly appeared at the door of her homewagon. "I'm coming. I'm coming. You didn't think I had the gems just sitting out on the table, did you? Took me a while to gather them up."

I had begun to inch away from where I was standing in order to bring me a bit closer to the ax Stodd had left stuck in a large tree stump where he had been splitting wood when Timir shouted that I should not move another inch. He moved the hand holding the knife away from Lakyle and pointed it where he wanted me to stand. As he did that, a great many things happened at once.

Lorcan seemed to come out of nowhere, sprang at Timir, and clamped his teeth on Timir's wrist causing him to drop the knife. The surprise of the attack by the hunting cat also caused Timir to pivot and lose his balance. Lakyle glanced at me, and I signaled him. He dropped like a stone to the ground, causing Timir to fully lose his balance. Lorcan released Timir's wrist and moved to sit on the man, placing his jaws very close to Timir's neck.

Meanwhile, just as Donnola was about to draw her knife, Kipp dropped off a tree branch that Donnola had been standing under and landed on her head and back. From the sounds of pain that Donnola made, I suspected that Kipp had all his claws fully extended. I rushed forward, kicking Timir's knife into the surrounding brush on the way. With several swift moves, I had the woman Timir had called Donnola on the ground, her hands behind her back.

Stodd rushed forward and handed me the rope he was carrying. I tied Donnola's hands and then Stodd and Sawyer took over, securing her so that she could not get away. I looked around for Kipp, to make sure he was all right. I found him sitting on Elder Iona's homewagon steps cleaning his hind quarters, just as calm as you please, as if nothing had just happened. I was distracted from Kipp's ablutions by the yelling coming from Timir.

"Get this cat off me," Timir yelled, not daring to move for fear that Lorcan might bite him.

Elder Iona stepped forward and looked down at the man who had threatened to harm Lakyle. "I've a mind to let Lorcan here have you for dinner. He would probably get a bellyache, however. I would not want that to happen to him. Instead, if you want to survive the next few minutes, I am going to ask Lorcan to back off. No, do not move. Once the hunting cat has backed a little way away, I will ask you to sit up and put your hands behind your back. If you try anything, anything at all, I will ask the hunting cat to get a taste of you. Are we clear?"

Timir nodded his head in acquiescence. Lying there was a man who had threatened to harm Lakyle. He had been, I am sure, quite willing to dispose of me for a fee, and he had the reputation for causing grown folk to quake in their boots with just a look. He did not look so fearsome now. As he glanced at Lorcan, I could read fear in his eyes.

I walked over to Stodd and asked him where I might find some more rope, preferably heavy-duty rope. He told me he would fetch some. Just then, Arnar and Rosilda came striding toward me out of the trees from the direction that Lorcan had come.

"Looks like, for all our careful slipping and sliding through the shadows and hiding behind trees and shrubs, we have arrived too late for the party," said Arnar, sadly.

"There is still the chore of tying Timir up and searching these three for anything that might help them escape," I suggested. "I want to go check on Lakyle."

I left the others to take care of tying up Timir and search pockets, boots, and cloaks for anything that might allow them to escape. Sawyer and Stodd went to take care of the horses. I took a moment to step inside of Elder Iona's homewagon and get something from my pack. I then went in search of Lakyle. I found Wright and Brodie fussing over him. Keitha was hanging on to her mother's leg with all her might.

"I wonder if I might talk to you all about how very sorry I am that I have brought this trouble to your doorstep …."

"There is no blame here," stated Brodie. "Life on the road always holds danger. I'll not hear you taking blame for the choices of others. It is I who should be thanking you, for you, Arnar, and Rosilda probably saved Lakyle's life by beginning to teach him kazan. I saw the signal you gave him. I have been watching his lessons. I think I would like to join them."

I told Brodie she would be welcome to join the early morning lessons. Then I turned to Lakyle. "Your mother is incorrect that we saved your life this day, Lakyle. You saved yourself by being a serious student of kazan. Though you are a beginner, you have taken to heart one of the first lessons, which is patience. Sometimes waiting, when you really want to do something immediately, can be the best choice. If you had squirmed or tried to fight when Timir held the knife to your throat, you probably would have been hurt. He most likely would have cut you. That pain would have caused you to lose focus. Instead, you held and waited. I imagine that was very hard to do. It was natural to be terrified in that situation, and yet you held when I signaled you to hold."

"I tried to be still like a deer when sensing danger, listening, not even flicking an ear."

"Can you actually flick an ear?" I asked, causing Lakyle to laugh.

"No."

"I have something for you. As Arnar has explained, it takes years to master all the levels of kazan. You certainly showed that you have mastered an important one this day. When I was young and learning the discipline, sometimes Arnar would reward me with something to commemorate what I had accomplished. I think you have earned this, this day."

With that said, I pulled a slim wrist band out of my pocket. It was made of metal and had an intricate design stamped into it. It was too small for my wrist now, though I had held on to it. It was one of the sentimental items I had packed in my pack when I knew I had to flee Bortfjell. I felt that I no longer needed to hold on to it. Lakyle was the one who should have it now.

As I handed it to Lakyle, I knew I had chosen right. I saw no puffed-up pride in the lad, rather I saw a deep humility.

"I will cherish this, Perrin. Thank you."

Before anyone could say anything more, we were interrupted by a shout from Rosilda.

"Riders coming."

CHAPTER TWENTY-THREE

I turned around at the sound of Rosilda's shout and surveyed the scene. The cookfire had been stirred up and wood had been added. A kettle hung from the tripod over the fire. Burle was chopping up vegetables. The horses were all being groomed and given grain. Stodd was stacking firewood. Elder Iona was just coming back out of her homewagon after going in to put away the gems that Timir had demanded. It all looked extremely ordinary, except for three tied-up folks, which might be a bit hard to explain to anyone stopping at this campsite this night. It was perhaps not the most welcoming sight.

When a patrol of royal guards rode into view, I became more than a bit concerned, since it was going to be our word against that of the three trussed up like geese over a spit. I felt a bit better when Stodd greeted the Leftenant by name.

"Well met, Leftenant Emera. You have arrived just in time to take three major problems off our hands."

Before Leftenant Emera could even greet Stodd or dismount, Grimur began trying to wheedle his way out of his responsibilities as to why he found himself tied up.

"I demand you have me untied and charge these rovers with trying to rob me. They, they, um, jumped me quite suddenly, yes, quite without warning, when I arrived at this campsite. They tied me up and stripped me of my belongings. I am in fear for my life. I am, after all, a noble from Bortfjell and should not be treated like this."

The Leftenant dismounted and signaled her patrol to dismount also.

Turning to Timir and Donnola, she asked if they were nobles from Bortfjell too. Donnola responded first.

"Timir and me was hired by this gentleman to track down a relative of his who had gone missing. That gel there ..." Donnola pointed her chin in my direction. "... he says she's not right in her mind, and her family wants her to be brought home. When we tried to get her, these rovers helped her attack us, tied us up, and took our belongings."

"I see. So according to you, I should believe that this lass is of noble birth, is not right in the head, and this nobleman hired you to bring her back to her home in Bortfjell. Is that correct?"

"Yes," agreed Donnola.

"And when you tried to get her to go with you, you were thwarted from doing so by her and these rovers?"

"That is exactly right. Grimur tol' us she is very clever, you know, and probably spun a wild tale to the rovers about being the heir to a large landholding and having to flee for her life."

"Grimur, did you tell your companions this?"

"Yes, yes. It's the truth. Be careful when you approach her to seize her, for she is trained in the discipline of kazan. Now I demand again that you untie me. Your commander is going to hear from me about your taking your time to release me."

The Leftenant reached into her uniform pocket and pulled out a folded piece of paper. She unfolded it and looked at it for a long moment, then looked up and took a long moment to study Timir. After glancing down at the paper briefly, she addressed him.

"The man's face drawn on this wanted poster, though a bit younger looking, bears a striking resemblance to you, Timir. Now the name Timir is one rarely if ever heard in Sommerhjem, and here we have you with a name and a face that matches the ones on this wanted poster. Fancy that."

"Taint me. Ya have the wrong man," growled Timir.

"Not according to the two street men who identified you, one of whom you paid for information. You forgot that time has a way of changing loyalties. Or whomever has the most coin. You seem to have lost some of your skills, Timir. Now then, in all fairness, I really need to hear the rover side of this tale and what the others gathered here have to say. Who wishes to go first?"

"I'll go first. I am Wright and this is my wife Brodie, our son Lakyle, and our daughter Keitha. The three who are not rovers and are not tied up are those we owe a debt to. When we were traveling back from a cold months commission in Bortfjell, we were chanced upon by a group of bullies who tried to tip my homewagon over with my son and my mother inside. These three, Perrin, Arnar, and Rosilda, stopped the bullies and sent them on their way. What Donnola told you about Perrin is also what she told us minus the part about her not being right in her head. What Donnola did not tell you is Perrin left because she overheard Grimur plotting with another man that they were going to do away with her so her baby half-brother would someday inherit the landholding. You really should let Perrin explain it to you."

"Perrin?"

"Recently, Prince Mallus has taken over the rule of Bortfjell. He declared that if you are not of pure Bortfjellian blood, you cannot hold a high office. My father is the Laird of Nytt Heimili, our landholding. I am his heir. However, because my mother was from beyond, meaning from beyond the Bortfjell border, I am now disqualified to inherit. What Grimur fears is that the rule might change and whatever prince becomes the next ruler, he or she might allow me my birthright again. Grimur and my stepmother felt eliminating me permanently would clear the path for my baby half-brother. I left home before they could carry out their plans. They followed me here."

"Those three who are now tied up," continued Wright, "who traced Perrin to here, arrived several hours ago, and they asked to camp here this night. They asked some questions, but very quickly Timir grew impatient and grabbed our son Lakyle, threatening to hurt him if we didn't produce the folk or folks he was looking for. He also told Elder Iona to fetch any gems she might have, since he noticed she is a gem smith. Their plan was to tie all of us up, rob Elder Iona and I am sure the rest of us, and take Perrin off somewhere to dispose of her."

Grimur had been talking the whole time Wright was speaking, trying to talk over him and denying everything Wright was saying. Leftenant Emera signaled one of her patrol to go and stand next to Grimur. She suggested to Grimur in no uncertain terms that he needed to be quiet, or she would have her sergeant stuff a rag in his mouth. He sputtered for a moment and then fell silent.

"Now that we have silence, please go on, Wright."

"It would appear there truly is no honor among thieves, for Donnola dropped Grimur to the ground and tied him up when Grimur balked at having to be the one to take care of Perrin. Donnola demanded that I bring her Grimur's belongings. While that was happening, Perrin was inching closer to an ax. Timir told her to move to the spot he pointed to with his knife, or he would hurt Lakyle. After that, things were a bit of a blur."

"If you do not mind, Wright, since I probably had the best view of what happened next, I would not mind taking over the narrative," suggested Elder Iona. Wright nodded acquiescence to Elder Iona's request.

"When Timir moved his knife hand away from Lakyle, Lorcan leapt at Timir and grabbed Timir's wrist in his teeth, throwing him off balance and causing Timir to drop the knife."

I almost burst out laughing watching the Leftenant looking at the three of us, trying to figure out if one of us was Lorcan and just why we would bite Timir.

"My apologies, Leftenant. A moment, please, while I invite Lorcan out from under my homewagon."

The hunting cat came out from under the homewagon, stretched his front paws out, and then his back paws, gave a huge yawn, and moved to sit beside Elder Iona.

"I see," said the Leftenant. "Any others I should know about?"

"Well, there was Kipp," I suggested.

"Kipp? Another hunting cat?"

"No, Kipp is a wild hill cat from the high hills of Bortfjell. He is that large, brown-striped cat sitting on Elder Iona's homewagon stairs."

"And what did Kipp do?"

"He leapt off a tree branch that was hanging over Donnola's head as she was about to draw a knife. He landed on her back and head, claws out I assume. Considering the pained noises Donnola was making, Kipp both surprised and hurt her. Kipp's action caused enough distraction for me to get to her and get her on the ground."

"So let me see if I have this straight. Timir grabbed the lad Lakyle and, using him as a hostage, demanded that you folks turn over Perrin, who was hiding in Elder Iona's homewagon with her companions. He also demanded Elder Iona turn over her gems. Meanwhile Donnola decided she did not need Grimur any longer and tied him up. Distracted by Perrin, Timir move his knife-holding hand away from Lakyle, and Lorcan, the hunting cat, took him down. While that was happening, Lakyle got away, Kipp the wild hill cat from Bortfjell jumped on Donnola, which allowed Perrin to drop her to the ground with some type of swift move. Once all three were tied up, life just went back to normal. Do I have the tale right?"

"Pretty much," agreed Stodd.

"I see. Grimur, in my judgement, you and your companions are very much at a disadvantage here, since I have known Stodd for a number of years. He and his have never been known to cause trouble. Not even in the leanest of years, have I ever heard of them trying to rob anyone. Their reputation is that of good, honest, hardworking folk. Your companion Timir is another matter altogether. I am surprised he was willing to cross over into Sommerhjem when there is a reward out for any information leading to his arrest. As for Donnola, since she seems to speak for Timir, I would suggest she is in as much trouble with us at this time as he is. The three of you are certainly going to have to go before the magistrate on charges of theft and attempted abduction with the intent to murder Perrin."

"Leftenant, sorry to interrupt, a lead scout just arrived. He says the holding cart should be here in about two hours' time, maybe longer due to the fading light."

"Thank you, sergeant. Well, we had better make ourselves comfortable while we wait. May we share your cookfire?"

Before Burle could answer, Grimur began talking loud and fast.

"You do not mean to put me in one of those cages on wheels, do you? I am a Bortfjellian noble and should not be driven through the streets like a common criminal!"

"No ..."

"Good. I'm glad you see it my way ...."

"... for you are more like an uncommon criminal. We do not have too many noble Bortfjellian criminals here. Not that that matters, for you will be secured for the return to Klippebyen in the holding cart."

Grimur just sputtered and then fell silent. The royal guard set about setting up camp for the night. Several of the patrol members joined Burle at the cookfire and began to prepare the evening meal. Soon the night was filled with the ordinary sounds of folks going about their business. After the meal, Leftenant Emera drew me aside.

"Just for my own satisfaction, was the tale about you that you and others told true?"

"Yes, other than not being in my right mind. I no longer have a place on my clan's landholding or in my family. All that I have been raised and trained for all of my life is now forbidden by the current ruling prince."

"What are your plans now?"

"I hope to find my mother's folk."

"Do you know where she was from?"

"Sadly, no. I know very little about her. Her name was Helka, and I do not know her last name or place name. Wright has suggested that the name Helka is quite uncommon here. He said he had only met one folk with that name in all of his travels."

"Where was that?"

"In a valley in the eastern mountains where a group of porcelain crafters live. It is where we intend to head next."

"You, the rovers, and your two companions?"

"Not the rovers. We will travel with them until they head off to their commission. I have not had a chance to talk to Rosilda or Arnar. Now that, hopefully, those who have been following me have been stopped at least for a while, depending on what happens with the magistrate, they could choose to return home. They have accompanied me because of loyalty to our clan. To them, at least, I am next in line. They see loyalty to clan the first choice and loyalty to Bortfjell's ruling prince, second. I think they have also accompanied me because they are my friends. Oh, and then we must not forget Kipp. I hope he will choose to stay with me."

"I wish you luck."

"I thank you for believing the rovers and us as to what happened here. It is a relief to know I will have a little time to disappear into Sommerhjem's interior."

It was not until much later that I had a change to bring up with Arnar and Rosilda the subject of whether they wished to return home, since those who were trying to dispose of me were at the very least delayed, if not stopped, or whether they wished to continue on with me farther into Sommerhjem. Arnar answered first.

"Don't seem to have anything or anyone back in Bortfjell that is calling me back. Besides, haven't felt this useful in a while. Seems to me seeing new territory and learning new things is quite a fine way to spend my days. If you are in agreement, I would like to continue on with you."

"Oh, definitely in agreement. I would be grateful if you would continue this journey with me. And what of you, Rosilda?"

"I did not return to the border guard, for I had seen too much being done in the name of our ruler that I just could not stomach. Left me with a sour taste in my mouth. Bortfjell is an uncomfortable place for me right now. I, like Arnar, am enjoying this new country, and I would not mind seeing more of it. I would like to continue with you."

"I would be honored to travel farther with you, my friend."

I settled into my blanket roll that night feeling better than I had since this journey began. Those that I feared were following me had been stopped for now. I could only hope they were the only ones after me. My companions were choosing to continue traveling with me, and Kipp was snuggled in next to the small of my back. I now had time to think of what might be ahead instead of always looking over my shoulder.

CHAPTER TWENTY-FOUR

The holding cart arrived an hour after dusk had slid into full dark. The waning moon gave little light. Accompanied by riders holding lanterns aloft, the cart and riders made quite a sight entering the camping area. Grimur and Timir were unceremoniously ushered into one section of the holding cart, and Donnola was placed in the other section. After their blanket rolls were thoroughly checked to make sure they hid nothing that could help the three escape, they were passed to the prisoners before the barred doors of the holding cart were clanged shut and locked.

I found I had little or no compassion for the three who were now caged and faced an uncertain future. I might have been more forgiving if Timir had not taken Lakyle and used him as a means to locate me. That the other two did not protest Timir using Lakyle as a hostage and holding a knife to the lad's throat made them just as guilty in my mind.

Another reason I was having trouble finding even a modicum of sympathy for their plight was the troubling thought as to what might have happened to the rovers had I not been there. Grimur and his companions appeared to have convinced themselves that Arnar, Rosilda, and I were with the rovers based on information they had gleaned from their sources in Klippebyen. They had added one plus one to arrive at two correctly. What if their one plus one had added up to three, and they had been incorrect in their assumptions? Would Lakyle have survived the meeting if I had not appeared out of Elder Iona's homewagon because I was not here at all? I found this line of thinking a very frightening one.

The true heroes of the day were Lorcan and Kipp. Each had taken advantage of extremely small windows of opportunity to turn the situation to our favor. I noticed that evening when we sat down to dinner, I was not the only one slipping them tidbits from our plates.

I slept better that night than I had since leaving home, knowing those who were after me were locked up for at least one night. I was up before dawn, rolling up my blanket roll and moving our possessions to where the pack horse was tied. I wanted to be ready to leave the minute the rovers were ready.

Once the royal guard had left with their prisoners, it did not take us and the rovers long to finish packing up and doing last minute chores. We had done most of the clean up and restocking of the campsite before Grimur, Timir, and Donnola had arrived. It felt good to be on the road again, even if I did not know quite where I was heading. When we stopped for a break at noon to rest the horses and to have a cold lunch, Elder Iona approached me.

"I was wondering if you might ride with me for a while this afternoon. I would like to talk to you away from listening ears. It has to do with the medallion you allowed me to put the firestar gem in."

Because I was curious as to what Elder Iona wanted to talk to me about, I quickly agreed to ride with her. After alerting Rosilda and Arnar that I intended to ride with Elder Iona for a time, I tied my horse to the back of Elder Iona's homewagon and climbed up to share the driver's seat with her. Kipp was much faster than I was and arrived on the seat before I did.

"Perhaps Kipp might enjoy joining Lorcan in the homewagon, out of the sun for a while. I keep the door behind me into the homewagon open when we travel, so Lorcan can come and go as he pleases. Would you like to go in, Kipp?"

To my surprise, Kipp jumped through the door. When I looked into the interior of the homewagon, I saw he had made himself quite comfortable on Elder Iona's bed next to Lorcan.

"What is it that you wish to talk to me about?"

"When I took the medallion from you to my homewagon in order to set the firestar gem in it, I wanted to accomplish that for you in the quickest amount of time. I felt if I took too long, you might begin to have misgivings and wonder if you should have trusted me."

When I started to protest that I would not have stopped trusting her, Elder Iona interrupted.

"You wondering what was taking me so long or worrying whether I was ruining the medallion would be quite understandable thoughts, considering the circumstances."

"You are probably right," I admitted.

"Upon looking at the firestar gem a bit closer, I noticed it was of an unusual cut and polish. The cut is what made me think that the gem belonged in the medallion, for it is a nine-sided shape, a nonagon rather than a simple oval, rectangle, or square. When I looked at the medallion, I saw it was designed to hold a nonagonal cut stone."

"You said it was of an unusual polish. What does that mean?"

"Gems which are clear are polished on the top and sometimes faceted. They are also polished and faceted on the bottom. That allows the gem to catch and reflect the light. A firestar gem is opaque and appears almost black, yet has colors within it. Most firestar gems are cabochons, that is a gem or bead cut in convex form and highly polished, but not faceted. In the case of a firestar gem, often the back side is flat and left unpolished. In the case of your firestar gem, the back is flat but highly polished. That has made me curious."

"How so?"

"What would be the purpose of spending so much time polishing the back of the gem when it would never show? Firestar gems are extraordinarily difficult to cut, shape, and polish. There are very few of us who have either the patience or the skill to do so."

"Perhaps the gem you set in the medallion was the right shape, but it was not actually the stone that was originally designed for the medallion."

"That thought has crossed my mind, yet ..."

"Yet?"

"... yet, I think it is the original stone. It has me so curious. I am wondering if I might look at it again this night after we stop. I would like to give the medallion a less rushed examination. Would you join me in my homewagon after dinner? I know you trust your friends, but I would ask you to keep silent as to why you are visiting me for the time being. I want to figure out if there is something I have not discovered about the medallion."

Since I had not shown the medallion to my friends, as of yet, I thought

I could stay silent a bit longer. I agreed to join Elder Iona in her homewagon after dinner this night.

Once the discussion ended about the firestar gem and the medallion, Elder Iona and I talked about the countryside we were traveling through. She told me we were heading toward the high hills and were now in a forested part of Sommerhjem, which was cared for by the forester clans. I found it interesting how different Sommerhjem was organized compared to Bortfjell. In Bortfjell, each laird controlled all that went on in their landholding, including any forest, lakes, rivers, and farmland. If the landholding bordered on the Rumblesea, the vast body of water that formed Bortfjell's western coast, the laird of that landholding also controlled the fishers, those who fished the waters.

It seemed to me that Sommerhjem's way of organizing various portions of the country's resources made more sense. The foresters were beholding to the king or queen of Sommerhjem and specialized in protecting and preserving the forests of the land so that they were not over harvested and could support the wildlife. In Bortfjell, the forests were cared for willynilly, with little or no thought to reforesting in some of the landholdings.

When we stopped to rest the horses and stretch our legs, I went back to riding my horse. My talk with Elder Iona left me a lot to think about. As we traveled along, I pulled my horse between Arnar's and Rosilda's horses so we could talk. I told them about what Elder Iona had said about foresters and fishers.

"I have been talking to the rovers about their life," said Arnar. "It seems that there are guilds in some of the larger towns pursuing some of the same crafts that the rovers ply. I asked how that worked. Was there not competition? Apparently, there is competition for the sale of items at the large summer fairs, but not so at the smaller markets or for those villages that are far away from the larger towns. In addition, a rover lad or lass is not obligated to learn the same craft that either of their parents pursue. They are free to follow their own path, unlike in Bortfjell, where from a young age we must learn our parent's trade. While the rover life is never easy, they enjoy the freedom of the open road. Interestingly enough, though they are fiercely independent, they are very loyal to the Crown. This is quite a different way of looking at how things should be done."

"I had a chance to talk to the some of the royal guard last night," stated

Rosilda. "Seems there are royal guards, border guards, home guards, and peacekeepers. The royal guards and the border guards are directly under the crown, whereas the town peacekeepers answer to the lord or lady whose landholding includes a large town. Joining a guard unit or becoming a peacekeeper is open to all who pass muster and wish to take the training, unlike Bortfjell where you are mandated to service by your laird."

Our comparing what we had learned made for interesting conversation as we rode, and the rest of the day flew by quite quickly. I was surprised when I saw Wright's homewagon pull off the lane we had been following, turn down a narrow track, and stop. Several folks slipped out from between the trees and approached Wright. These folks were dressed in clothing that was a mix of brown, green, and gray colors, allowing them to blend into the forest. I suspected they were foresters. The conversation must have been a positive one, for soon we were traveling again. When I passed the place where the folks had talked to Wright, I could see no sign of them.

We camped in an established campsite about an hour after we had left the foresters. Once dinner was over, I excused myself from around the fire and followed Elder Iona to her homewagon. I had told Arnar and Rosilda that I was going to talk to her about gems. They were aware that I had carried gems out of Bortfjell in addition to gold, silver, and coins. While I had not lied to my friends, I also had not told them the whole truth.

Once I entered Elder Iona's homewagon, she motioned me to join her at the table. She had hung a bright lantern overhead, giving us good light to see by. I lifted the chain that held the medallion over my head and handed it to her. Then I sat down and waited.

Elder Iona handled the medallion with great care, turning it this way and that, looking at it along its edge, until finally she handed it back to me.

"I think there is a seam that is barely visible that runs around the middle of the edge. I do not want to pry at it, for I do not want to ruin the piece. I suspect there is a better way to see if it opens. I think it might open for you."

"Why would it open for me and not you?"

"Because the firestar gem is yours. It has chosen you."

I still did not quite understand how a gem could choose someone. I guess I just had to take Elder Iona's word for it. I took the medallion back and looked at Elder Iona questioningly.

"Just try twisting the front and the back. Or you could try touching or pressing the firestar gem. I really don't know. I am just making guesses here."

I tried twisting the front and back. Nothing happened. When I put my finger on the firestar gem, I felt it warm under my touch. When I applied a soft amount of pressure, the back opened. I discovered that the back swung all the way around to the front and closed over the front of the medallion. The front of the medallion had now become the back, and a new front was exposed. The design on this new exposed medallion was quite different. In addition, the firestar gem, while there, was covered with a very lacy filigree. I handed the medallion back to Elder Iona.

"Oh my. I have heard of this medallion inside of a medallion design before. I have never actually seen one. And what a one this is."

"What is it?"

"What you are now holding is a seeker medallion, which suggests that perhaps your mother was a seeker."

CHAPTER TWENTY-FIVE

Elder Iona very gently placed the medallion back into my hand. I had no idea what she was talking about. I was still surprised that the medallion had another medallion hidden inside it. Finally, I asked her the obvious question.

"What is a seeker?"

"Seekers are folks who spend their lives in pursuit of the old knowledge, trying to find that which has been lost. They are the folks who seek out the land's mysteries. A seeker is a scholar, and it is said, so much more. A long time past, a wise woman began to realize there was more to Sommerhjem than we knew. She was aware that others had occupied this land before our ancestors settled here. For that matter, little or nothing was known as to where we came from or why. These mysteries both bothered and intrigued her. She set about creating the Order of the Seekers and used her holdings to provide funds for the first of several scholars to begin to try to find the answers to her many questions. In her lifetime, she continued to gather more like-minded folks, and they became the first members of the Order. At the time of her death, there were about ten to a dozen seekers. When she died, she willed her holdings to the Order of the Seekers. The seekers are always small in number. I imagine it is not an easy life, for seekers are on a permanent walkabout, as it were. It's difficult to have a family when one is constantly on the road. Perhaps your mother gave up the seeker life for a new home and family."

"Maybe not, at least not at first, if she was a seeker. When my father married my mother, he was second in line for our landholding. My aunt was the laird. I suspect that, from what Wright and other rovers have been teaching us, a laird is similar to a lord or lady in Sommerhjem, in a way. A laird is also the head of a clan in Bortfjell. Anyway, my father was always interested in learning new things and traveling. Perhaps that was going to be what they intended to do, before my aunt died in a riding accident, and my father became laird and had to return home."

"Possible. The fact that this medallion allows the wearer to hide the seeker symbol does raise some questions as to why it was designed that way. In Sommerhjem, there is an unwritten rule, or tradition, that no harm is to come to seekers."

"And that holds true?"

"By all accounts, it seems to. Somehow, over the years it became accepted that seekers really only wish to find the old tales, legends, and knowledge before it is lost. They not only scour the countryside, but also spend time in the royal library and the libraries of manors, or anywhere they can find books, scrolls, papers, and other written material. They also write down any tales they are told. They often spend time with the elders of a clan or group to write down the tales and knowledge the elders impart."

"How do the traveling seekers, who seem to spend a lot of time perusing dusty old tomes, keep themselves safe on the road? It would seem to me that unwritten rules or traditions do not always stop folks intent on harm."

"Very true. However, enough rumors and tales have grown up about the seekers that most folks do not bother them."

"What kind of rumors and tales?"

"Oh, everything from they can make themselves invisible to how they can change themselves into animals."

When I just raised an eyebrow, Elder Iona went on.

"Remember I was telling of some of the rumors and tales. It is also said they can transform themselves into someone else so you would never know it was them. That is woven into the tale that if you harm a seeker, or try to do something harmful to a seeker, they can change themselves so completely that you would not recognize them if they came to find you to return the favor. Retribution is a strong deterrent to harming a seeker."

"There is almost always a wee bit of truth in the old tales and legends. That might also be true of what is said about seekers."

"I think you have the right of it, Perrin."

"What I know for sure is that the medallion I am holding was my mother's. Whether she was a seeker or not is certainly a question that might need an answer. I can see two possibilities. The first, and more reasonable, is that while the medallion was hers, she did not know that another medallion was hidden within."

"And the other possibility?"

"That my mother was a seeker and belonged to the Order of the Seekers here in Sommerhjem. Having a way to disguise the seeker medallion within the outer medallion could suggest that she might go places where having a seeker medallion found on her would cause her danger."

"That is a good assumption. Go on."

"I never knew what side of the border my father met my mother on. I know he was serving in the Bortfjell border guard on the southern border at the time he met her. His posting was not at the major pass at Høyhauger, but rather at a narrow pass farther to the east. He could just as well have met her on the Sommerhjem side, or she might have been traveling in Bortfjell."

"You just thought of something else."

"Yes. My mother always spoke Bortfjellian and spoke it quite fluently. I never recall her speaking in the language of Sommerhjem, but ..."

"But?"

"... perhaps that is not correct. I think she might have spoken your language when I was very, very young. Sometimes I catch myself humming snatches of melodies, and I cannot place them. I caught just a few notes of a song Brodie was singing to her daughter Keitha one night at Keitha's bedtime. It reminded me of something I had heard before. I could not put my finger on when or where."

"Mayhap, your mother sang songs to you when you were an infant or talked to you in her own language when she was alone with you."

"Mayhap. Also, I just remembered how astonished my tutor in your language was that I picked it up so quickly. I remember him saying it was almost as if I had grown up speaking the language. I guess I might have. I have a question."

"Go ahead."

"I know the climate in Bortfjell at this time is not one that welcomes foreigners ...."

"Ah, you are wondering if there have been other times in the recent past that that was also true."

"Yes."

"There has always been tension between our two countries. Border clashes now and again. Never all out conflict, mind you. However, the folks of Bortfjell tend to be a bit more secretive and less than willing to share information, even if it might be mutually beneficial to both countries. Let us just say, they have been less than willing to share what is stored in their royal library and other repositories of learned material. That could cause them to not welcome a seeker in those places."

I noticed that Elder Iona was looking quite weary and thought it best we continue this conversation another time.

"I thank you for asking me here tonight, and for the discovery of the secret design of my mother's medallion. It grows late, and I have a feeling that dawn is going to come especially early on the morrow. I think I need to return my mother's medallion back to the way it was earlier. Do you think I just flip what was the former back of what was the back of the medallion back?"

I had to laugh for the last sentence that had just come out of my mouth sounded both confusing and funny.

"Yes. Try gently putting your finger on the filagree that covers the firestar gem and see what happens."

I did as Elder Iona suggested and thought I heard a faint click. When I touched the back, it moved in my hand and opened a crack. I then reversed the process that had exposed the seeker medallion. Once the back was in its new position, I pushed gently and heard a click. I placed the medallion chain over my head and tucked the medallion under my shirt.

"One question before I head out. Would it be wrong for me to continue to wear the medallion if I am not a seeker or a member of the Order of the Seekers?"

"Do you think it is wrong to wear that which is a gift from your parents?"

"Perhaps not."

I thanked Elder Iona once again and left her homewagon. I had a lot to think about.

I did not head to the lean-to right away, for I realized as I followed

Kipp down the steps of Elder Iona's homewagon that I had way too much on my mind to sleep. I settled in on a log next to the glowing embers of the cookfire. Kipp settled in next to me. As I absently stroked Kipp's back, I began to think about what I had learned this night.

My mother's medallion was just another unknown about my mother, especially because it contained a secret and gave me more questions than answers. Had my mother known there was a seeker medallion inside of the medallion? If she had, did that mean she was a seeker? If she was a seeker, had she ended up in Bortfjell because she was seeking some type of knowledge? Had she come disguised as something other than a seeker? Had she given up the seeker life to marry my father or ....

I had to stop myself for a moment. I was not sure I even wanted to think about the next part of my questioning. I know my father had adored my mother. Had my mother adored my father, or was he, and for that matter was I, just a means to discover some information that she was seeking?

I think I preferred to think about the idea I had presented to Elder Iona that my mother and father had intended to travel together exploring and learning, that they were going to just follow the road, lane, or path to the next question or the next answer.

I realized as I sat there that while I had many childhood memories of time spent with my father, I had only a vague recollection of time spent with my mother, from even before the time she lost the baby and became lost in her own world. While most of my childhood days were filled with lessons both inside and outside the manor house, I do not remember my mother being a part of them. Had she been as involved in her own pursuits, as had I, in a way that our paths just did not cross all that much? She would have overseen the running of the manor in addition to standing by my father's side during clan business, not to mention a multitude of other duties. Maybe she filled her other hours in the manor's library or, well, I do not know what. I wished at that moment I could sit down with my father in the garden and ask him a whole flurry of questions I should have asked long ago.

After a long while, I realized the coals in the cookfire were almost gone, and the air had grown quite chilly. It was time to put myself to bed.

157

All my questions would still be there in the morning. Sadly, I did not think any new answers would suddenly appear at dawn.

By morning I had reached a few conclusions. Despite finding the seeker medallion, I had made the decision as I lay in my blanket roll to not change course and immediately head toward the Order of the Seekers landholding. Going there might tell me more about my mother's life, if she had indeed been a member. Traveling on to the valley that held the porcelain crafters might connect me to her side of my family.

I had debated as to whether to tell Arnar and Rosilda about both the medallion and what Elder Iona and I had discovered about it. I had decided not to at this point in our travels. One step at a time. The first step had been accomplished when we got over the border pass into Sommerhjem, leaving Bortfjell behind. The second step happened when Grimur and his two companions were driven away in a holding cart, heading for the magistrate in Klippebyen. The third step would be to see if this Helka that Wright had met was related to me, or if she was just someone who had the same name as my mother.

Instead of continuing to mull over my questions, I decided that I was going to enjoy the day and take in the changing scenery. We were traveling along the base of the foothills to the high hills that bordered the eastern mountains. Sometimes we were traveling through forested land that was maintained by the forester clans. Sometimes we were traveling through small villages that were the cold months homes to sheep herders and surrounded by small farms.

Over the next fortnight, we fell into a routine. Each day we travelled from early morning to several hours before dusk, stopping along the way for a noon meal and to rest the horses. Each evening after the dinner cleanup was done, we practiced kazan with Lakyle. It would be more correct to say, we practiced kazan with any of the rovers who wished to participate. Most nights we had all of us out in the campsite clearing going through the movements and learning a new lesson.

All too soon, it was time to part ways with the two rover families. They needed to head higher up into the high hills to fulfill their commission for Lady Jegerinne. The last evening, Arnar and Rosilda called Lakyle over and presented him with a leather-bound journal. Brodie had made the cover, and Arnar, Rosilda, and I had a hand in filling the interior with pictures, diagrams, and text of the first several dozen movements of kazan so Lakyle could keep practicing. He very solemnly thanked us, hugging the journal to his chest. I was going to especially miss the lad.

I hoped that we would be able to run across the rover families sometime in the future. They had become more than casual traveling companions; they had become friends.

It was quite quiet in the campsite the next morning as we packed up and got ready to depart. I tied my backpack and satchel down on the back of the horse and then attached what I had come to think of as Kipp's shelter. When we could delay no longer and had said our goodbyes, admonished each other to try to meet again, wished each other safe journey, and started and stopped a few more times, we finally parted and went our separate ways.

I could only hope this next leg of our journey would not bring disappointment.

CHAPTER TWENTY-SIX

There was not much conversation during our morning travels, with all of us lost in our own thoughts. Near the noon hour, I spotted a rivulet of water running over some rocks and suggested we halt, give the horses a chance to rest and drink, and stretch our legs.

"Perrin, I have something for you," Arnar stated. "Elder Iona gave it to me just as we were pulling out of the campsite. She said she was tired of farewells and asked me to give this to you when we stopped. She seems to have taken quite a shine to you and admonished me to look after you. Well, at any rate, she wanted you to have this."

Arnar handed me a small leather cylinder. It was about ten inches long and three inches in diameter. The hinged top was fastened by a thin leather thong that wrapped in a figure eight around two leather tabs. The cylinder was not new, for it was scuffed and scratched and had a well-worn look. I was certainly curious as to what was inside.

I dismounted and found a tree to lean against while I worked the leather thong off the two tabs. I opened the cylinder and looked inside. There was what looked to be paper rolled up tight inside. I very gently pulled the paper out and began to unroll it. Before I had unrolled it very far, a smaller piece of paper fell out. There was a message from Elder Iona on the small piece of paper.

Dear Perrin, it has been an honor getting to know you. I can only hope that our paths will cross again, and we can sit around a campfire and catch up. The travels ahead of you are difficult

*enough not knowing exactly where you are
going in this new to you land of Sommerhjem.
At the very least, I thought this map might help
your journey be less difficult. May Neebing luck
continue to ride with you. Safe journey, Iona.*

I unrolled the paper and then unfolded it, taking care to try to remember the order of how I had done it, so I would be able to put it back. Once it was fully open, I just stood there amazed at what a gift Elder Iona had given me.

"What is it?" Rosilda asked.

"It is a map like the one Wright had. It shows the main roads and lanes plus many of the side lanes. Come look. There are farms and campsites marked, towns and villages, some landholdings, rivers, streams, springs."

"It looks old. Some of the ink is so faded that it is almost invisible. Other marks are sharp and new as if they have just been added," remarked Arnar. "What a treasure!"

What a treasure indeed. I felt a small tear begin to run down my cheek and hastily wiped it away. What Elder Iona had given me was more than a map, for I understood just what the map really was. It was filled with information gathered over a long period of time as to where good markets were, where good and safe campsites were, where the small side roads would take one. I expect many folks had had a hand in making it. I suspect these maps were closely guarded by each rover family, and yet this rover elder, who I had known for so little time, had given me one.

Pulling myself together, I suggested to Arnar and Rosilda that we take some time to figure out where we were and then see what the most direct route to the valley of the porcelain crafters might be. Once we had discussed the way we wished to travel and tried to memorize the route, I carefully folded and rolled up the map and put it back in the cylinder. I tucked the cylinder down into the bottom of one of the saddlebags, for I wanted to know it was secure.

"Just one question before we start out," said Rosilda, as she drew her horse next to mine. "What in the world is Neebing luck? For that matter, what is a Neebing?"

"I have no idea."

Late in the afternoon, we turned down a lane that led to a small farm. I felt the rover way of asking permission to camp on a farmer's land and offering to help with any chores or needs in return was a fair and good custom that we should adopt. I hoped we looked better than we had when we crossed the border disguised as mercenaries. During our recent travels, we had had the opportunity to replenish the small amount of clothing we had left Bortfjell wearing. We now looked much more presentable. We had also discussed what we would tell folks, should they be curious about who we were and why we were at their farm, on the road, or in their village.

We halted our horses in the farmyard and held them still as several dogs came racing around the cottage, barking fiercely. They did not charge the horses, and we did not move forward. A young man came around the corner of the cottage and inquired as to whether he could help us.

"We have traveled a long way this day and are weary. We are wondering if we might camp on your farm this night. We would be glad to help you with anything that might need help," stated Arnar.

"Where have you come from this day?"

Arnar told him we had been traveling with several rover families and had parted ways with them this morn.

"Traveling with rovers you say."

"Yes. We traveled with Wright and his family, his sister Sawyer and her family, and the Elder Iona. We are following their advice that some farm holders might allow us to camp on their land."

"I know Elder Iona. She has camped here a few times. My children look forward to her coming this way, for she tells the best tales. There is a level, sheltered spot down by the creek behind the barn. You are welcome to camp there. You will have to walk beyond the fields to gather firewood. Once you have set up, come back and you can help me milk the cows and goats."

Every day in Sommerhjem provides a new adventure, or I learn something new. This day it would seem, I am going to learn how to milk a cow or a goat. My skills and knowledge just keep expanding, I thought with a chuckle.

I actually enjoyed milking the cow. Milking a very ornery goat was not as enjoyable. The farmer gave us some of the cheese made from their goats' milk for our dinner. The greatest gift he gave us, however, was an invitation to use their bath house. They had the great good luck to have a natural warm spring on their farm. I think if it had not been too impolite, I would have slept in the bathing pool. It had been a long time since I had felt warm after a bath, since we had been bathing in nearby streams at night. This high in the hills, the water in the streams had been more than a bit brisk.

Our travel over the next fortnight was relatively uneventful. As we moved higher into the hills, the narrower the lanes became, and we saw fewer folks. My favorite place on the journey so far was the forester village that was nestled in, around, and above the magnificently large trees. One of the foresters said we were in an ancient quirrelit grove. Some of the cottages were built into what was left of large quirrelit tree trunks. Other homes were actually built up in the trees with suspended walkways connecting them. One thing I found particularly interesting was that despite the number of folk who lived and worked in and around the forester village, there was a feeling of peace within the quirrelit grove. I was told that I would most likely find that same peace in other quirrelit groves I might happen across in my travels.

As we drew closer and closer to the village of the porcelain crafters, I became more and more anxious. I hoped I was not on a wild goose chase, that I had not come all this way only to find that my Helka, my mother, had no connection to anyone in the porcelain crafter's village.

When we finally got to within what looked on the map to be a several hour ride from the porcelain crafter's village, it was late afternoon. I suggested we halt for the day. I am not sure I suggested that because I did not want to arrive at their village at dinner time, which I worried might be rude, or because I wanted to put off for a few more hours either the good news that I had found my mother's family or the bad news that the villagers had never heard of her.

As it was, I should not have worried so much about arriving at dinner the night before. We had underestimated how difficult the lane into the porcelain crafter's valley was going to be and how long it would take for us to get there, so we arrived at noon. We found out later that we had taken the back way to the road leading to the valley. Had we traveled a bit farther south, we would have been able to enter the valley on a well-maintained lane with much less difficulty.

The passage into the valley and the village housing the porcelain crafters was very narrow and closed off by a stone wall and a substantial wooden gate, which while open was watched over from a gatehouse.

Our greeting at the valley gate was not like what we had come to expect during our travels in Sommerhjem. Now, mind you, when we had traveled with the rovers, those that we met were always polite and many were welcoming. The folk who stepped out from his spot guarding the village gate looked at us with suspicion.

"Halt, come no farther. What brings you to our valley?" asked a tall, reed-thin lad sporting a sparce, scraggly red mustache.

I figured he could not stop anyone who might want to move through the gate. At most, he probably was a good runner and could run to get help. I spoke up in a quiet, calm voice, since I did not want to send him down the lane alarmed. I told him the truth, that we were here because I was looking for my mother's folk.

"We mean no harm to you and yours. We have travelled a long way, for I am searching for information about my mother's folk. Her name was Helka, which I understand is a most unusual name in Sommerhjem. I was told by a rover named Wright, who visited your valley a few years back, that there is an elder here by that name. I would very much like to talk with her."

Just then another folk came bustling down the main lane toward the gate house, talking demandingly in a loud voice.

"Just what is going on? Who are these folk? Why have you not sent them back down the lane?"

When she reached the gate and looked up, she took a good look at the three of us. I saw the blood drain out of her face and go deathly white. She stumbled forward, one hand clutching her chest, the other reaching out for the young lad.

My first instinct was to slide off my horse and rush to help the woman. I thought better of it, however. The young lad steadied the woman, who slowly gathered herself together, though she still looked quite pale. The first words out of her mouth, though shaky, gave me pause.

"Helka? No, no, you canna be. You're too young. Who, who are you? Why are you here?"

"She says her mother's name was Helka, and she wanted to talk with Elder Helka."

"Explain?" the woman demanded.

"Would you mind if we dismounted? I am uncomfortable sitting high up here on my horse talking down at both of you. I would be happy to tell you what I told the lad and to answer any questions. My name is Perrin. My companions are Arnar and Rosilda."

Just as I finished the introductions, Kipp made his way over my shoulder and sat down in front of me, looking intently at the two at the gate.

"Pardon my manners, my furry friend here is Kipp."

"Fine, get down, but donna you come any closer," the woman admonished.

"Thank you." I signaled to Arnar and Rosilda to dismount. It felt good to be standing. Kipp, on the other hand, did not join us on the ground but continued to sit alert on my saddle.

Clearing my throat, trying to slow my heart rate, for it seemed I might be in the right place to learn more about my mother's family, I began again.

"As I said, my name is Perrin. I know very little about my mother, other than her name was Helka, and she was from Sommerhjem. She met my father, who was a Bortfjellian border guard, and they married. When he was called back to our landholding at the death of his sister, they settled there. My mother died when I was about thirteen. She did not talk of her past, and my father did not share much information."

"So, why are you here now?"

In for a copper, in for a silver, I thought to myself.

"The newest prince of Bortfjell has taken a strong dislike to anyone who is not pure Bortfjellian. Some folks on our landholding thought the land would be better off without me. Since I no longer have a home, and really nowhere to go, I thought I would come to the country of my mother's birth and try to find out a bit more about her."

"How do I know that you are not just spies here to try to steal our secrets? You come with this tall tale about trying find your mother's folks and worm your way into our village. Next thing we know, you are riding down that trail with our craft secrets to sell to the highest bidder."

"No matter what I say concerning whether I am a spy or not, I will never convince you that I am not if you are determined to think that way. I would ask you a question. Why did you turn white and say my mother's name when you first saw me?"

CHAPTER TWENTY-SEVEN

My question hovered in the air like a griff falcon circling on the wind. Time seemed to stop while I waited for the woman to respond to my question. I could see her struggling for an answer. I was both afraid she would not answer or, if she did, she would lie. Or maybe, I only thought that to protect myself from an answer I did not want to hear, having come so far to find what I hoped were my mother's folk.

Finally, the woman spoke. "I was taken by surprise, for at first glance you look so very much like my childhood friend, Helka."

"My father has told me I take after my mother in looks. He used to tease me, saying it was a good thing, since he thought I would look pretty funny looking like him, a lass with a beard."

I hoped my use of humor might soften the woman's attitude toward us. It seemed to work, and I watched her posture unstiffen a bit. The lad beside her tried to continue to look solemn with little success.

"Please. We do not even have to enter through your valley gate. We can just turn around and find a place to camp away from your valley. I just want to find out if you are my mother's folk, and if anyone can tell me a little bit about her life."

"I will talk to the others," stated the woman, who then turned her back to us and swiftly headed down the lane toward a second stone wall and the gate to the village.

"Zasha is very protective of the secrets of our craft. Others have tried to steal our secrets, for we make the very finest of porcelain in Sommerhjem."

"What are you called, lad?" Rosilda asked.

"I am called Hiatt."

"Are you a porcelain crafter?"

"I try. To be honest, I am mostly a fumble finger and not good at the craft. I think I am more suited to working with those who guard our valley."

"Each of us has our own calling. My family wanted me to work the land as we have always done. I was too restless, so when assigned, I went into the border guard. Now I am on an adventure to see what is next. By the way, I think you show promise. You did not flinch or back away when we arrived."

I saw Hiatt turn a very deep shade of red when Rosilda complimented him. I felt he was pleased, however embarrassed he looked.

"Thank you. If you move a little way back down the lane, there is a small shady area with a wee spring. You might be more comfortable there while you wait."

We thanked Hiatt, turned our horses around, and walked back to the place Hiatt had pointed out. Once we arrived, it was apparent that this place had been used by others before us as a waiting spot. The small shady area was more than just a place to wait for a little while. It was a groomed glen cut into the surrounding woods, large enough to accommodate two rover homewagons with carts. There was an established fire ring and a stack of firewood nearby.

"From the looks of this place, you should feel a bit better that we might not be the only ones who have been turned away," suggested Arnar.

"You are right, from the looks of this place. I wonder if they allow anyone into their valley. When merchants, long haulers, or other folk come, I wonder if they must camp out here when they arrive late in the day and cannot return to the nearest village after finishing their business with the folks here," I said, as I tied my horse to the nearest tree.

"Is the crafting of porcelain a highly skilled trade?" Rosilda asked.

"It is an ancient one and finely made porcelain cups, bowls, plates, pitchers, vases, and other items are highly prized and costly. Their value also increases if the artisans who paint them are highly skilled. My feeling is that this group of crafters must be very good if they are guarding their valley and secrets so tightly," I suggested.

Our conversation drifted off as we all settled in to wait, each of us lost in our own thoughts. I slipped into a light doze and began to have disturbing dreams. At one point I jerked awake, and Arnar asked if I was all right.

"Just a disturbing dream. I was dreaming that I was standing in a glen much like this one. I was in a fighting stance holding a shiny silver needle, the only thing I had to defend myself with. Charging out of the surrounding woods were large hairy slobbering creatures who were wearing dirty, tattered tunics that had the words 'what if' written on them."

"Sounds like you were dreaming your fears," Arnar remarked.

"You have the right of it. We have traveled all this way, may have actually found my mother's folk, and yet, I have been asking myself 'what if' questions. What if they disliked my mother and were glad she left? What if they refuse to talk to me? What if they meet with me, but will not tell me about my mother and her family? What if they do not like me? I know, I am just borrowing trouble where there might not be any."

I settled back and practiced some calming exercises Arnar had taught me. Several hours passed, and I was beginning to think that Zasha had decided not to return, leaving us outside the valley without answers. Finally, I saw Hiatt walking toward us.

"If you will follow me. There is a guest cottage and stable attached to the gatehouse. You are welcome to stay there. The gate to the village will remain closed. Zasha has informed me that she will meet you at the cottage in an hour's time, and she will be bringing Elder Helka with her."

I felt some, but not all, of the tension leave my shoulders. At least we were not being turned away. The guest cottage was an attractive stone building with a slate roof. The stable was clean with fresh straw in the stalls. Once we had the horses settled and our gear secured in a small storage room next to the pack horse's stall, we grabbed our packs and entered the guest cottage. Kipp followed us as we made our way from the stable.

Like the stable, the guest cottage was clean and well maintained. The furnishings were sparse but comfortable looking. A fire had been lit in the fireplace, and surprisingly, there was a steaming kettle already hanging over the fire. Hiatt explained that the sleeping rooms were at the top of the stairs. We would have to provide our own food. We thanked him, and he left us to settle in.

"I don't know about the rest of you, but I could do with a cup of tea.

Anyone else?" I asked Rosilda and Arnar. They both answered yes. "Since we are responsible for our own meal, I will go back out to the stable and gather the supplies for both tea and a meal. I need to do something while I am waiting. Want to come with me, Kipp?" He just looked up from the chair he had settled on by the fire, yawned, and curled into a ball.

It did not take me long to find what I needed amongst our supplies and head back. I was accompanied by an orange tabby cat, who slipped through the door into the guest cottage just ahead of me. I handed off what I was carrying, and before I could close the door, a silver tabby cat and a black and tan cat hustled in.

As the cats settled in on the hearth rug, Rosilda remarked, "I wonder, is it you or Kipp, or the combination of the two of you, that attracts cats?"

"I have no answer. Maybe they are just the guest cottage cats, and this is their home."

Rosilda did not seem to accept my answer. When the door opened, and Zasha and an elderly woman entered followed by two more cats, there was no more time to discuss the gathered cats.

The cats moved directly toward Kipp, touched noses, and jumped up on the chair next to the fire that I had just vacated. The two women stood just inside the door. The older woman swayed and clutched Zasha's arm.

"Please take my seat," I suggested gently to the elderly woman, as I turned to brush the two cats off.

Zasha escorted the woman over and gently helped her sit. I offered tea, which both women accepted. Once we were all settled, Zasha introduced the elderly woman as Elder Helka, the woman I had traveled so far to find. I took a long moment to look at her while my two companions introduced themselves. Elder Helka was certainly in her later years, her skin wrinkled, her face lined, her hair snow white, and yet, I thought I saw a similarity between her and how I remembered my mother looking. That might have been wishful thinking on my part. I brought my attention back to what was being said and realized it was my turn to introduce myself.

"I am named Perrin Leifursdotter of the Nytt Heimili clan of Bortfjell." I do not why I went so formal. Maybe to bolster my courage in talking to this elder. Maybe to hold on to what little I had left of my family. "My mother was named Helka and was, as we say, from beyond, meaning she was not from Bortfjell. As I told Zasha yesterday, she died when I was thirteen," I stated gently.

I could think of no soft way of easing the conversation around the fact that my mother was dead. I watched Zasha's eyes fill with tears and Elder Helka's eyes fill with sorrow. Their reaction had me thinking that we had found my mother's folk.

"I am sorry I delivered the news of my mother's death so bluntly."

Elder Helka spoke for the first time. "You have the look of her, and it would seem, her habit of straight speaking. I have hoped these many years that my granddaughter, my namesake, Helka, would return, that age would have brought wisdom and forgiveness to all of us. I will answer any questions you have, great granddaughter, but first, please tell me of your mother."

I could not speak for a long moment, taking in what Elder Helka had just said. It felt incredulous to me that following the slimmest of clues, I had actually found my mother's folk, and I was sitting in a cottage with my great grandmother.

I cleared my throat to begin to speak and had to clear it again. Kipp startled me when he jumped up on my lap, circled twice, and settled down. While I could not hear his purr, I could feel the vibration and found it soothing.

"I am afraid I know little. From a very early age, I spent my days training, for I am, or was until recently, the heir to the landholding Nytt Heimili. I do not have many memories of time with my mother. I probably spent more time with my father, who is the laird of our landholding. I have vague memories of my mother spending time in our library. When we would venture to Fyrstaborgin, the capital of Bortfjell, when my father had business at the court, my mother would spend the days at the royal library. Sometimes she would take me with her and settle me in a corner with a stack of books while she spent the day looking through dusty old tomes."

I had to smile at the memory of the time I spent at the royal library. I had thought I was going to be bored having to spend the day inside when I would rather have been outside. It had surprised me how my mother had known just which books to put in front of me that would capture my interest or imagination. I had forgotten that.

"When I was about ten years old, my mother gave birth to a child who lived only a few days. After that, she was never the same. She withdrew from the world. I do not remember much about her from that time. She died when I was thirteen. It has been suggested that the loss of the child was too much for her to bear. In my mind, it felt like my mother faded away, and then she was gone. I lost my father at that time too."

When I saw the look of shock and sadness on the two women's faces, I quickly went on.

"Oh, no, my father is very much alive. It is just that he adored my mother. I am not sure he has ever gotten over his grief and despair at her passing. I am sorry I have so little to tell you about my mother."

"Please do not apologize. You have given me a gift this day."

I am sure Elder Helka could see the look of puzzlement on my face. How had I given her a gift when I had brought the news that her granddaughter had died?

"How have I given you a gift?"

"You have answered my long-held questions as to what happened to my granddaughter. You have given me family, for you are my great granddaughter."

"You are sure I am your great granddaughter?"

Elder Helka laughed when I asked that question.

"If I had not been convinced before, as you have the looks of our family, I would have known for sure because of the cats."

"Because of the cats?"

"Look around you. You have a cat the likes of which I have never seen before on your lap, and when we entered here there were three other cats, and two more came in with us. Your mother always seemed to have cats near her, following her, gathering by her. Used to annoy the others of the village, since they wanted their cats doing their jobs and keeping the vermin out of their houses, shops, and barns. Everyday, your mother would have to tell the cats to head back to where they were needed. Now youngling, it is time for you to ask your questions."

"I do not know where to start. What was she like when she lived here? Why did she not stay here? What needs to be forgiven?"

Chapter Twenty-Eight

"I think you had best ask Zasha the questions about what your mother was like, for the two were like two peas in a pod when they were young."

"Your mother and I had a good childhood. We had lessons in the morning and then training in the craft for several hours after the noon meal. Your mother was a very good student and was always asking questions that often times our tutors could not answer, which frustrated your mother. As for training to work in the porcelain craft, your mother was attentive and tried hard. The craft did not come easy to her like our lessons and book learning did."

"And what of you?"

"I was the opposite of your mother. I did not have the interest in the lessons or the book learning like your mother. I did passable work, but I was not brilliant. As for the craft, I would have cheerfully stayed all day learning there. Especially when it came to painting on the designs after the glaze."

"Zasha is one of our most respected artists," commented Elder Helka.

Zasha thanked Elder Helka for her kind words and went on with her narrative.

"This valley is very protected and quite safe, so as children we had the run of the valley. Your mother loved to explore, always wanting to go farther and farther away from the village, often causing us to be late getting back home. Getting home late was something my family was not pleased about, but your grandparents did not mind. So, I got in trouble, Helka did not."

I did not hear any bitterness in Zasha's voice about the different reactions from the two sets of parents, for which I was glad. It also struck me at this moment that I had not asked what had happened to my grandparents. Why were they not here and part of this conversation we were having about my mother? I decided I would ask that question once Zasha had had her say.

"As we grew older, sadly as often happens when one's interests change, your mother and I did not spend as much time together. I was given an opportunity to learn from our best porcelain painter, and so I began to spend my days with her. Your mother worked at glazing and other tasks. I do not think her heart was in it though. She was often restless. I know she would spend her evenings with you, Elder Helka."

"Your mother often visited me in the evenings, from her early childhood on through to the time she left the valley. She was interested in all the old tales and legends I knew. She was such a curious lass. I had hoped she would continue to learn from me and eventually be the valley tale keeper and historian, so the tales would not get lost. Fortunately, after she left, two more children of the valley began to visit me for the tales and history of our valley. I have great hopes for both to carry on when I am gone."

"I am curious as to what happened to my grandparents, for you have not mentioned them."

"They are alive and well," Elder Helka answered with a sigh. "That brings us to the question you asked about as to what needs to be forgiven."

"Go on."

"Like Zasha said, your mother loved to explore and learn about what she had found, be it a type of rock, a newly discovered plant, or an animal she had not seen before. She was so very curious. She also was, as I said, especially interested in the old tales and legends."

"Sometimes she would get lost in an old book she had found out someone had and be late to our lessons. In later years she was often late to work, which created trouble for her. We are all called to do our part here in the valley. Our livelihood depends on it," stated Zasha.

"Her curiosity and need to explore and discover, her need to learn, became an issue of deep disagreement between your mother and her parents," stated Elder Helka. "Your grandparents finally insisted that she, as they put it, stop her foolishness, and get on with the task of finding what she was best at to support the village. They had many arguments about it.

Finally, one day, your mother just packed up the few possessions she had, came and said goodbye to me, and left. That was the last we heard from her, or about her, until you showed up at the valley gate."

"I am so sorry that I came as the bearer of sad news for you. If my grandparents are alive and here in the valley, why are they not here with the two of you so I can also meet them?"

"Sadly, it is because they have never forgiven your mother for what they thought of as her disobeying them. They gave her an edict, fully believing they were right, and she left. I think they somewhat blame themselves for driving her from the valley, and they somewhat blame her for not doing what they felt was best for her. Now, I am afraid, if they back down from their anger toward their daughter by acknowledging you, they would have to acknowledge they might have been too harsh or wrong," suggested Elder Helka. "I am so sorry. Now, I am afraid I grow a bit weary, so we need to leave for this day. I would like to meet with you again, if you could find it in your heart to stay several days. In the meantime, Zasha and I will each individually talk with your grandparents and see if we can convince them to change their minds."

With the agreement of Rosilda and Arnar, I told Elder Helka and Zasha that we would stay a day or two more at the guest cottage. Once the two women left, the three of us settled back to talk over what had been told to us.

"I can understand your mother leaving," Rosilda stated. "Being locked into a certain job or skill just because your parents and their parents before them did that job or did that craft can cause problems. Not each and every child grows up wanting to do what their parents did. Eventually, the next generation will either abandon the land, job, or craft until you do not have folks left who know what they are doing, or you do not have folks left to do what needs to be done who are really invested in what they are doing. I think the rovers have the right of it, encouraging their younglings to seek what they want to do and then find someone to teach them."

"Remember, there are the guilds in Sommerhjem," suggested Arnar.

"Guilds?" I asked. "Tell me more about the guilds."

"Wright told me about them. There are guilds for many crafts, such as glassblowing or glassmaking, metalsmithing, wood smithing, and many, many other skills. These guilds take in younglings and others who are interested in and have a talent for the particular craft. They start as apprentices and can work their way up to journeyman or journeywoman and finally to master. I wonder if there was some other craft or interest that your mother chose to pursue after she left here. Could she have sought out a guild?"

"Well, one thing we did learn today was that your mother had the same affinity with cats. Good thing I like cats," Rosilda said laughingly, "since if I stick with you, cats will always be near."

Rosilda's statement lightened my mood. I had so much to think about now that I knew a little more about my mother and where she came from. I was thankful that Zasha had returned to talk with us, and that she had brought Elder Helka.

Sleep did not come easy that night. One of the thoughts that kept circling around and around in my head was what would my life have been like if I had been born in Sommerhjem? What would I have wanted as a craft or a trade? If I had been born on a farm, would I have wanted to stay there or would I have been like Rosilda and had restless feet? I knew from what I had heard, that if I had been born into a forester clan, there were many different skills needed that I could have chosen from. Might I have wanted to enter a guild? Or would I have wanted to be a fisher, living on my boat and being at sea? Would I have grown up in this valley? Would I have been content to follow the craft like my family?

Up until I had been forced to flee Bortfjell, my life had been all planned out, not unlike my mother's life had been planned out by her parents. Nytt Heimili had been my gated valley in a sense. I was destined to become the next laird. I had never thought otherwise. In my mind, it was not about choosing what I was to become, it just was what was. I wonder if I had been allowed to stay in Nytt Heimili whether I would have come to resent that path which I had not chosen.

The problem now is I had too many choices, for which I was either starting quite late or did not even know if I could join or become. I did not know if I had the inclination or the desire to learn a skill or a craft. I cannot imagine many landholders saying "why sure, you can come in and inherit the landholding since you are trained for that. My children will just step aside for you."

The one choice I did not think I had was to stay in the valley of the porcelain crafters. It did not matter that I was related to Elder Helka and others here. I had neither the desire nor the skills to work in the porcelain craft. I had not grown up here, nor did I feel I would be totally welcome. I felt Elder Helka would be welcoming. I did not know if my grandparents would be welcoming.

Dawn arrived much too soon. I knew I was not going to get any more sleep, so I got up. Since we were able to stay in a dry, sheltered place for several days, we would be able to catch up on some neglected chores. I dressed and headed out to the stable where our gear was stored. The day before, Hiatt had shown me where there was a clear stream where I could bathe and where there was a wash tub behind the guest cottage. He had also shown me a place to string a clothesline. Taking advantage of the early hour, I got washed up and began on the dirty clothes. Rosilda joined me about an hour later.

"Very good plan, Perrin. Arnar is in the stable cleaning and oiling the tack and saddles. Kipp seems to be earning his keep in the stable and watching over Arnar to make sure he does a good job. I have brought more dirty clothes if you are so inclined to do them. I am going to string a few more lines and hang out our lean-tos, empty packs, blanket rolls, and saddle blankets."

"That would be fine. Would you mind hanging out my cloak and my rain gear? Everything has gotten a bit musty."

It felt good to have chores to be busy with. Washing, wringing out the clothes, and hanging them up was a mindless activity for which I was grateful. I had spent too much time thinking and not enough time sleeping the night before. It felt good to be out in the sunshine, smelling the fresh pine-scented air, and not spending the day on horseback.

After the noon meal, Elder Helka joined us once again. She suggested we might want to sit outside in the shade of the guest cottage porch. I was hoping she would have arrived with my grandparents, but she had come alone. Arnar and Rosilda greeted her and then excused themselves to go back to their chores.

"Zasha needed to get back to work this day. Yesterday was her normal day of rest. Today she needed to get back to painting pieces for a large commission. You see, once a piece is glazed and fired, then Zasha and other artists paint the pattern, design, or scene onto the piece in a process called overglazing. Most porcelain colors are painted over the fired glaze and fired at a much lower temperature. Mind you, I am not giving away any trade secrets here, for what I have told you is common knowledge. Do you think you might be interested in learning to make porcelain?"

"I do not think that is my calling. I am sorry."

"Now, Perrin, do not apologize. It was just wishful thinking on an old woman's part. I was very fond of your mother. Now that I have found I have a great granddaughter, I had hoped you might find some reason to stay."

"I noticed my grandparents did not come with you."

"Ah, well, yes, they did not. I fear they cannot find it in their hearts to bend even a little bit. I am sorry. I think my son, your grandfather, might be willing, but your grandmother is very vocally not willing. I hope you know I would welcome any time you would choose to spend with me. I hope this will not be your only visit to this valley."

I did not know how to answer this request from Elder Helka to return at some point to this valley, since I did not know where I was heading next or what I was going to do with the rest of my life.

Elder Helka spent some time talking to me about my mother's family, past and current. It seems we were never a very large family in any one generation. It was interesting to know about the history of my mother's family. The knowledge, while giving me some background, did not make me feel any more connected to my mother's family than I had before I had come here. That feeling might have been caused by the fact that my remaining living relatives, other than my great grandmother, did not want to meet me.

I had just asked Elder Helka to tell me some of the tales and legends that she had told my mother when Rosilda and Arnar rejoined us. We settled in for the next hour or so, as my great grandmother spun some tall tales. I asked if there were any tales about folks partnering with wild animals, and she told me that there were.

"It seems to happen most frequently when it is time to choose a new ruler, although not always. I have heard of folks pairing with hunting cats like this Elder Iona you mentioned. They have also paired with mountain cats, bog foxes, griff falcons, the dogs that have evolved into our border dogs, and on exceedingly rare occasions, night wolves."

"Night wolves?"

"Never seen one myself. They are said to be large wolves, black as midnight, with the tips of their hair sparkling silver in the moonlight like the stars on a crisp dark cold month night. Always wanted to see one, though," stated Elder Helka wistfully.

Finally, in the late afternoon as the sun was reaching the golden hour, which came earlier in the high hills, when all of the green in the forest seemed to become brighter and the tree trunks took on a slight golden glow, Elder Helka bid her farewell. I felt a wee bit sad to see her go.

As pleasant as the afternoon had been, I realized that it was time to move on. Other than Elder Helka, there was really nothing for me here in the valley of my mother's folk. As to just where I was to go next, I did not really know. I did have one idea that I would need to talk over with Arnar and Rosilda.

Chapter Twenty-Nine

After Elder Helka left, I went to see if there was anything left of the chores we had started earlier in the day. I followed Arnar and Rosilda out behind the guest cottage and helped take down the last of our gear and fold or roll it into good packable sizes.

"Did you have a good talk with Elder Helka about your family?" Rosilda asked.

"I did. Did you enjoy the tales she told?"

"I did indeed. I have always liked hearing old tales and legends. Did you notice that some of the tales she told were similar to Bortfjellian ones?"

"I did notice that. Do you ever remember hearing tales about folks pairing with wild animals?"

"Not that I can recall. Arnar?"

"I have never heard any tales of folks pairing with wild animals in any of the Bortfjellian tales or legends. Wait, that is not true. I know of one."

"You do?"

"Why yes, Perrin. I know of a lass who has paired with a wild hill cat from the high hills of Bortfjell. This cat travels with her on the back of her horse."

"What, wait, no …."

"You think your traveling with Kipp is any different than Elder Iona traveling with Lorcan, other than the size of each cat?"

I did not know what to say after that. I was going to have to think about what Arnar had just said. We continued to work on packing our gear into the bags the pack horse would carry. After that, I went into the guest cottage and sorted through my freshly cleaned laundry, deciding what I wanted to carry in my saddle bags and what I would pack in a bag to be carried by the pack horse.

After dinner and cleanup, I settled in a chair by the fireplace with a cup of tea to think. Arnar and Rosilda joined me after they had finished up with their packing.

"Since we left Nytt Heimili, we have taken a fast and dangerous route to elude those who might be trying to follow me and do away with me. Hopefully that danger ended when Grimur, Timir, and Donnola were arrested and detained. You both chose to accompany me to this valley as I followed a very slim lead that my mother's folk were here. That lead paid off, allowing me to meet at least one member of my mother's family and learn of my mother's early life here. It also gave me some information as to why she left. The one other thing this visit here has taught me is I do not belong here, and quite frankly, probably would not be very welcomed."

"I would agree, since your grandparents did not come rushing over to greet you with open arms," Rosilda suggested.

"They did not." I went on to tell Rosilda and Arnar what Elder Helka had told me about the rift between my mother and my grandparents. I am sure they could hear the slight hurt in my voice, even though I tried to hide it.

"So where to next?" asked Arnar.

I was touched by such a simple question, for it implied that Arnar was at least thinking of continuing to travel with me. I looked at Rosilda.

"In for a copper, in for a silver, as they say. I have traveled this far with you. Seems we are not done."

I took a deep breath and discreetly swiped at a small tear that threatened to fall down my cheek. These two had come with me out of loyalty to the clan and to do their duty to protect the heir of the clan. That was not completely the reason they continued to ride with me now, for they had become friends, or in the language of the old tales, boon companions.

Clearing my throat, which I found was feeling a little tight, I began. "As you know, my father had surmised I might be in danger because of the edict by Prince Mallus that folks not of pure Bortfjellian lineage could not hold any positions of power. My becoming the next laird of our clan and landholding becomes possible only if a new ruler reverses the edict. My father rightfully feared for my life and told me to be prepared. You also know that he left me a small fortune in the hollow of what we called the wishing tree …"

A stray thought entered my mind at that moment, and I wondered if he had found the note I left in the wishing tree for him just before I headed to the old keep to wait until darkness to leave to meet Rosilda and Arnar at the old broken down mill.

"… and he left me something else."

I reached into the neck of my shirt and pulled out the chain that held my mother's medallion.

"This medallion was my mother's. My father told me she never took it off. She always wore it hidden under her clothing."

"Did you show it to your great grandmother, Elder Helka?" asked Rosilda.

"I did not. Something held me back. Let me try to explain."

"On the day just before Grimur and company showed up at the campsite, I had wandered into the surrounding woods to sit by myself and take some time to think. Shortly after I had sat down, I was joined by Elder Iona and her hunting cat, Lorcan. I have to say, Lorcan was only one of the surprises that afternoon."

"Only one of the surprises. I would think not much would top a large hunting cat stepping out of the woods," suggested Arnar.

"Yes, well, what Elder Iona had to say was equally surprising. She told me that some folks in Sommerhjem were what you might call sensitives. She explained that those folks could sense objects of power, and she was one of them. Elder Iona told me that she sensed I was carrying one or more objects of power."

"Go on," said Arnar quietly.

I looked at him and was about to ask him if he knew of folks who were sensitives. He just waved his hands in a hurry up motion, so I went on.

"Elder Iona looked at the medallion and told me that there should be a gem in the middle. Then she asked if I had a gem on me that was black with sparks of color inside. I did, so I pulled it out from where I had hidden it in my boot. Once I had it in my hand, something happened that almost made me drop the gem. A light arced from the stone in my hand to a stone in a ring on Elder Iona's finger. She told me I was holding a firestar gem. She explained that one of the interesting properties of firestar gems is that when one firestar gem is near another firestar gem, and it is in the possession of someone with good intent, it will arc, of like to like. Also, when a firestar gem is near an object that is more than what it seems by its outward appearance, it grows warm. Perhaps the most interesting property of firestar gems is that they seem to choose who will wear them."

"They choose those who wear them?" Rosilda questioned.

"Apparently. After seeing the firestar gem I held send an arc of light to the stone in Elder Iona's ring, I tend to believe what she has told me. At any rate, Elder Iona asked to take both the medallion and the firestar gem, for she thought that the two belonged together. She left for a short while and returned the medallion to me after she had set the firestar gem into it. She was just about to talk more to me about the medallion when Lakyle came running to fetch us. You all know what happened after that."

"We do indeed," Rosilda exclaimed, rubbing her hands together in glee.

"The next day after we settled into the camping site, Elder Iona asked Kipp and me to join her and Lorcan in her homewagon. Once there, she told me she had noticed something about the medallion that she wanted to study closer. To make a long tale short, she was right about there being something more about the medallion. Let me show you."

I placed my finger on the firestar gem as I had that night in Elder Iona's homewagon and again felt the firestar gem warm. As had happened that night, the back opened to reveal the seeker medallion inside.

"What you see here hidden inside my mother's medallion is what Elder Iona calls a seeker medallion. When I asked what seekers were, she explained that seekers are folks who spend their lives in pursuit of the old knowledge and trying to find that which has been lost. Apparently, there is an Order of the Seekers, and they have a landholding. Elder Iona told me a great deal more about the seekers. She could not, however, tell me if my mother had been a member of the Order of the Seekers, only that she had been in possession of a seeker medallion hidden inside another medallion."

"You are thinking your mother might have been one of these seekers," suggested Arnar.

"I think it might be possible. From all I learned here from both Zasha and Elder Hilka, my mother had a restless spirit and an unquenchable curiosity. It seems she would get lost in a musty old tome to the point of missing work. I remember my mother spent hours at the library in the capital of Bortfjell and in the library at the manor. Who knows? Maybe she joined the Order of the Seekers. Being a seeker might explain how her life led her to the border of Bortfjell where she met my father. I know it is another slim clue ….."

"Yet look where the last slim clue led us," declared Rosilda.

"True. Sometimes I just feel adrift in the middle of the sea with no land in sight, not knowing which way to set my sails or what direction to head. Maybe my bringing this up is just a way to delay the inevitable issue of what to do next, for the small wealth my father left me is not going to last forever. Maybe I, or we, need to give some serious consideration to how we are going to survive in this new country."

"All very weighty issues to be sure," commented Arnar. "However, I think if you do not follow up on finding out if your mother was a seeker, you will always have that unanswered question hovering in your mind. I, for one, think we should travel to this landholding of the Order of the Seekers. The very worst that can happen is they will turn you away at the gate. In the meantime, we will see more of Sommerhjem and learn more about this country and where we might fit in."

"You do know that both of you can head back to Bortfjell at any time, do you not?"

"I am not sure that is true, lass. Rosilda and I have aided you in escaping Grimur's fate for you. I feel that what happened to him near Klippebyen has either gotten back to his sister, your stepmother, or will eventually. I do not feel we would be welcomed back to Nytt Heimili with open arms, since we have aided and abetted a foreigner. That being the case, Sommerhjem is a better choice for us now. I think we should just continue to travel on together."

"I agree with what Arnar said," stated Rosilda. "I suggest we make sure we pack up everything and not leave anything behind. We also need to take time to sweep, clean up the guest cottage, carry in a good supply of wood for the next guest, and get some sleep so we are ready to head off early. By the way, do you know where this seeker landholding is located?"

CHAPTER THIRTY

I answered Rosilda's question as to whether I knew the location of the Order of the Seekers landholding by going to my saddlebag and pulling out the cylinder that held the map Elder Iona had given me. She had marked the spot where the Order of the Seekers had its landholding. Elder Iona had shown me it was close to the north end of the bluffs, tucked away in a large, protected valley surrounded by foothills. The holding had good farmland and good foothills pastureland for the raising of sheep. While it was not a large holding, it was a productive one and was known for its honey. I rolled out the map on the table under the lantern. We all gathered around it. I pointed to the map to show where we were now.

"As you can see, we are north of the village of Mellomdaler. Where we want to head is farther north. The landholding of the Order of the Seekers is located on the east side of the north end of the bluffs. While I know it sounds strange, we can head south and then swing west around the south end of the bluffs, where we can take a ferry across this large lake and then head north. Our other option is to head west down out of the high hills and travel north between the foothills and the bluffs. While we might save some time with the first option by traveling on the ferry, we also might lose time if the weather becomes stormy, and we have to wait for the ferry to be able to cross the lake."

"Much as I hate to admit it," said Rosilda, looking a bit embarrassed, "I am not fond of traveling by boats. I get a bit queasy."

"You have both given good reasons for why heading north by horseback might be a better choice," suggested Arnar.

"I agree." I asked Rosilda her opinion, and she also agreed we should head north. "If folks ask where we are going and just what we are about, we should have something to tell them. I do not think we should tell folks we are heading toward the landholding of the Order of the Seekers."

"Let us just say we are on a walkabout," said Arnar. "I know that walkabouts are normally done by young lads and lasses in Sommerhjem. Stodd did tell me that sometimes they are done by older folk. They take a summer off and travel about the country. Or, if whatever they might have done to earn their keep is suddenly no longer available, they go on a walkabout looking for a new place to find work. We could tell the truth. That we no longer had a place in Bortfjell and are trying to find a place in Sommerhjem."

"I find I like your idea of sticking to the truth," I remarked. Rosilda agreed. "That is settled then. We will take the land route. All we have left to do in the morning is to tie the packs to the pack horse, saddle up, and be on our way. I suggest we get an early start."

"If that is going to be the case, we should turn in now," Rosilda said with a huge yawn.

I told the others that I would take one last look about the stable to make sure we had not overlooked something. When I entered the stable, I found Kipp sitting on our pile of gear.

"Guarding our meager possessions, are you?"

Kipp gave me a look that suggested it should be obvious what he was doing and did not need my comments. I sat down on the bench that was in the small storage room that held our gear. Kipp settled back down atop the packs.

"We are a long way from home, Kipp. I thank you for traveling with me. We are headed north again to a valley that has some bluffs and foothills surrounding it. I wonder if the land will look anything like home. We both seem to have left hearth and kin behind. Well, perhaps not a hearth for you. A family den maybe. Do you miss the high hills of home?"

Kipp, of course, did not answer. He did climb down off the packs and settled in on my lap. As I stroked his soft fur, I was comforted by his presence. I realized I was homesick. I think my feelings of loss and loneliness were compounded by what had transpired here in the valley of my mother's folk. Though I had not wanted to admit it to myself until now, a part of me had hoped that I would find a welcome here. Now, I was just sad, for I felt, though I had family, I could not be with them. In a sense, I was an orphan. It was not a good feeling.

Finally, when my chin bobbed on my chest for the sixth or seventh time, I concluded it was time to head into bed. I got up and ambled back to the guest cottage. Either Arnar or Rosilda had left a lantern burning on low to light my way to the door. Inside the cottage they had left a candle lit on the mantle. Not for the first time I was grateful for having such caring and thoughtful companions traveling with me.

The next morning, just as we were checking the straps and cinches on our saddles, packs, and tack, I glanced down the lane heading toward the village gate. I saw Zasha moving briskly toward us. I left the others and turned to greet her. I know I felt a small glimmer of hope that she was rushing to catch us to tell us not to leave, that my grandparents had changed their minds and wished to meet me.

"I am so glad you have not left yet. I am sorry I could not spend any time with you yesterday. I just wanted you to know that I did try to persuade your grandparents to come to the guest cottage and meet you. They remain too stubborn for their own good and will not change their minds."

"Zasha, I appreciate that you tried."

"I wanted to come this morning, hoping to catch you before you left, to tell you I would welcome more time with you, if you choose to return to our valley. Also, last night I remembered I have something of your mother's that I thought you might want as a keepsake. It has a good tale behind it."

"I would like whatever it is very much, although I think the tale is going to be an even greater gift. Let me tell my companions that we will be a little delayed."

I tied my horse up to the hitch in front of the guest cottage and took a seat on the porch. Zasha joined me, as did Arnar and Rosilda.

"Your mother was not wildly interested in any phase of the making of fine porcelain, as you now know. She was a decent glazer when she put her mind to it. Unfortunately, her mind was often elsewhere."

Zasha took a small bundle out of her leather apron pocket. She carefully unwrapped it. Inside was a figurine, I think. It was not in great shape. The glaze had hundreds of tiny cracks running through it, and whatever it was supposed to be was hard to distinguish, for it looked as if it had melted.

"Your mother is responsible for this dubious piece of art. It was supposed to be a figurine of a graceful swan. As you can see, it is not in good shape because your mother got lost in a book and forgot to watch the time and temperature. This is the only piece from that firing that survived somewhat intact. The others exploded, for your mother let the heat get too high. I have held on to this piece to use to tease your mother when your mother had younglings, and they made a mistake learning the craft. I could say, 'well now, if you think that is bad, you should see what your mother was capable of.' Since you are that youngling, albeit all grown up, I thought you might like this."

I was touched by Zasha's thoughtfulness and thanked her for the melted, oddly shaped piece of porcelain that had cracks running every which way through the glaze. I wrapped it back up and placed it in my saddlebag.

After Zasha left, we mounted and headed through the valley gate. Hiatt was once again on gate duty. We thanked him for his kindness and traveled on down the lane. The lane was decent to travel on, and we made good time. For the next few days, we left after dawn and tried to find a place to camp by dinner time.

Before we arrived in the area between the foothills and the bluffs, we traveled for a time out of the high hills through an area that was tended by foresters. I admired how well they were able to blend in with their surroundings and to slip noiselessly through the forest. One did not know that they were nearby unless they wanted their whereabouts to be known. It was during this section of our journey that we rode through several quirrelit groves. Something about these trees called to me. I always felt a great sense of peace whenever we wended our way through a grove of these magnificent old trees. There was something special about them.

The weather held as we headed north. The days were mild, and while the nights still had the bite of cold to them, the farther we moved out of the high hills, the warmer the nights were. I had hoped the weather would remain mild and dry until we reached the seekers' landholding. We almost made it. Just as we were approaching what I hoped was the lane that would take us to the manor house, the wind picked up, lightning flashed, thunder rolled in a continuous cacophony of rumbles, and the rain pounded down. At times we had to find shelter among the trees, for we could not see more than a foot or so through the pounding rain. By the time we arrived at the manor house, we were soaked and chilled to the bone. Kipp was probably the only one of us who was warm and dry, having slipped into the modified pack Brodie had made for him.

I was surprised to find the manor house dark. I thought with the storm raging around us and the dense gray clouds blocking out the sunlight, someone would have lit the outside lantern by the door. I suggested we try to find the stable before we knocked on the manor house door. If nothing else, perhaps we could get the horses out of the rain.

There was a lit lantern by the small door at the end of the stable. I knocked. No one came to answer the door. I tried the latch, and the door opened. I went in to find anyone who might help us. A lit lantern showed me that to the left of the entrance was a stair. I assumed it led up to the quarters for those who took care of the stable, horses, and carriages. I called a hello and heard movement above me.

I heard a young voice saying he was coming right down before I saw the scrawny form moving slowly down the stair. It was the look of fear in the young lad's eyes and the way he was holding himself as if he expected a blow at any moment that concerned me.

"Ah, lad, no harm here, no harm here. We've come a long way in the rain this day and hope to seek shelter and to talk to a seeker."

"Yer, yer, not with them's folks headed by Desna?"

"Who is Desna?"

"She and five others came ridin' in about a fortnight ago an' tooks over this place. They been holdin' Seeker Alden and threaten ta harm him if'n we don'ts do as she says. Been bossin' us all around, she has. Ye had best be movin' on. They's mean ones. Say's this is their landholdin' now."

"I see. What is your name lad?"

"Blain."

"Well, Blain, let me talk to my two companions. Can I trust you not to go running to Desna or her companions?"

"I'll jus' go back upstairs."

"Is there anyone up there with you?"

"No, they sents all the rest of those of us who works at the stable out ta the crofters, makin' them works the land."

"And no one has fought back against this?"

"That Desna threatened ta harm Seeker Alden and made everyone sends one member of their family ta the manor. If'n everyone does as they says, then no one will get hurts. They locked them up in the cellars …."

At this point the young lad pulled even farther into himself, if that was at all possible, turning his head down to look at the stairs, but not before I saw the tears brimming in his eyes.

"Who in your family are they keeping, Blain?"

"I don't have anyone septin' the marshal who tooks me in an' gave me a place here at the stable. Theys locked away the marshal along with the steward, and others."

"Instead of going upstairs, why don't you wait here? I am going to invite my companions inside so I can tell them what you have told me. Will you wait on the stairs?"

"All right."

I left Blain huddled in a ball on the stairs and opened the door to signal Arnar and Rosilda to quietly enter. Once they were inside, followed by Kipp, I introduced them to Blain and told them what I had learned.

Arnar asked a question of Blain that I had not thought to ask. "Are they just here to take over the landholding, or are they here for other reasons too? I wouldn't think they could control the landholding for very long. Word would get out."

"They's waitin' for the return of the other seekers. Once a year at the end of sprin', they all returns for a fortnight or more afore goin' back out. They's think that the seekers are bringin' back coin and treasures. They's donna understand that the seekers donna go lookin' for treasures."

"So, they are going to be sadly disappointed," suggested Rosilda.

"Are Desna's horse and her companions' horses stabled here, Blain?"

"Yes sir. They's tooks the best stalls."

"Is there a place where we could move our horses in out of the rain? Somewhere they would be out of sight should someone walk into the stable."

"Ya could put yer horses out back in the lean-to. They's donna go back there."

"As long as this gully washer of a rain continues, I do not think others will be venturing out. So far, I do not think our presence here has been noticed. I think we are safe here for the moment. I certainly do not want to continue riding right now, nor do I think I want to just ride off and not have a chance to speak to a seeker. Rosilda and Arnar, are the two of you willing to stay?" Both agreed to stay.

"Why don't we all go get the horses and move them into the lean-to? Blain, would you lead the way? Once that is done, we need to take the time to learn more and decide what we want to do."

We were successful getting the horses into the lean-to, and just in time. I did not think the rain could fall any harder than it had been. I had been mistaken. While it was cold and miserable in the lean-to, it was at least dry and protected from most of the wind and rain. Blain hovered in the small doorway leading into the main part of the stable to maintain a lookout. I had suggested to him that he grab what he would need to muck the stalls, so if someone were foolish enough to head out in the bad weather and come into the stable, he could look like he was working.

"I know that look on your face, Perrin. I remember that look from our early years. If I remember rightly, when you got that look, we often got in trouble. Just what do you have in mind?" asked Rosilda.

"For one thing, I am getting tired of folks being bullies. I am tired of traveling to find out more about my mother and my mother's folk only to be disappointed with the outcome or turned away. We have traveled all this way to talk to a seeker concerning the medallion I wear, and what that might have to do with my mother. Six folks are holding this entire landholding hostage and keeping me from talking to Seeker Alden. I think I have just about had enough."

"And ...."

"And I think there are five of us and six of them. And we have the element of surprise."

"Five?" questioned Arnar.

"The three of us, the lad, and Kipp, of course. Not bad odds."

Chapter Thirty-One

Those had been pretty brave words spoken by me in a moment of anger and frustration, and yet, neither Rosilda nor Arnar stepped forward to try to dissuade me.

"Obviously, we need a plan. It would not do to rush off unprepared," suggested Arnar mildly. "Blain, what can you tell us about this Desna and the five folks with her?"

"They's all rough and tough type of folks who ya cans tell has fought a few fights. Gruff and growly type of folks. Quick ta hits and slaps folks around."

"Do they have a routine or set assignments to keep the folks on the landholding under control?" asked Rosilda.

"Theys mostly stays in the manor house. Two of thems rides out each day ta threaten the crofters and beekeepers that theys best not say anythin' or their families will gets hurt."

"I know that this is going to be a strange question, but Blain, do you know any secret ways into the manor?" I asked.

I saw a flash of surprise on Blain's face before he turned away and looked anywhere but at me.

"I donna know what ya're askin'."

"I grew up in what you call a manor house. It was big, had a number of wings and additions added on to the original old keep. My ancestors were not trusting of others at one time and so had ways of entering and leaving the keep unseen in times of trouble. I think that is probably true of many manor houses, even those in Sommerhjem. I asked, because it might be a way to get into the manor house unnoticed and allow us to take care of Desna and her crew one folk at a time."

I watched Blain glance back at me before turning away quickly and fiddling with the pitchfork he was holding. I went on.

"I will, and Arnar and Rosilda will, pledge on our honor we will never reveal any secrets about the Order of the Seekers' manor."

"On your honor?"

"On our honor."

Blain took his time thinking over what I had said. "So, you wants ta sneak inta the manor an' capture Desna and the others one at a time?"

"I guess the best way to put it is that I want to disappear them, just snatch them up one at a time and tuck them away somewhere. That might begin to frighten them and have them jumping at shadows."

"Seeker Alden showed me a ways ta gets inta the manor from the stable. Says it was a ways in the ol' days that folks could get ta the animals without goin' outside ina rain or snowstorm."

"Where does it enter the manor?"

"Downs below ina cellar storeroom."

"Is that anywhere near where they are holding the folks of the landholding?"

"There's a slidin' panel that lets ya inta a corridor jus' down from where they's holdin' folks."

"Do they have a guard posted where the folks are being held?"

"Yes'm. Has one there at all times. He has a chair an' a table that faces away from the corridor ya would enter from."

"Blain, when do they feed the folks they have locked up?"

"Cooks and me only takes the porridge and water down at the dinner hour. That's also when theys change the guard."

"Arnar? You look like you have an idea."

"Here is what I am thinking. If we go soon, we might be able to remove the guard in the cellar, get the holding doors open, and release the folks that are being held. Blain is there another place in the cellar that the folks can hide in while we try to tie up the guard?"

"Theys locked up the bottler an's mad at him 'cause he wouldn' give 'ems his keys ta the wine and mead cellar. He slipped 'em ta me. They could hide in that cellar an' he could locks it from the inside."

"Who would that leave in the manor?"

"Just Seeker Alden, Cooks, an' thems four that's left."

"Do they stick together?" I asked.

"One sits outside Seeker Alden's library makin' sure he doesn't escape. The others sits around cleaning their nails with their knives and eatin' up the best food in the kitchen. They keeps Cooks pestered with demands for vittles and sweets while all our folks gets is porridge once a day."

"It seems to me," suggested Rosilda, "that we need to get in without being seen, take care of the cellar guard, and move the folks out soundlessly. While that is happening, Blain needs to go about his usual routine. When Blain, Cooks, and the replacement guard come down, we snatch the replacement guard. Those first two parts of the plan should work fairly smoothly, barring unseen complications."

"It is the next part that will be a bit trickier. Should we go for those in the kitchen first or the guard at the library?" I asked.

"The guard at the library. Once we have removed the folks that are being held, and we have Seeker Alden safe, we will have removed all the possible hostages, except for Cooks and Blain. Blain," Arnar asked, "what do you usually do once you help Cooks deliver the porridge?"

"I's sent back ta the stable."

"So only Cooks is left?"

"Yes sir."

"At that point it will be four against three," I suggested.

"Four against three?" Blain questioned.

"It never does to discount Kipp."

We talked a while longer, refining our plan as much as we could. We gathered what tools we might need. Arnar suggested we might try to find some oil, in case we needed to oil some hinges so as not to alert Seeker Alden's captors with loud squeaks and squeals.

Even though it was still an hour or so before Blain was due at the kitchen door, we decided we needed to move into the underground passageway that would lead us to the cellar under the manor house. Blain led the way to stairway where I had first encountered him. Just before we reached the stairs leading up, he stopped at a panel on the same side of the corridor as the stairs. Reaching up, he did something I could not see to the coach light that hung there, and the panel swung inward.

"There's a lantern hangin' just ta ya're right. Ya can see the stairs that leads down ta the passage that will take ya ta the manor."

"Are you going to be all right waiting here by yourself? There is no guarantee that our plan is going to work. It is possible that folks might get hurt."

"At least we would have tried. I ..." Blain took a moment to pull himself together before he went on. "... I dinna know what ta do and felt awful I couldn' help. Nows I can. I'll be all right."

I could hear the determination in the lad's voice and knew he would do his best. After I got the bottler's keys from Blain, I gave his shoulder a reassuring squeeze as I passed him and entered through the paneling. Kipp slipped by me, but Arnar and Rosilda waited their turns to enter after me. Blain closed the panel behind us.

It was obvious that this route into the manor had not been used for a long time, based on the amount of dust and cobwebs. Once we reached the bottom of the stairs, we turned left and then turned left again to follow the passage as it headed toward the manor house.

We walked for what I estimated was the distance from the stable to the manor house, and then the passage changed from carved rock to laid stones. Our way was blocked on three sides of the passageway by wooden panels like the one we had encountered in the stable. Blain had told us the entrance to the corridor was the panel straight ahead. I was about to push it open a crack when I realized Kipp was no longer at my feet. I turned around and held the lantern aloft. Looking back beyond Arnar and Rosilda, I saw Kipp pawing at the panel to my left. Speaking in a whisper, I told the others I was going to check out what was holding Kipp's interest.

"What is it, Kipp?"

He batted a paw against the panel. Then he stood on his hind legs and pushed against the panel with both front paws.

"Let me look, Kipp."

Remembering how Kipp, or a cat just like him, would show up in the women's work room, the sleeping cupboard, and other places around the home I had grown up in, I wondered if he thought there was another hidden passage behind the panel he was pushing against.

Arnar came over, took the lantern, and held it aloft so I could see better. I felt along the edges of the paneling and found an indentation halfway down the right side. I pushed my finger in the indentation and heard something click as the panel swung inward. Before I could stop Kipp, he slipped through the opening.

"Kipp, come back." He did not heed my words. I was torn as to what to do. Rosilda solved my dilemma by reaching into her pocket and pulling out a glow lamp.

"Thought we might need this. Here, take it and see where this passage goes. Arnar and I will handle the guard and get the folks out. Follow Kipp. If it leads you to somewhere useful, either take advantage or come back this way."

After handing the bottler's keys to Rosilda, I did not hesitate to follow Kipp, who sat waiting for me just beyond my reach. Once I had stepped through the panel opening, Kipp turned and began to move forward. This passage was even dustier than the other one and was so full of cobwebs that I got out my knife and began to cut them down. I had to put my hand over my mouth to muffle a laugh, for as Kipp moved forward, cobwebs attached to his fur, and soon, he was trailing cobwebs behind him like a long lacey cape.

The passageway we were following led to a stair. I noticed I could see a faint flickering light at the top of the stairs, so I closed down the glow lamp to give a minimum of light, just enough to see the stair tread directly in front of me. We slowly climbed up the stairs, sticking to the side of the treads in order to minimize the chance of the stairs squeaking.

When we reached the landing, I realized the flickering light was coming through several small holes in the paneling. The holes were just slightly above eye level for me, so I had to stand on tiptoe in order to peer through. I found I was looking into what must be a formal parlor. I could see the flickering light was caused by lightning flashing outside the tall windows across the room. There was no one in the room. By looking closer at my side of the wooden paneling, I saw that there was a latch, and I could enter the parlor if I wanted to. I tucked that information away for later.

I opened the glow lamp a bit more and could see Kipp had moved on down the passageway. I moved swiftly to catch up with him. As we moved along the passageway, I was able to look into other rooms. While shrouded in shadows, I thought all of them were empty. Finally, we came to the end of the passageway where there was a ladder that I assumed led to the next level. In the panel to my left, there were peepholes once again. I looked through and quickly pulled back for this room had an occupant.

Almost not daring to breath, I looked once again. I surmised that I was looking into a library. The walls were lined with floor to ceiling shelves filled with books and a variety of interesting items, some of which I could not identify. Sitting at a desk across from me was a man who might have been what would have been called a strapping lad in his youth. He still looked to be in fine shape for his age, if a little time worn. His snow-white hair was tied back, and his beard looked as if it had been neglected of late. He had a lined face with deep grooves around his mouth and rays of lines at the corner of his eyes, either from laughing or squinting in the sun for a lifetime. While he might have looked like he was concentrating on the book in front of him, I sensed an alertness about him. It would seem that Kipp and I had stumbled upon Seeker Alden.

I again opened the glow lamp a bit wider to give me more light to look at the wall before me. There was a latch at about waist high. I worried that it might not work, for there was a very thick layer of dust on it. I tried the latch, and it did not budge. At first, I thought it might have rusted shut, and I would not be able to open the latch. It was then I remembered the oil I had brought along. I used a bit on the latch, and for good measure, I also oiled the hinges I had located. I tried the latch once again. It still did not move. It was then I hunkered down and took a close look at the latch. It was designed with a locking lever. I oiled it, waited for a few moments and moved the locking lever upward. I had to apply some pressure before it slowly moved. After that, I was able to move the latch.

I heard a soft click and froze. Taking time to look back through the peep holes, I saw that Seeker Alden had looked up. I very slowly pulled on the panel. It did not swing inward toward me. I then very lightly pushed the panel away from me. At first it did not move. Then ever so slightly, it moved forward. I took a quick look again through the peephole. Seeker Alden had stood and was rounding his desk.

It was at this point three things happened at once. The panel, which I realized was a bookcase, moved forward leaving about a six-inch opening into the library, Kipp slipped through, and there came a voice from outside the library. I was not fast enough to grab Kipp, I could not shout for him to come back, and it sounded like the someone just outside the library scooted a chair back. I quickly pulled the bookcase back. I hoped I had done it fast enough.

CHAPTER THIRTY-TWO

Before anyone could enter the library, or Seeker Alden could make it completely around his desk, I saw not one, not two, but three cats enter the room. Kipp sat patiently in the middle of the rug in front of the desk. Just as a tough, burly, barrel-chested man framed the doorway, the cats, who had just entered, jumped up onto various chairs and hassocks and settled in. Kipp lifted his hind leg and began grooming the underside of his tail. Seeker Alden stopped moving toward Kipp and where I was hiding behind the bookcase.

The burly man stayed where he had stopped. After three or four of the loudest sneezes I have ever heard, he began to question Seeker Alden. "Where did all these cats come from?"

"They are a few of the cats that keep the vermin out of the manor. Good hunters they are, good hunters, yes indeed."

Too bad they are not big enough to rid the manor of the large vermin standing in the doorway, I thought.

After several loud sneezes, the man wiped his running eyes and his dripping nose on the sleeve of his shirt and told Seeker Alden to close the door and keep the darn cats in the library. Seeker Alden did as he was told. After he closed the door and took a moment to listen to the muffled sneezes coming from the corridor outside, he moved across the room and stood in front of the bookcase I was standing on the other side of.

Very slowly, I swung the bookcase open. Standing in the shadows, I whispered, "How soon before he will come back?"

"Probably not at all, thanks to the collection of cats in the room. He will sit outside until they change the guard, which is not until they have fed those they are keeping in the cellar and have fed themselves."

"I have come a long way with a question for you, and I cannot get that answered until we get you and your folks safe. Will you follow me?"

"Yes. Following you seems a better option than remaining locked in this library by an annoying, sneezing thug. Besides, I have a question for you. I want to know how a wild hill cat from Bortfjell ended up in my library. Oh, and how did you got here through a bookcase I did not know opened?"

"Hopefully, there will be time to explain all of that. Right now we need to hurry."

Kipp had already entered the passageway though the open section of the bookcase, as had the other three cats. After Seeker Alden entered, I closed the bookcase back up and opened the glow lamp up just a fraction more, which lit up my features, giving Seeker Alden a chance to see me for the first time. I saw a look of surprise on his face. He looked like he was about to say something and then thought better of it. I turned away and headed back down the passageway.

When we were at the top of the stairs that would lead us to the panel that would let us into the passageway to the stable, I halted.

"Here is what has hopefully happened. My two companions were going to immobilize the cellar guard and try to release your folk. Blain suggested they hide in the wine and mead cellar, and that the bottler lock them all in. That way, when Cooks, Blain, and the replacement guard bring down dinner for the folks who are being held in the cellar, we can disappear that guard too, along with Cooks and Blain. The added bonus is that when they come to find you, you will also have disappeared. That will leave only four of them, and hopefully, they will be very disturbed by the fact that all of you have vanished."

"Very clever. You will have taken away their hostages temporarily. This will only work if you can gather up the remaining four. Have you explored this passageway?"

"Only to your library. There is a ladder leading up to the next floor just beyond the bookcase entrance we just came through. I am thinking that if my companions have taken care of the first guard, and we can rescue Cooks and Blain while taking care of the replacement guard, then perhaps we can get the guard outside of the library door. That would leave only three."

"I like the way you think. Among those who you hopefully have rescued, there are a few folks I think could help us. However, much as I see the advantage of using this passageway for folks to move around undetected within the walls of the manor, I have a few thoughts about that. I have known some of these hidden ways within the manor, but not this one. Much as I would like to bring others to sneak around, when this action clears the manor and the landholding of Desna and her crew, the hidden ways would no longer be a secret."

"I fully understand. I know that the more folks who know a secret, the less a secret it is. I have learned from traveling with rovers these last few weeks that giving one's honor is a high oath. So, I would propose that only my companions and I use the passageways. We already know of their existence, and I trust my companions not to reveal the secret. We would gladly, on our honor, keep the secret of the passageways. Think on that while we go down the stairs and see what has transpired."

When we reached the bottom of the stairs, I stepped close to the panel and put my ear next to it. I did not hear anything from the other side. Opening the panel a crack, I took time to listen. Again, I heard nothing. I opened the panel wide enough for me to slip through, almost stepping on a cat's tail. I turned back to Seeker Alden and asked him to wait behind the panel while I checked out what was happening. He agreed.

I moved to the panel that Blain had indicated opened up to the corridor that led to the area of the cellar where the folks from the landholding were being held hostage. I opened the panel a crack and listened. Suddenly, the panel was jerked open from the other side. I had already taken a defensive stance when I realized I was looking at Rosilda, who had taken the same defensive stance. We both had to cover our mouths to muffle the laughter. What a pair we made.

We both spoke at once. She was asking me what I had discovered while I was asking her if she and Arnar had been successful.

"One of Desna's folks is now trussed up like a harvest festival goose, unable to move or make a sound. He is tucked away behind a locked door, thanks to the bottler's keys. Two of the landholding folks are locked in there with him so he will not make a disturbance and attract attention once he comes to."

"And what of the folks that were being held?"

"All have been released and moved into the wine and mead cellar. They understand that they need to remain quiet, so they are not discovered. They are all very loyal and fond of Seeker Alden and do not want him harmed. Now what did you and Kipp find?"

"Seeker Alden. Oh, and the three cats milling at your feet. I had best let him know that his folk are safe."

With that, I turned and walked back to the panel that Seeker Alden hid behind. Rosilda and Kipp followed. The other three cats did not. I opened the panel that Seeker Alden was behind and motioned that he should join us.

"I think introductions might be in order. Explanations can come later. I am Perrin, and this is my friend Rosilda. Rosilda, this is Seeker Alden. Oh, and the wild hill cat at our feet is Kipp."

"I am happy to greet all three of you. Perrin, I have been thinking while you were away. Do you think you and I could take care of our sneezy, sniffly friend?"

"I would think so, since we definitely have the element of surprise on our side. If we invite the cats to join us, maybe his eyes will puff up even more, and he will not be able to see well," I suggested. I saw Seeker Alden smile.

"I have one more idea. Have any of Desna's crew seen any of you?"

"No. We would be strangers to her. Why?"

"The weather has been bad all day. It would not be unusual for travelers to come down our lane seeking shelter. Most travelers would head to the kitchen door rather than to the darkened front of the manor in a storm such as this. If your companions can get Cooks and Blain to safety, and you and I get ol' sneezy under wraps, we could try to separate Desna and the other two, who will most probably be in the kitchen, by knocking on the outside door to the kitchen."

"So, you are suggesting we grab the one who comes to the kitchen door, wrap him or her up, so to speak, and then go in after the other two?" stated Rosilda.

"Yes."

"I think it will work better if we have a three-pronged approach," Rosilda continued. "You said you had some folks in mind who could help. Once we get the second guard taken care of, they could be at the top of the cellar stairs, ready to grab anyone who might come to check why Cooks and Blain have not returned. That might reduce the number in the kitchen by one. Arnar and I will try to get at least two of the three remaining in the kitchen, and you and Perrin will approach the kitchen from the library. That way, if the final folk gets away from us, you two can take care of him or her leaving the kitchen. If no one runs from the kitchen, you two can come help."

"Ah, my yes, a much better strategy. Much better. Let us get this done, because I have so many questions. I think if we have a bit of time, I need to talk to my folk. I will hurry. My marshal and others would be willing to help. We need to fill them in on the plans."

That was another good suggestion, and so we took the time for Seeker Alden to talk with those who had been held captive, letting them know he had not been harmed and was free. He recruited the marshal, the steward, two men, and two women to help with the capture of the remaining members of Desna's group. The rest settled in the wine and mead cellar to wait and hope our plans worked.

Chapter Thirty-Three

Several hours later, Seeker Alden, Arnar, Rosilda, Cooks, Blain, the marshal, the rest of the manor staff, Kipp, and I were all gathered in the kitchen. The last of those who had been held captive had just been sent on their way home to their families. The plans we had made in the cellar to capture Desna and her crew had gone off with only a few missteps, and a number of bumps and bruises.

"Well done, all of you, well done," stated Seeker Alden. "I am most anxious to hear each of your tales as to how you overcame our captors. Now start at the beginning."

Blain, Seeker Alden, Arnar, Rosilda, and I had had a chance to talk over how we could explain how the three of us had gotten into the cellars without being discovered. We wove a tale of Blain leading us to a side door to the manor, and we chanced not getting caught. When Seeker Alden called upon us to be the first to tell how we had come to rescue him and those locked in the cellar, we were ready.

Sticking close to the truth, so as to be believed, I began by telling them that Blain had led us to a little-used door into the manor which had allowed us to split up, and for Arnar and Rosilda to find their way to the cellar and for me to find my way to the library.

"How did you manage to sneak around the manor without being seen or heard?" the steward asked.

"I think I will let Arnar explain," I told the others.

"I am a master of the discipline of kazan, which is part meditation and part martial arts. Part of the discipline is to train yourself to move silently across any surface. Perrin and Rosilda are two of my best students. Also, we learn to become still and to find a way to blend with our surroundings.

"Once we found our way into the cellar, we chanced upon the guard. He had become too accustomed to not having to pay attention to his duties, for he felt they had everything under control. It was easy for Rosilda and I to take him by surprise. Once we had him tied up, we searched for the keys to the rooms your folks were locked in. Unfortunately, he did not have them. I will let Rosilda tell the rest of this tale."

"Sometimes skills one learns out of sheer boredom can come in quite handy. When I was a young border guard, I was assigned to a post in the high mountains. It was a good assignment only because it paid a bit more than most posts. Unfortunately, the higher pay did not really offset the fact that there was really little to do there. After one had read all the books off the small shelf of books two or three times and played cards way too often, one began to look for other things to do. One of the other guards challenged us to open all the locked doors, cupboards, chests and crates, or anything else with a lock. My fellow border guards began to place wagers on who could open the most and the fastest. One of my fellow border guards whose tour was almost up, and who wanted to leave with a good bit of coin in his pocket, came to me and offered a deal. He would teach me to use lock picks and then bet that I would be able to do better than the others. It seems he had not told anyone he was a metalsmith by trade and had only joined the border guard to earn enough money to open his own smithy. It worked like a charm, and both of us left that post a great deal richer."

Rosilda got a good laugh from the others in the kitchen when she finished her tale. After the harrowing few weeks they had spent under the thumb of Desna and her crew, a number of good laughs would begin to make things less tense.

"I have never stopped carrying the lockpicks that I learned to use at that far away post. They certainly came in handy this day."

"I heard a cut off yelp," stated the steward, "and looked out through the bars on the small window of the door we were locked behind. I saw these two take down that brute so fast I thought I was seeing things. When Rosilda came to the door, she told us to be really quiet, for she and Arnar were going to get us out. I cautioned her that if we left the room we were locked in, they would hurt Seeker Alden. She assured me that that was being handled. There was such a quiet authority in her voice that I believed her."

Picking up her tale, Rosilda told those gathered that once they got everyone moved to a safe place, she had headed to find Perrin. "I had just reached a door, hoping it led to a stairway, when I saw it begin to open. Since there was no time to get away and no place to hide, I decided to use the element of surprise and yanked the door open. Perrin and I had a good laugh, for we were mirror images of each other, having both struck the same defensive pose. It was then that she introduced me to Seeker Alden, who was behind her, along with Kipp and three other cats.

"That is when I came to talk with you all, and we put together the next part of the plan," stated Seeker Alden.

"So how did you escape the library, Seeker Alden?" asked Cooks.

"I had best turn that tale over to Perrin."

"Blain had told me that Seeker Alden was usually in his library guarded by one man. I quietly moved from shadow to shadow to get as close to the library as I could. I met no one on the way. Just before I was to make a move, Kipp and three other cats came and surrounded the guard. The man started sneezing and sniffling, and his eyes started running. The cats just would not leave him alone, even though he swatted at them and kicked at them. Finally, he stood up and unlocked the door to the library, quickly stepping inside to avoid the cats. Seeker Alden, alerted to the noise outside, stood behind the door when the man entered. I rushed forward, and between the two of us, we had him trussed up in no time."

That was the version Seeker Alden and I were sticking to. It was fairly close to the truth. The real version was that Seeker Alden and I had gone back to the library through the passageway. We had both reentered the library, and I went to stand with my back to the wall next to the door. We could hear the guard still snuffling and sneezing on the other side of the door. Seeker Alden pounded on the door to get the guard's attention. He had demanded that the guard open the door so Seeker Alden could let the cats out. The guard reluctantly did as asked. Because the guard had grown complacent about guarding Seeker Alden, because he assumed the seeker would not do anything since his folk were being held captive, he was not prepared when Seeker Alden reached out, grabbed him by the shirt front and yanked him into the library. I then stepped in, and we had him subdued in seconds. After tying him up, we placed him in a closet in the library, locked the library, and moved into position to catch any who might escape from the kitchen.

The folks who had captured the guard who had entered the cellar with Cooks and Blain deferred to Blain to tell the next part of the tale.

"Cooks and I loaded up the porridge and water likes we did every night. I dinna have time ta tells Cooks what was happenin' …."

"And it was good ya dinna, young man. I surely woulda given it away."

"Anaways, we went down the steps ta the cellar just likes we always did, and whens we got ta the bottom, I quickly stepped ta the side. The marshal swung Cooks ta the side likes she was lights as a feather …."

"Course I's light as a feather, ya young rascal."

I had to stifle a laugh, for Cooks would never be described as a thin petite woman, having generously sampled her own cooking over the years.

"As I was sayin' afore I was interrupted, Marshal swung Cooks aside, and someone else lunged for the guard's legs, caught one, toppled the guard, and dragged him down the steps. Those waitin' made pretty quick work of the guard. Then we went ta hide with the rest 'til ya comes and lets us out."

"So now three of Desna's crew were under control at this time. In addition, all of the folks that she had held hostage were now safe," stated Seeker Alden. "Perrin and I were ready to capture anyone who headed toward the library or escaped the kitchen. Steward and others were waiting for anyone who might have been sent to see what had happened to Cooks, Blain, and the other guard."

"I think I would like to tell this next part," stated the marshal. "I decided to get as close to the kitchen as I could, so I took the servant stairs up two floors and then came back down the stairs that lead to the pantry. I hid there, waiting to see if I could help. I arrived just as Desna was sending one of her men off to check why Cooks, Blain, and the cellar guard had not returned."

"She was destined to be disappointed about finding out what had happened to Cooks and Blain, not to mention her man, since we took care of him right quick as soon as he entered the cellar," commented the steward.

"So, at this point, we were down to Desna and one other of her thugs. I had a good view toward the back door. Even though I had been expecting a knock and to see Arnar, I was momentarily taken aback when there was no knock, just someone opening the door and walking in. I felt a moment of panic, for I thought, oh no, here is someone else who could become a hostage."

"Who was it?" asked Blain, looking confused.

"Well at first, I thought it was one of the returning seekers. That had me very worried that he was walking into the kitchen and did not know he was walking into danger. The trouble was, I did not recognize the stooped, older man who had walked in and was asking Desna why the place was so dark and where was Cooks. He said 'Havin' no light out front twernt no way to welcome me home, and now Cooks is missing, and there is no kettle on! Well, lass, what have you got to say for yourself?' I have to tell you," the marshal went on, "I thought all this time locked up in the cellar must have done something to my mind. Here was this stooped-over stranger claiming to be a seeker, soaking wet from the rain, pounding what looked like a walking stick on the kitchen floor, demanding attention."

At this point, I think you could have heard a mouse squeak, had one dared to enter the kitchen, since besides the folks listening to the marshal's tale, there was Kipp and at least six other cats now.

"What happened next is that Desna advanced toward the stooped 'seeker', intent, I think, upon overpowering him. I really cannot explain what happened next. All of a sudden, Desna was on the floor being held down by a walking stick, Rosilda had suddenly appeared in the kitchen, I presume through the outside door, and she had the remaining member of Desna's men also on the floor. Before the sound of his body hitting the floor with a thud had died away, Perrin and Seeker Alden showed up. I came out of the pantry and started back to make sure the guard sent to check on what was going on in the cellar was under control. I was met by Cooks and Blain, who were leading our folk up out of the cellar.

"I have to tell you, Arnar, that performance as a stooped, old, demanding, returning seeker sure had me fooled. Are you a member of a street player group? That was some performance."

"Ah, no, not a street player. Just a skill I learned while working for the border guard. Came in handy when I needed to gather information in the seedier sides of border towns or seaports, places where the guard was not welcome."

"And what of those moves you all seem to know how to do that allow you to take down someone who is bigger, taller, and weighs a lot more than you do?" asked Seeker Alden. "Is that part of the discipline of kazan?"

"Yes."

"I do not know how we can ever thank you for what you folks have done for the Order of the Seekers and this landholding. Without your assistance, I do not know what would have happened to us here and to the other seekers who should be returning over the next week. What I do know is we were, and still are, not adequately prepared to defend ourselves against this happening again. I know I was not prepared to be in charge here when I said I would take over the running of the landholding. We have lost so many of the old crofters and retainers in the last few years. Our master beekeepers are aging with few to take their place ...." Seeker Alden sighed and slumped in his chair. "I am sorry, I find I am tired, and I have been remiss in offering our hospitality to you three who have saved us."

"I think you folks did a good job of saving yourselves this day. Perrin, Rosilda, Kipp, and I could not have done it alone. If you truly wish to thank someone, none of this rescue would have even gotten started if it had not been for Blain."

I turned to look at Blain and watched a blush start at his chest and rush up to above his ears.

"True, true," agreed Seeker Alden. "On the morrow, I will send someone off to the nearest royal guard station and have them send a patrol to remove our unwanted guests from the locked rooms in the cellar. A number of folks have volunteered to sit guard duty until the royal guard can arrive. Now then, as I said before, I have been remiss about offering you the hospitality of our home. Our housekeeper, once she had recovered and had a chance to reunite with her family, has been busy with airing out rooms for each of you."

"I have had several of the stable hands remove your tack and saddles and groom your horses," stated the marshal. "They are now in the stable proper. Your gear has been taken off the pack horse and placed in a mouse-proof storage room. I have had your packs sent up to your rooms. I hope that was all right."

I assured both Seeker Alden and the marshal that we were grateful for their care. The group gathered in the kitchen broke up at that point, with folks heading to their respective quarters. Arnar and Rosilda headed out to the stable to gather a few more items that they wanted from our gear. I was about to follow when Seeker Alden asked to speak to me.

"I hope you and your companions will choose to stay with us for a while. Know you would be welcome here. I think we have much to discuss, the least of which is how you came by Seeker Helka's medallion."

CHAPTER THIRTY-FOUR

I quickly glanced down and saw that during the several scuffles I had been part of over the last few hours, my mother's medallion had slipped out from under my shirt and was hanging askew, partially hidden by my vest. I was about to speak when Seeker Alden told me it could wait until morning, that he was tired and just wanted a peaceful night in his own bed. He bid me goodnight and left me sitting in the kitchen alone, waiting for Arnar and Rosilda to return from the stable.

Upon entering the kitchen, Arnar must have seen something in my face or body language, for he asked me if I was all right.

"Seeker Alden drew me aside when you two were heading to the stable. He had a question for me."

"And that question was?"

"He asked me how I had come by Seeker Helka's medallion."

"Ah, well, that certainly answers one of the questions you came here to ask."

"And raises a whole lot more, which I hope might be answered in the morning."

I thought I would have difficulty getting to sleep. I did not. Once I had stretched out on the softest bed I had slept in since leaving home, and my head hit the pillow, I was asleep. When I finally woke up the next morning, I found it was way past dawn and way past breakfast. I could not remember sleeping this late in years.

After quickly washing up in the washbasin that had thoughtfully been left in the room along with a pitcher of water, I headed downstairs to the kitchen. I found Arnar and Rosilda, looking relaxed, sitting at the table, and drinking tea. In front of them were empty plates, indicating that they had eaten breakfast already.

"Ah, the last of our little band has finally decided to join us. Kipp, Rosilda, and I have been here for hours," suggested Arnar, and then had to stifle a yawn.

"Now, donna ya believe him," scolded Cooks. "The only early riser of this group was the cat, Kipp. I say, he's a big one, inna he? Are all the cats where ya come from big like him?"

"No. The cats who take care of the vermin in our homes, stables, barns, shops, and granaries are very much like the cats that I saw here in the library and kitchen last night. Or should I say, like the two that are sleeping by the hearth. Kipp is a wild hill cat. Normally, wild hill cats are only found in the high hills of Bortfjell. I do not understand why he has chosen to travel with me, but I am grateful he has."

"Every once inna while, I has heared tell of wild animals traveling with folks. Never thought I'da meet one, much less be feeding one breakfast. Now then, I needs ta fix you some vittles."

"Please, don't go to any bother. I am terribly late."

"Now lass, ya jus' sits yerself down. Tea's hot, and food will be on the table afores ya know it."

I decided it was not in my best interest to argue with a woman who was emphasizing her wishes holding a sharp knife, which she had been using to slice a hunk of bread off a fresh loaf.

"Seeker Alden was here earlier and said he had a number of things to do this day. He apologized and begged off talking to you about the medallion, Perrin, until after the evening meal," said Rosilda. "He did request that once you are up and have eaten, that we join him for a ride around the landholding. He wants to make sure everything is back to normal. In the meantime, I had occasion to talk to the housekeeper and asked where we might hang our gear out and do laundry. She would not hear of us doing laundry, and I was told quite strongly that we should get what we want cleaned to her this morning."

"Marshal has informed me that his stable lads and lasses are taking good care of our horses and that they had already set about cleaning and oiling our saddles and tack," stated Arnar. "He said to let him know when we want our mounts ready for our ride with Seeker Alden. I will go now and tell him we will be ready to ride in about a half hour."

While I was disappointed that I would not get to talk to Seeker Alden about my mother, I found I was looking forward to seeing the landholding that belonged to the Order of the Seekers.

I am afraid it was my fault that our ride about the landholding took twice as long as it might have. I found myself talking to the crofters about their land and their crops, to the beekeepers, to the families of the shepherds, and many others. I did not realize I had fallen into the patterns of how I had interacted with the folks who had lived on the Nytt Heimili landholding. It came easily, for it was what I had been trained for from birth.

It was when I got into a discussion with the head miller at the grain mill, that Arnar and Rosilda begged off staying at the mill while the head miller and I discussed grains, fine and course ground flour, and the fair distribution of the flour.

"Ahem, Perrin?" said Arnar, clearing his throat several more times to get my attention.

I absently looked up. "Yes?"

"Rosilda and I are going to ride ahead with Vander. He is the head of the home guard, such as it is. We want to look over the border of the landholding and discuss what, if any, defenses are in place. What happened here to Seeker Alden and the folks of this landholding should never have happened. Apparently, the tales and legends concerning seekers have worn a little thin. They need more to protect the folks here than tales about being able to be invisible, becoming animals, and taking revenge for being harmed."

"I am grateful that you and Rosilda are willing to look things over. You both come with training and expertise that we could use. Alas, over the last twenty years, we have grown old as a group. Our young folks often move on to find work or adventure in other parts of Sommerhjem. They seek training and trades that are more suitable to larger holdings, larger villages, or towns," stated Seeker Alden. "We are a different type of landholding, for we are not ruling lords or ladies. Folks choose to take up living here. While you are out riding trying to shore up our defenses, if you could come up with a way to find more folks who would want to settle here …."

"I have an idea or two," suggested Arnar. "Let us see what is in place, who is doing what, and then talk over dinner."

I felt a bit chagrined that I had been monopolizing the time and conversation. When I started to apologize, both Arnar and Rosilda reassured me I was just being myself and should never apologize for that. Seeker Alden agreed.

Arnar and Rosilda left with Vander, the yeoman in charge of the home guard who defend the landholding. Seeker Alden and I remounted our horses, and Seeker Alden asked me to tell him how I knew so much about the running of a landholding.

"Now I want you to start at the beginning and tell me more of who you are and where you are from. I think we actually have not been formally introduced," Seeker Alden stated. I noticed that he had a twinkle in his eye when he said that.

"I am named Perrin Leifursdotter of the Nytt Heimili clan of Bortfjell. My father is the laird, and up until several months ago, I was the heir to the landholding and clan. I have been raised and trained to take over Nytt Heimili after my father."

"It is obvious you were a very good student. You are knowledgeable of the workings of a landholding ..."

I was about to interrupt when Seeker Alden held up a hand to stop me.

"... and more importantly, you are good with folks. You listen to what they have to say, and you have good suggestions. You certainly know more about grain and crops than I ever have. With all the questions you asked the master beekeeper, you probably now know more about beekeeping than most."

"I am sorry if I overstepped."

"I assure you, you have not overstepped. Today has been enlightening to say the least. It has given me much to think about and much to talk over with the returning seekers."

Since it was just the two of us riding on together, I really wanted to take this opportunity to talk to Seeker Alden about my mother, and was just about to, when several riders came galloping toward us. Without a thought, I moved my horse in front of Seeker Alden's and tensed, prepared to defend us both.

The first rider was of middle age and sat his horse well. The second rider had just left youth behind and was hanging onto his saddle for dear life. The contrast between the two was almost comical. The first rider was pudgy and pasty, as if he spent all of his time sitting indoors. He sported a reddish sunburn, which looked to be painful. The second rider, a much younger man, was rail thin but had faired better with the sun. Before the older man had even come alongside and halted his horse, he began to rant.

"What's all this about being held hostage? What is wrong with you that you cannot keep the landholding up and running, much less safe? I was never convinced that you were the one we should have left in charge. Why, we could have lost our home and our livelihood. Mark my words, I will be talking to the other seekers about this …."

"And good day to you, Seeker Hambir," said Seeker Alden mildly. "Good to have you back."

I knew Seeker Hambir's kind: a complainer and a know-it-all who thinks he knows better, but when challenged to take on a task, would find a great many excuses as to why he could not.

Seeker Alden went on. "You are correct, I have definitely failed in my duties as the one left behind in charge of the landholding. When all of the rest of the seekers arrive and we hold our annual meeting, I will be more than willing to step down. Since you seem so passionate about what I have not done, might I put your name in as the next one of us to take over the task? Your words suggest you have better ideas than I as to how to run the landholding."

Seeker Hambir began to sputter and backed away from his rant by changing the subject.

"Now, now, let us not be hasty. I am sure we can work something out. Now then, I have been remiss. The young man traveling with me is Garan. He is interested in joining our ranks. He has served as an assistant to the head royal librarian. He …."

"Welcome, Garan," Seeker Alden said graciously. "Have you found the royal library too confining?"

The young man seemed startled that Seeker Alden had cut Seeker Hambir off and addressed him directly.

"Aye. I have enjoyed discovering ideas and lost knowledge in the books and scrolls in the royal library. I liked learning how to repair the old and worn books. All of that was fine. Mostly I missed fresh air and wanted to go and see the places I was reading about."

Seeker Alden nodded his head and suggested he understood the need to be out and about and see places. He then suggested he had been remiss and introduced me. "Pardon my bad manners, the young woman riding with me is Perrin, who is one of the four who came to our rescue when we had been taken hostage by Desna and her crew. Oh, and the wild hill cat sitting behind Perrin is Kipp, another of our rescuers. I have been showing Perrin the landholding. We are almost done. I suggest, Seeker Hambir, that you take young Garan back to the manor house and get him settled in. Perrin, Kipp, and I will be along in a few hours."

I could tell that Seeker Hambir was less than thrilled with the suggestion. Garan looked relieved. After several more exchanges, the two men rode off. I turned to look at Seeker Alden, and he had a very thoughtful look on his face.

"Are all of the returning seekers going to be in a rage like Seeker Hambir?"

"Thankfully, no. Most of the other members of the Order are calmer thinkers. They will be worried about what happened, and they will be compassionate about what our folk have gone through. Now on to another subject, for I fear that with the arrival of Seeker Hambir, others will not be far behind. We need to have a chat about the medallion you are wearing. It belonged to Seeker Helka, who left long ago heading north to seek out the tales and legends of the border country and never returned. How did you come by the medallion?"

"According to my father, it belonged to my mother, who never took it off. Her name was Helka, and my father met her on the border between Bortfjell and Sommerhjem. I think maybe when they met and married, they intended to travel and explore together. That all changed when my aunt was killed in a riding accident, and my father had to return to become the laird of our landholding and clan."

"That explains much."

"What does it explain?"

"Why we never heard from Seeker Helka again. Back when she disappeared, there was much unsettled between Bortfjell and Sommerhjem. Getting information across the border was tricky and dangerous."

"Is that why the seeker medallion was hidden within the other medallion?"

"There was some suggestion at that time that seekers were especially looked upon with suspicion by those in power in Bortfjell. They did not understand that we are just extremely curious folk who are looking for lost knowledge, legends, and tales. They thought we were spies out to gather information about their plans toward Sommerhjem. Tell me about your mother. Is she still in Bortfjell? Is she safe?"

"My mother died when I was about thirteen years old. She had a second child when I was about ten who died shortly after birth. I do not really know what happened to my mother after that. I suspect the loss of the child weighed heavily on her. She became a mere shadow, lost in her own world after that. She seemed to fade away more and more each year until she was gone."

"I am so sorry, Perrin."

"Thank you. Can you tell me what she was like? I really know so little about her."

"I remember when she first came here. It was the year that I did not travel out from the landholding, for I had broken my leg when a carriage I was riding in tipped over."

When I raised an inquiring eyebrow, Seeker Alden went on.

"That is a tale for another time about foolish mistakes and taking a dare. At any rate, I was here when she arrived. She had left her home and family because she knew she would wither and shrivel up in the valley of the porcelain crafters, since she had no interest in the craft. She told me her folks had demanded she get her nose out of a book, that it was time to grow up and start earning her keep and taking her place in the valley. I remember she arrived here with just what she carried in her pack. That and a lot of determination."

"That certainly fits what my great grandmother Helka and my mother's childhood friend, Zasha, told me."

"Your mother spent the next year here studying, reading, and learning all she could to prepare herself to take to the road. I remember there were times that she just radiated joy in all she had learned. I also recognized that there were times she seemed sad or lost, but those were few and far between. The one thing I could tell was she was going to be a great asset to the Order of the Seekers."

I was glad to hear my mother had found a place where she seemed to have fit and was comfortable, a place where she appeared to be welcomed.

"How many years was my mother a seeker who returned here each spring?"

"She left after the spring meeting after the year she spent here. We actually traveled together for a short time. I was on my way to the forester settlement of Trelandsby along the Raskalt River in the Skoj Fjell Forest. There was an elder there I wanted to talk to. We parted ways there. Your mother intended to travel farther north. That was the last time I saw her. Ah, time is getting late. We had best be heading back. We will talk more about your mother. I would like to learn more about her life in Bortfjell, and I am sure you would like to hear more about her time here."

"I just have one question before we head back. Should I give her medallion back to the Order of the Seekers?"

"I think we should not be in a rush to make any decisions concerning the medallion this day."

Chapter Thirty-Five

I was glad Seeker Alden and I had had a chance to talk about my mother and her time here. When we arrived back at the manor house and entered the kitchen, I saw that in addition to Seeker Hambir and Garan, there were several more folks that we had not yet met. Seeker Alden had informed me that there were currently fewer than a dozen seekers, and he expected all of them to arrive within the next week.

Seeker Alden introduced us, including Kipp. Each of the two new arrivals introduced themselves. I was relieved that the new arrivals were more concerned that everyone was all right, and that Desna and her crew were securely locked up awaiting the arrival of the royal guard. They did not blame Seeker Alden for what had happened, rather expressed concern as to what could be done so it would never happen again.

"I think once all of the others get here, we need to discuss a number of pressing concerns about our safety and about maintaining the landholding. I have some ideas," suggested Seeker Alden. "Meanwhile, I think we should spend our time getting all of you settled in and catching up on your travels."

I started to edge my way out of the kitchen, since I was beginning to feel like an intruder at a family gathering. I noticed that Arnar and Rosilda were also heading toward the kitchen door. Just before we could make our escape, Seeker Alden called for our attention.

"Perrin, Rosilda, Arnar, please do not go. We are very informal here, and as other seekers arrive, we will move into the larger dining room for our meals. For this night, we will eat in the kitchen. Please stay and join us. After all, the others need to get to know the folks who came up with and carried out the plan that stopped Desna and her crew from doing more harm."

While I was a bit uncomfortable and would have preferred to leave, it was hard to refuse Seeker Alden. One of the newly arrived seekers was an older woman. She kept looking at me with a thoughtful look on her face.

"Perrin, I feel as if I know you, though I am certain that we have never met," stated Seeker Yuna. "I rarely forget a face."

"Perhaps you knew my mother. You would have known her as Seeker Helka. It is said I look a great deal like her."

"Oh my, of course. Your mother, is she here with you? She has been gone for so long."

I wondered if I was going to answer these questions over and over again as the seekers arrived throughout the coming week.

"I am sorry, no, my mother is not with me. She passed away a number of years ago. Maybe I could go into the details when all of you have arrived, so I only need to tell the tale once. I know very little of my mother's past and came here on the chance that she had been a seeker."

"On the one hand, I am sorry to hear of her passing. On the other hand, I am glad her disappearance is no longer an unsolved mystery. It will be good to have closure. I will respect your need to not tell the tale over and over again to the seekers who knew her when she was with us. Should you wish, I would be happy to talk with you about what I know of your mother."

I thanked Seeker Yuna and was thankful she did not press me for any more information at that time. When the meal was over, I was glad to leave the kitchen, for Seeker Hambir had sporadically kept up his litany of complaints and accusations throughout the meal. Unfortunately, throughout all that negative verbiage, he did not make even one suggestion on how to solve any of the problems facing the seekers or the landholding. Rosilda and Arnar left with me. Arnar suggested we might want to stretch our legs and take a walk.

"Basically, this is a good landholding," stated Arnar.

"I would agree. There is good farmland, though not enough tenants. Unfortunately, some of the land is laying fallow, for there are not enough folks to tend it. Though the village is small, it is well kept. However, it is missing a blacksmith and a cooper," I suggested. "In addition, when I talked with the master beekeeper, he introduced me to the brew master of the mead. While they have a good production of honey, for they have good forest land and the high meadows are fill of wildflowers that provide nectar, they need more barrels and bottles for storing the mead. In addition, when I talked with both the master beekeeper and the brew master, they lamented that they had no one interested in their craft to train."

"When Arnar and I rode with Vander to look over the border of the landholding, we talked to him about the defenses that are in place. Once again there is a lack of folks to really set up a home guard, due in part to the shortage of folks to take care of the land," stated Rosilda.

"So, in other words, this is a fine landholding with great potential that has been not so much neglected but lacked consistency in leadership, since who is in charge changes more frequently than is normal. The other issue is that the seeker in charge might or might not be knowledgeable about the various needs of the landholding."

"I have wondered something else," stated Arnar.

"What?" Rosilda and I both queried at the same time.

"Just what kind of training is given to the seekers themselves before they leave to venture out for the first time? In addition, what kind of training do they continue to get from year to year? Do they spend time when they return here discussing practical things they have learned, or do they just tell each other what their seeking has turned up?"

"Seeker Alden told me that my mother came here and stayed a year learning all she could of a practical nature, so she would be prepared to venture out on her own. She needed to learn about taking care of her riding horse, tack, pack animal, living off the land, and living out-of-doors. From Zasha's tale concerning the melted swan figurine, my mother certainly did not need to learn about building fires," I said with a smile.

"Another thing," said Rosilda. "Are they trained to defend themselves if they need to? They often travel alone. Do they know how to change their appearance like you do, Arnar? If they did, it would allow them to either gain entrance to places and fit in or leave someplace quickly and change appearance. Could they have muddied their trail as we did when we left Bortfjell? Would they need these skills?"

"These are all good questions that I would like a chance to sit down with Seeker Alden and ask," I stated.

Before the conversation could continue, I noticed Kipp, who had been walking in front of us, had stopped and was staring back the way we had come. The others noticed too. As I looked back in the dimming light, I could just make out someone moving swiftly toward us. We waited to see who it was.

"Well met, you three. Or perhaps you four would be more accurate," said Seeker Yuna. "Do you mind if I join you? I need to stretch my legs and give my ears a rest."

"Your ears a rest?" inquired Arnar.

"Seeker Hambir."

"Ah, yes. I understand. By all means, join us."

We walked in silence for a time before I asked Seeker Yuna a question.

"Can you tell us what the requirements are for becoming a seeker, and what type of training you receive after you are accepted into the Order of the Seekers?"

"Are any or all of you interested in becoming seekers? Other than Kipp of course, for I suspect he may already be one," Seeker Yuna said, and I could hear the humor in her words.

"I agree with you concerning Kipp. For myself, I am just curious at this time. If the answers to my questions are closely guarded secrets, I am all right if you do not answer them."

"The answers to your questions are not closely guarded secrets. As to who can become a seeker, that is a hard question to answer. Some come thinking this would be a fairly easy way to make a living. Just wander around the land with no worries because they are being supported by the Order and would essentially be on a constant walkabout."

"In other words, they think they really do not have to do any work," suggested Arnar.

"You are correct. They do not have the drive or the curiosity to lead them to new places in order to learn the old tales or legends, find old lost books and tomes, or find hidden places and long-lost knowledge. A seeker needs to have intelligence, perseverance, patience, an innate curiosity, self-sufficiency, compassion, and a bit of wanderlust. They need to have the ability to adapt to all different kinds of environments and situations. A seeker needs to be able to think on his or her feet. Seekers are the kind of folks who wonder about the world around them."

"So, how do you sort them out?"

"Sometimes we have an applicant travel with one of us. That works as part training, part evaluating. Sadly, that has happened less and less frequently as our ranks have diminished and we have grown older. When the Order first formed, there was at least a year of training for a new seeker before they traveled out. Then they were paired with another seeker for a year or two. I have long thought we should go back to the old ways."

"I have another question."

Seeker Yuna chuckled at my query. "Are you sure you are not looking to become a seeker, Perrin? One other common trait of a seeker is they are folks who are always either asking questions or seeking answers. Do not mind me. Go ahead and ask your question."

"It concerns the landholding."

"Go on."

"Arnar, Rosilda, and I were just talking about what a fine landholding this is …."

"I hear a 'but' coming."

"Not so. We all agree that this landholding has much potential. We felt that the issues it faces now are not due to neglect, but rather a lack of consistency. How is a seeker picked to be in charge of the landholding? Do you have a governing body that takes a vote? Sorry, that was two questions."

"We used to have a governing body when we had more members. That has fallen by the wayside, like so much else. To answer your question about how one comes to be called upon to supervise the landholding, there are various ways that happens. At times, a member might volunteer to come back to the landholding and live here year-round, for they had grown tired of the life on the road. At other times, a member might be asked to volunteer for a year or two, and then another member needs to take his or her place and serve for the next several years, and so on. This having the landholding supervised higgledy-piggledy has most probably created some of the concerns we now find ourselves facing."

"Thank you for answering my questions."

"Thank you all for letting me join you on your evening walk. You have given me much to think on."

Seeker Yuna departed after that, and Arnar, Rosilda, and I walked a bit farther in comfortable silence before turning back. When I arrived back at the room I had been assigned, I found my clothes clean and neatly folded. They had been placed on top of the clothes chest set at the foot of my bed.

I lay awake for a long while thinking about what I had learned about my mother and her time here. I looked forward to talking to other seekers who might have known her. Once they arrived for their annual visit, and I had had a chance to speak with them, what I had come here for would be completed. I needed to begin to think about what to do next. I still faced the problem of what to do in this new country and how to survive, since there was no guarantee that I could ever return home to Nytt Heimili.

Morning arrived, and I was no further in my thinking than I had been the night before. I found myself feeling a bit adrift once again and more than a little directionless. So much had happened at such an urgent pace since leaving Nytt Heimili to cross the border. Then there was the kerfuffle with Grimur, Timir, and Donnola that hopefully ended the chase after me and the threat to my life. After that, all my focus was on getting to the valley of the porcelain crafters to find out if my mother's folks were there. While I had met my great grandmother and learned more about my mother, I knew that the valley of the porcelain crafters was not where I was destined to stay. My focus then became to find out the history behind the seeker medallion. I had felt useful helping capture Desna and her crew and freeing the hostages. Now I just felt adrift once again.

CHAPTER THIRTY-SIX

The next day, several more of the seekers arrived. It was interesting to note that two more of them arrived with someone in tow who professed to want to become a seeker. It was half past noon when I took a stroll in the overgrown manor garden and came upon Garan, pacing back and forth muttering to himself.

"Garan, are you all right?"

"I'm fine!" Garan spat out.

"Ah, I can see you are just brimming with sunshine and good feelings toward folks."

I watched Garan's shoulders droop, and his eyes filled with tears. He swiped at his eyes and kept his head down.

"If you would like, we could take a sit on that bench over there by the fountain. I am a good listener."

Garan took a deep breath and walked over to the bench, sitting down with a thump. I sat next to him and waited. Finally, he began to speak.

"I grew up in the capital. The family I come from is not a wealthy one. One of my teachers noticed that I always had my head in a book. He was friends with a librarian at the royal library. One day he invited me to go to the royal library with him and introduced me to the head royal librarian, who informed me that there was a system in place where young folk, who were interested in scholarly pursuits but did not have the means, could receive training and work at the library while being provided room, board, and a small stipend. I was told that those who showed great promise in one area or another often rose up the ranks. My teacher recommended me, and I was accepted into the training. For a while I was content. Lately, however, I had become restless."

Garan had trailed off, so after a few moments, I urged him to go on.

"I have heard about the Order of the Seekers all my life. Since I was a wee lad, I have dreamed of joining the Order. When Seeker Hambir came to the royal library, I was excited to meet a real seeker in person. He spun many a tale about his grand adventures as a seeker, so when he asked me to travel with him on the chance that he might help me become a seeker, I left my position at the royal library and went with him."

"Have you been told, now that you are here, that you cannot pursue becoming a seeker?"

"No. However, I have discovered what Seeker Hambir told me was all part of my training was really not. Doing all the fetch and carry, all the chores, all the laundry, and paying for all of my expenses out of my meager savings has all been a ruse. He just wanted a servant for the journey back here. I now know this because I spent this morning talking with the two new arrivals who came with the other seekers. Their experiences have been vastly different from mine. I have been played for the fool. I have lost my position at the royal library, and Seeker Hambir really had no intention of training me," Garan spat bitterly.

I felt sorry for this young man who had had his dreams crushed at a very high cost. I also felt extremely angry on his behalf.

"Do you still wish to become a seeker?"

"With all my heart."

"Then come with me."

I stood up and asked Garan to follow me. Kipp, who had been patiently sitting nearby, led the way. I noticed as we walked back down the garden path toward the manor, we were joined by several more cats. I led all of us to the library where I had first found Seeker Alden. I hoped he might be there now. Once we reached the library door, I knocked, and a voice called out telling us to enter. I heard movement behind me and turned to see Garan beginning to slip back.

"There is no reason for you not to enter the library," I suggested gently.

"Isn't it Seeker Alden's office?"

"Yes. I think he needs to hear what you have told me. Seeker Alden strikes me as a highly intelligent, caring man. Let us give him a chance."

With that said, I swung the door open and stepped into the library. Garan reluctantly followed. The cats showed not a bit of reluctance to enter.

"Ah, Perrin and young Garan, welcome."

As I looked farther into the room, I noticed that Seeker Alden was not alone. There were several other seekers gathered, among them Seeker Yuna.

"I hope we are not intruding. We can come back at another time."

"No, no, please come in. What brings the two of you here?"

I turned and looked at Garan who looked as if he wished to be anywhere else but here. I whispered to him that nothing was going to change by itself. If he truly wanted to be a seeker, he needed to speak up for himself. After all, Seeker Yuna had told me that seekers are folks who ask a lot of questions and seek answers.

"Garan, please tell these kind folks what you just told me," I urged.

"What is it, lad? You seem nervous and perhaps troubled. What can we do to help?" inquired Seeker Alden.

Garan stood up straight, cleared his throat several times, and then clearly and concisely told how Seeker Hambir had treated him and how disillusioned he was concerning his "training" after talking to the two newcomers who had come with two of the other seekers. I thought he handled himself well.

Seeker Yuna was the first one to speak up. "I can assure you, and I think I speak for the rest who are assembled here, that you certainly come with the qualities that we are looking for in those who wish to join our ranks. How Seeker Hambir has treated you is shameful and will be dealt with."

I saw the other seekers gathered nod their heads in agreement. Seeker Yuna went on.

"Garan's bad experience is a perfect example of why we need to go back to the old ways in how seekers are trained."

"But Seeker Yuna, we are so short-handed now. How are we going to achieve that?"

"First things first. Garan, are you still interested in becoming a seeker?"

"Yes, ma'am."

"Good. I suggest you go and gather your possessions up and find the housekeeper. We have moved the other two who are also interested in becoming seekers into a suite of rooms. Will you be willing to join them?"

"Very much so."

"Take your time to get settled in, and we will see you at dinner."

Garan thanked the gathered seekers and me, turned, and hurried out of the room. As I turned to follow him out, Seeker Alden asked me to stay.

"Thank you for bringing Garan and his troubles to our attention. The Order would have lost a potentially fine new seeker if you had not done so. I fear the young man would have left us."

There were murmurs of agreement from the others who were gathered in the room.

Seeker Alden went on. "I would have a favor to ask of you. Would you, Arnar, and Rosilda join us the day after all of the seekers arrive? We intend to hold a meeting and would like input from all of you."

"From us? What is it you want from us?"

"You all come to here with experience at such things as running a landholding and defense of such. You come with fresh eyes. You all come with some very specialized skills, such as the discipline of kazan and the ability to disguise oneself. These are all areas we wish to get your insight about."

I told Seeker Alden and the others I would be honored to speak with them. I would extend the invitation to Rosilda and Arnar, but I could not speak for them.

I spent the rest of the day on horseback, wandering along the foot of the high hills, exploring. I needed time to myself to think. Kipp had come with me. Midafternoon, I spotted a spring trickling out of the rocks at the edge of a rock outcropping and dismounted. I found a flat rock warmed by the sun to sit on, and Kipp stretched out on the rock with me. I had brought a journal along and opened it, pausing for a long moment, pondering before I began to write. I wanted to organize my thinking about what I had noticed around the landholding that was working well, and what in my opinion needed to be fixed or changed. I tried to imagine what I would do if I were in charge. I also jotted notes and ideas as to how others might be recruited to fill places and positions that were empty.

Before I left for my solitary ride, I had told Rosilda and Arnar about

Seeker Alden's request. We had agreed to meet after the dinner hour to exchange ideas.

For the next week while we waited for the rest of the seekers to arrive, Arnar, Rosilda, and I met early to practice the moves of kazan, as would have been a normal routine at home for the other two. I had tried to keep up and often practiced in my rooms either early morning or late at night, since my stepmother did not approve. Each day we were joined by more folks. At first, it was the marshal, the porter, and the steward. Then when the seekers began arriving, I noticed that Seeker Yuna came each morning. After Garan had joined the two others who wished to be seekers, the three of them were with us each morning, also.

After breakfast, Arnar, Rosilda, Kipp, and I would ride and explore another part of the landholding. Often folks would take time to talk to us, although I think part of the attraction was Kipp sitting behind me on his special pack.

By the end of the week, all of the seekers had arrived. I had thought we would be called upon the next day to speak to the assembly. However, Seeker Alden informed me that the seekers had some business they needed to discuss and handle before they would invite us to talk to them, and it would be another day or two before they would call us in.

I found Garan and the two others still sitting in the kitchen looking a bit lost. I realized that since they were not seekers yet, they had not been invited to the meeting.

"Do you folks have plans for the day?"

"Nothing in particular," answered Galena.

Galena was a small woman of middle years who was a widow. She had left home and hearth, for as she explained, there was nothing holding her there and a whole wide country to explore. She had grown up in Springwell-over-Hill. She and her husband had owned and run a small press that printed and bound books. She told me she had read every one of the books and pamphlets they had printed.

The man sitting with Garan and Galena was called Cleary. He was from a farm on the rolling grass prairie. He was the youngest of seven brothers and the least interested in farming. He had told me he drove his family crazy with his always asking questions. He had jumped at the chance to travel with one of the seekers and hoped to become one.

227

I suggested that they follow us to the stable and saddle up. When they had left the kitchen, I asked Cooks if she could spare some bread, cheese, and perhaps some fruit for us to take along on our ride.

"'Tis good of you ta get them outta the manor. Theys is twixt and between. Not who they's have been and not yet who they's ta become."

Very much like Arnar, Rosilda, and me, I thought.

We spent a really pleasant day meandering about the landholding. The sun was shining, there was a light breeze, and the green and growing plants seemed to almost glow under the blue and cloudless sky. That pleasant and relaxed feeling came crashing to an end when we returned to the manor.

We arrived just as the royal guard, which I assumed had shown up just shortly before we reached the stable, were escorting Desna and her crew out of the manor and to the holding cart. Desna was protesting at the top of her lungs, and her companions were struggling against the royal guards. Just before they pushed Desna into the holding cart, she sent such a scathing look of hatred toward Arnar, Rosilda, and me that I felt just a bit scorched. I was glad that they were leaving.

Shortly after the royal guard had left and we were just finishing up rubbing down our horses, Seeker Hambir came storming into the stable looking to pick a fight. He began ranting at Garan, calling him an ungrateful cur and telling him that he did not appreciate him making up tales about how ill-treated he had been.

"I spent so much of my time and precious knowledge training you, and you have betrayed me. You have cost me my position as a seeker. They have taken away my medallion. I should have you strung up by your ...."

"Hambir, enough!" stated Seeker Alden, who had just entered the stable. "Must we try for the truth with you once again. How you misled and treated Garan was the last straw added to a long litany of the misuse of your seeker status and the exceedingly long litany of complaints we have received over the years. Enough is enough. You will cease berating this young man whom you have harmed. You will put your pack on your horse and leave. Once again, you are blaming someone else for your irresponsible choices. The assembly has voted, and you are done here."

When it looked as if Hambir was about to start speaking again, Seeker Alden shot him a look that would have made strong folks shake in their boots.

"If the rest of you do not mind, would you please leave the stable while we send Hambir on his way? Marshal will have his folks finish up with your horses. Dinner will be a bit delayed this night. We will assemble in the dining room in an hour's time."

What we had just witnessed was certainly an unexpected turn of events. I wondered what else had been discussed and decided in the seeker's meeting this day.

CHAPTER THIRTY-SEVEN

The time finally arrived to meet with the members of the Order of the Seekers. I found I was not at all nervous. After all, I held no illusion that the seekers would listen to a young stranger and consider what I had to say relevant. Seeker Alden could just be humoring me.

The steward met Arnar, Rosilda, Kipp, and me at the foot of the stairs in the entry hall and suggested that we follow him. I had expected that we would meet in the dining room or perhaps one of the more formal parlors. I had not expected that the steward would lead us up two flights of stairs, down a short hall to a large double set of carved wooden doors.

"The seekers are assembled within. You are expected," he told us as he opened one of the doors.

The room we entered was a large one and bright, for it had tall windows lining both sides of the room. The back wall was covered floor to ceiling with bookshelves, so tall that one would have to use the sliding ladder to reach the top shelf. In front of the bookshelves was a long, slender u-shaped table that could have seated several dozen folk on its outer side. The small group of seekers were seated facing us.

Seeker Alden stood and motioned us forward. "Thank you for coming. The other seekers and I have had many hours of discussion over the last few days about how easily I was captured by Desna and her crew. What Desna's actions brought into exceptionally sharp focus was that this landholding is in trouble, as is the Order of the Seekers. If we do not find a way to fix what has gone wrong, or what has been mismanaged or neglected, we fear that in not too many years, there will no longer be an Order."

When Seeker Alden had finished speaking and sat back down, Seeker

Yuna stood and addressed us. "The debacle of Hambir's mistreatment of Garan brought home to us very sharply that we need to go back to the formal and proper way of training those who would wish to join our ranks. What our founder set up worked for years, and we have moved too far away from the instructions she laid down. That brings us to why we have invited the three, or more correctly, the four of you here. Seeker Alden and I have had the opportunity to spend time with each of you. We would like you all to give us your observations and any suggestions as to what might help us change the very rough road this landholding is at present traveling down."

"Arnar, Rosilda, and I have been talking, and if it is all right with you folks, we would like to talk about the landholding first. This is a beautiful holding with great potential. You have good farmland, good high meadows for raising sheep, and are well known for your honey and mead. It seems to us that one of the greatest needs is the folks who dwell here are aging and few have come to learn from them and take their places in the future. In addition, there just too few folks to do all the jobs that need to be done. Besides the need for farmers and laborers, you have need of highly skilled folks such as a metalsmith, a cooper, a potter or two, and a glassmaker."

One of the seekers spoke up at this point. "We are well aware of the need for more folks, but where do you propose to find them?"

"As you are aware, Perrin left Bortfjell because the ruling prince has stated that no one not of pure Bortfjellian birth can hold high positions," said Arnar. "That bias has been expanded and many in Bortfjell have concluded that anyone who is considered a foreigner does not belong in the country. I think Perrin, Rosilda, and I are part of the first wave crossing the border into Sommerhjem. As the antiforeigner furor increases in Bortfjell, more and more folks are going to be arriving at the border crossing at Høyhauger. I might suggest that you send someone to the border to recruit skilled folks who come through there."

I saw several of the seekers nod their heads. One even hit his forehead with his hand and questioned why they had not thought of the idea of looking to castouts from Bortfjell who might have the skills that the landholding needed.

Once the murmuring between the seekers quieted down, I continued. "One of the issues we have had a chance to discuss with Seeker Alden was how the folk who oversees the landholding is chosen among you folks. It seems it is a bit higgledy-piggledy and has lacked consistency over the years. At times, you have a seeker who is very skilled and vested in the job, and at other times you have a seeker who is perhaps resentful and feels stuck with the job. A third possibility is the seeker chosen is indifferent or does not have the skills to handle running the landholding. I mean no disrespect when I make this observation."

"And none is taken," suggested Seeker Alden. "Unfortunately, we are sadly more than aware that our higgledy-piggledy way of handling the landholding is not working. Go on."

"I think which seeker you choose to oversee the landholding needs to take a more active part. It is all well and good to go over accounts and have various folks report to you what is happening in the village, on the farms, with the bees and honey production … well, you know what I mean. What folks who live on a landholding really need is to see you, to know you care about them. When my father ceased to travel about the landholding, our folks became sullen and resentful. They felt as if the laird of their land no longer cared about their wellbeing. I appreciate that it is easy to get lost in the latest discovery, mystery, or puzzle, thinking that when you get the next question answered, you will get around to checking on the folks on the landholding."

"You are right again," stated a seeker whose name I could not recall. "When I was in charge here for several years, I did exactly as Perrin has described. I would get caught up in my research and weeks would go by before I would leave the library to meet with the reeve, the steward, or the marshal. Fortunately, we had good folks in those positions, thank goodness. I shudder to think what might have happened while I was so focused on what I wanted to pursue, because I was unaware of anything around me."

"I appreciate your candor. Thank you. I have spent the last week riding about the landholding, observing, and talking to folks. I have spent my evenings writing down my observations and have put together a list of suggestions. I am going to turn this discussion over to Rosilda and Arnar, who have some good ideas concerning defense and training. Rosilda."

"You have a good man in Vander, who does the best he can," suggested Rosilda. "Again, the problem is not having enough folk, particularly youth, to train and form a home guard. Consistency is an issue here also. To have an effective home guard, besides the initial training, they need to meet and work together as a unit at least once a week. This could be done by dividing the landholding up into sections and forming patrols for each section. This system would work if you had a fulltime trainer. I would recommend that."

"Seeker Alden asked me what type of training I think would be important for seekers to have," stated Arnar. "Each seeker comes to you with different experiences, different skills, and different knowledge. That means that the training for each one who aspires to become a seeker must be adjusted to meet individual needs. Some will already be fine horsemen or horsewomen. Some will know how to live off the land and others will not. Some will know how to camp, to cook, and to take care of their equipment. Others will not. All will need to know how to survive on the road. Having knowledge of what to do if they become injured or ill is also important."

Rosilda took up the conversation at that point. "Each and every one of you need to know how to defend yourselves. I have appreciated those who have joined us for the practicing of kazan each morning. Some type of discipline like kazan would be essential to be included in seeker training."

"One of the reasons Arnar, Rosilda, and I were able to muddy our trail leaving Bortfjell was in good part due to the ability to change our appearance. Arnar's great performance as a demanding returning seeker created an opportunity to take down Desna and the one remaining member of her crew in the kitchen. Knowing how to take on different personas might be helpful to a seeker. One other thing. Arnar has a way of using his voice that commands attention or can create fear in the folk he is speaking to. I have often wanted to learn how he is able to make his words sound like they are wrapped in ice. Do you include any of the suggestions we have made in your current seeker training?"

"Unfortunately, we do not," stated Seeker Alden. "I thank you for all of your suggestions. Please take a seat, all of you, that is if you can find an empty chair that does not have a cat on it."

I had been concentrating on our presentation, so I had not noticed the number of cats who had drifted into the room. As I moved a long-haired gray cat off the nearest chair, I heard one of the other seekers inquire, "What is it with all the cats?"

The meeting lasted through the noon hour. Cooks finally sent food and drink up. The seekers asked us questions, debated what could and should be done, gave suggestions, and hashed things out. Finally, about midafternoon, Seeker Alden suggested we all needed to get up and go out for some fresh air. The assembly would reconvene in the morning.

Over the next few days, the seekers sought us out individually or in small groups. They approached us to ask us questions, to clarify some of our suggestions, and to learn about each of our backgrounds. They sat with us and offered ideas, told tales, and generally included us in their day-to-day life, with the exception of the meetings which happened daily in their assembly room. At meals they did not talk to us about what they were discussing or debating.

Even though the days were long, and discussions went late into the night, I found I thoroughly enjoyed the conversation and the banter back and forth. I had enjoyed working with the seekers and listening to them work with each other. While they were all very different folks from a variety of backgrounds, I felt that they were very loyal to the Order of the Seekers, and that the landholding had become more than a home base. For them, it was truly their home. Since I could not at this time return to my home, Nytt Heimili, I hoped I would find someplace in Sommerhjem that I, like the seekers, could call home.

CHAPTER THIRTY-EIGHT

It was midafternoon, and I had just sat down with Rosilda and Arnar to have a cup of tea on the terrace overlooking the back garden when Seeker Yuna approached us. She seemed very solemn and serious. I also noted that she was not wearing her usual comfortable clothing. She was wearing a brilliant blue robe. Hanging down from a chain around her neck was her seeker medallion.

"Your pardon, I do not wish to interrupt your tea, however, we would ask you three, or rather the four of you, to join us in the assembly room."

Arnar, Rosilda, Kipp, and I got up from our chairs and followed Seeker Yuna back to the kitchen door. Cooks met us there and took our teacups. I looked at her face to see if I could tell anything from her expression. I could not. As we followed Seeker Yuna up the stairs leading to the assembly room, I began to worry. Had we overstayed our welcome? Had we said or done something wrong or offended the seekers with our ideas and suggestions?

I knew we could not stay with the seekers on their landholding much longer and felt it was probably time to move on. I had hoped to have a few more days, hear a few more tales about my mother before I had to leave, and I was not ready to leave yet. It was with great trepidation that I walked through the doors leading into the assembly room.

I became even more concerned when I saw that all the seekers were dressed in brilliant blue robes and were wearing their seeker medallions. Their faces all had serious and solemn looks matching Seeker Yuna's. As we entered the room, all the seekers rose.

"If all of you would please be seated," requested Seeker Alden.

He waited until all of us had taken our seats before continuing. Kipp chose to sit alertly on the table in front of me. I found a wee bit of comfort in having him close by.

"This gathering of seekers has spent the morning talking, debating, arguing, discussing, pacing, and deliberating as to what are the qualifications and the duties of a seeker. We have looked into our past, and we have looked toward our future. We have determined that we need to go back to the old ways where aspiring seekers spend at least a year in training before venturing out with a mentor. We have determined that part of that training needs to be on how to defend oneself and how to blend into different situations. We have determined that the landholding needs a consistent and steady hand to ensure that those of us who live here can prosper and grow, and those of us who leave to wander and return once a year or more, can have a home."

I wondered where Seeker Alden's speech was leading, and why we had been asked to this assembly to listen to it.

"When we looked back at our past, we realized that whoever took on the task of training aspiring seekers or whoever would oversee the landholding needed to be members of the Order of the Seekers because they would be more invested."

This was beginning to feel to me a rather formal way to let Arnar, Rosilda, and I know that our services here were at an end. Maybe they just wanted to thank us in a more formal way for what we had done while we were here. I began to position myself to leave when Kipp turned around and placed a paw on the hand I had just placed on the table. He pricked my hand with his claws and then turned back toward Seeker Alden. I remained seated.

"In our discussion this day we realized that while most seekers generally have traveled beyond the landholding looking for knowledge, that has not always been the case. Our founder was a true seeker in all senses of the word, yet she rarely left the landholding. There have been others over time who ventured forth occasionally, but for the most part, served the Order of the Seekers as trainers here. That led us to ask the question, could not a member of the Order be someone who brings knowledge and experience to the landholding rather than leaving the landholding to find such? We concluded that there was certainly both room for and a need for those types of seekers. We had forgotten that over time."

Seeker Alden then turned to Seeker Yuna and asked her to continue.

"We recognize the need for someone to be in charge of the landholding, and we recognize that we need experienced and skilled folk to develop training for both aspiring seekers, but also for continuing training for returning seekers. We are firm that those who do these tasks need to be members of the Order of the Seekers. We as an assembly have picked the folks we wish to take those positions. The problem we face now is whether those we have picked will be willing to join the Order."

I was so lost in my thoughts that I did not hear my name being called by Seeker Yuna.

"Perrin."

Arnar nudged me. "Seeker Yuna is asking for you."

"Perrin."

"Sorry, yes?"

"I know your journey to Sommerhjem was not one you freely chose to take. It, however, has brought you to us at a time that we are in great need of someone of your skill and training. We would invite you to join the Order of the Seekers and take up the reins of overseeing the landholding. Please take a moment to think upon our request."

"Rosilda," said Seeker Alden, "we would invite you to join the Order of the Seekers and share your knowledge of kazan and your knowledge gained in the border guard to help protect our landholding and train aspiring and returning seekers. Please take a moment to think upon our request."

"Arnar," said Seeker Yuna, "we would invite you to join the Order of the Seekers to share your knowledge of how to blend into any situation and to also use your knowledge as a former border guard to help protect our landholding, train aspiring and returning seekers, and continue training us in kazan. Please take a moment to think upon our request."

I was stunned by what I had just heard. Rather than being politely thanked for our services and asked to move on, the seekers were inviting us to join the Order. I was not sure if I had heard right, but I think they had also just asked me to take over for Seeker Alden and take on the task of overseeing the landholding. In addition, they had just invited Arnar and Rosilda to become seekers with the express purpose of designing the training for aspiring seekers like Garan, Galena, and Cleary, and continuing training for the returning seekers. Also, they wanted Rosilda and Arnar to work on shoring up the defenses of the landholding.

I looked to my two friends, who out of loyalty to our clan and Nytt Heimili had traveled all this way with me. I saw that they were looking at me.

"I, I …." Clearing my throat, I tried again. "Would it be proper for us to excuse ourselves and talk this over?"

"Take all the time you need," answered Seeker Alden.

I walked back out of the assembly room to the landing and turned to look at my friends. I noticed that Kipp had remained behind on the table, lying down with his front paws tucked under his chin.

"Looks as if Kipp has made his decision," quipped Rosilda.

"You both have been good and true friends. Your loyalty to me has brought both of you here, and I do not think I would have made it here without you. I want each of you to make your own decision as to whether you wish to join the Order or not."

"Once we accomplished finding your mother's folks, and then coming here and finding out she was a seeker, we have come to the end of the first leg of our journey," stated Arnar. "We are now faced with what do we do next, where do we go next? I have felt more useful here these last few weeks than I have in a long time. I like the idea of becoming a trainer of seekers and helping to protect this landholding. I would choose to stay."

"I had grown disillusioned with the Bortfjell border guard and what was being asked of us. I could no longer stand by and watch the members of my patrol or unit harm innocent folks just because one prince or another disliked the group they belong to. I have grown to like what I have learned about this new country. To be able to serve the Order of the Seekers suits me. Training others suits me. I would choose to stay," said Rosilda. "And you Perrin?"

"In the past few weeks, I, like Arnar, have felt needed and useful. It has been a joy to be able to use what I have been trained for. I have thought long and hard over the weeks we have traveled about whether I would ever feel comfortable back in Bortfjell and back home at Nytt Heimili. While the conclusion I came to was not the one I would desire, I feel that there really is no going home again for me. I have worried about what I would find to do to survive here in Sommerhjem."

"So, what will you choose?" asked Rosilda.

"When I crossed the border into Sommerhjem, I was determined to find my mother's folk. I did not find the feeling of family in the valley of the porcelain crafters. Ironically, I found that feeling here, which gives me all the more reason to accept the offer from the Order. Shall we return and let the assembly know our individual decisions?"

When we returned, each of us, one by one, accepted the offer to join the Order of the Seekers. Arnar went first, and they presented him with a seeker medallion and a brilliant blue robe. He looked somewhat embarrassed putting on the robe. I think he might even have blushed.

Rosilda stood guard straight when she donned the robe and when Seeker Alden placed the seeker medallion over her head. And then it was my turn.

Seeker Yuna helped me on with my robe. Seeker Alden stepped forward, but he did not have a medallion in his hand. Instead, he suggested that I might adopt my mother's medallion as my own. I was pleased with that idea.

Before the rest of the induction ceremony was over, which I cannot talk about, Seeker Alden announced that there was one more folk who needed to be inducted into the Order. He walked over to where Kipp was sitting upright and placed a small chain that held a small seeker medallion over Kipp's head.

Epilogue

So much has happened since that fateful day when Arnar, Rosilda, Kipp, and I were asked to join the Order of the Seekers. It is now late fall, most of the leaves have fallen, and it is a gray, cold, rainy afternoon. I am certainly glad for the warm fire in my office, and a warm wild hill cat on my lap.

Shortly after we joined the Order, Rosilda, Seeker Skelly, and Cleary traveled north to the border crossing out of Bortfjell at Høyhauger. They made arrangements with Captain Shala to stay at the Sommerhjem border guard encampment. The suggestion Arnar had made to recruit skilled folk and workers of the land from the castouts coming out of Bortfjell proved fruitful and also made Captain Shala's life a lot easier, for she had somewhere to send some of those who were fleeing Bortfjell.

Rosilda was a good judge of character and obviously spoke Bortfjellian. Seeker Skelly spoke some Bortfjellian and was a good interviewer. They had taken Cleary along, for he had grown up on a farm and while he did not want to work the land like the rest of his siblings, he along with Rosilda could make good decisions about who might fit in well to farm or work the land at the landholding.

Over the summer and into the fall, Rosilda, who I still have trouble remembering to call Seeker Rosilda, stayed at the border encampment near the pass into Bortfjell, along with Seeker Skelly, and Cleary. They had chosen wisely and sent a number of castouts to the landholding. We now had a good metalsmith and his family, a cooper and her family, not one but two glassblowers, and a number of excellent farmers and laborers. While we had not filled all of our needs, we had a good beginning. Most of the castouts arrived with families, and so that boded well for folks growing up on the landholding and hopefully wanting to stay.

With the influx of folks fleeing Bortfjell, the language here on the landholding was often a comic mix of Bortfjellian and the language of Sommerhjem. What had pleased me most was that those folks who had lived on the landholding for generations, or a number of years, did not resent the new arrivals. That is not to say there have not been a few tussles and misunderstandings along the way.

Another surprise was that all of the seekers had decided to stay on after their normal spring meeting. They decided they would not venture out again until the following spring. They pitched in wherever they were needed on the landholding and began to train with Seeker Arnar. More and more of the folks on the landholding, when they could spare the time, joined Seeker Arnar and I in the morning practice of kazan.

Seeker Arnar has not begun formal training for the aspiring seekers. Cleary, having gone with Seeker Rosilda and Seeker Skelly, would not begin until he returned. I expected them any day now that the air was beginning to smell of snow. Garan had suggested he wanted to wait to begin training until Cleary returned and had set off each day to help wherever he could.

Galena surprised us all when she told us she had changed her mind about becoming a seeker. She had discovered an old broken-down printing press in an outbuilding near the manor and realized that printer's ink still ran in her veins. Galena chose instead to mend and use the old printing press to print and preserve the tales and legends the seekers discovered and brought back.

As the cold season was almost upon us, I was looking forward to a less hectic time. The other day as I finally unpacked my saddle bags that I had set in a chest in my room months ago, I discovered the melted swan and have it proudly in place on my desk. I also rediscovered the journal of my mother's that Elder Nambi had given me all those months ago. I hoped now that the snowy season was almost here, I would have time to figure out what was written within.

As I had settled into the day to day overseeing of the Order of the Seekers landholding, I realized this was not the landholding I was raised to oversee, but then again, maybe it was. My name is Seeker Perrin, and this is my tale, so far.

The End

CPSIA information can be obtained
at www.ICGtesting.com
Printed in the USA
FSHW011502221221
87127FS

9 781663 232281